I0824657

Poppy Montgomery Gets Even

Poppy Montgomery Gets Even

GORDON JACK

THE MYSTERIOUS PRESS
NEW YORK

To my two *much* older sisters, Lisa and Sheila

❖

POPPY MONTGOMERY GETS EVEN

Mysterious Press
An Imprint of Penzler Publishers
58 Warren Street
New York, N.Y. 10007

Copyright © 2026 by Gordon Jack

First edition

Interior design by Maria Fernandez

This is a work of fiction. All characters, organizations, and events portrayed in this novel are either products of the author's imagination or are used fictitiously.

All rights reserved. No part of this book may be reproduced in whole or in part without written permission from the publisher, except by reviewers who may quote brief excerpts in connection with a review in a newspaper, magazine, or electronic publication; nor may any part of this book be reproduced, stored in a retrieval system, or transmitted in any form or by any means electronic, mechanical, photocopying, recording, or other, or used to train generative artificial intelligence (AI) technologies, without written permission from the publisher.

Library of Congress Control Number: 2025950466

hardcover ISBN: 978-1-61316-774-8
eBook ISBN: 978-1-61316-775-5

10 9 8 7 6 5 4 3 2 1

Printed in the United States of America
Distributed by Simon & Schuster

First Victim

The phrase "life passing before your eyes" takes on new meaning when you're falling from a tenth-floor balcony. It's true that time seems to telescope, bringing things into sharper focus. In my case, these things aren't moments from my past—birthday parties, weddings, or births of children, etc.—but scenes from my neighbors' lives. As I fall, I catch glimpses of those living in the apartments below me. In the darkness of night, I'm sure they don't notice me speeding past their windows, but to me they appear like slides in an incredibly boring presentation on the nocturnal habits of old people.

There's Ginny Anderson in the apartment directly below mine, illuminated by the glow of her microwave as it heats up a cup of tea. I wonder if the ruckus that preceded my tumble woke her up. Not that I put up much of a fight. The whole experience of being thrown off a balcony felt like a dream, which makes me wonder if I was drugged at dinner. I guess I should be grateful that my murderer put me in such a relaxed state, but maybe if I had my wits about me I could have screamed or scraped some of his DNA under my nails. Best I can hope for now is to come back and visit Ginny as a ghost, like Hamlet's father. Ginny told me she's seen her husband at her bedside twice since he died, so I think she's comfortable with a bit of haunting. She's a kind soul and needs to be warned.

Violet Pratt appears next. Poor woman has chronic back problems that make it impossible for her to sleep. She should try whatever narcotic was slipped into my glass at dinner. Who cares if you turn into a drug addict at ninety? We should all be heroin addicts here at Xanadu, or at least given the option. I'm glad those kinds of physical ailments will be over for me soon. No more waking up with sore hips or swollen knees. Half the people in this retirement home lose their minds before their bodies and the other half lose their bodies before their minds. Very few of us keep both in tip-top condition. I'm lucky to still have most of my cognitive functions intact, thanks to a steady diet of puzzles and cozy mystery novels.

Speaking of mystery novels, what a funny thing to leave this world as a crime victim. Honestly, I never saw that end coming. Xanadu is such a peaceful retirement community, but I suppose you could say the same thing about Cabot Cove, which had the body count of a major metropolitan city. I never got in any trouble during my entire law-abiding life. The only way I would be murdered would be if an assassin killed me by accident. But this was no accident. I know exactly who pushed me and I know why. If I tilt my head sideways just a tiny bit, I can probably see the face of the man peering over the side of my balcony. I hope he straightens up my apartment before he leaves. I'd hate for my neighbors to see all the sugar packets I've swiped from our cafeteria.

That man's face is *not* the last thing I want to see as I leave this world. Even with time slowing down in this way, I know I'm going to hit that pavement soon and then I'll be reunited with all my loved ones. I'm looking forward to it, actually. Too many people I've known and loved have left this world before me. That's why I started dating Steven. He reminded me so much of my older brother Tim. I hear how that sounds, even falling at this velocity, and no, I wasn't interested in my brother romantically. I just mean Steven and I understood each other's sensibilities, almost as if we were raised in the same house. Of course, I know now that I was tricked into believing that. If I have one regret, it's that I didn't have time to tell everyone at Xanadu what was going on right under their noses. But that's not for me to worry about anymore. Let them solve their own problems. I'm about to be problem free.

I must be passing the third floor because I see Wanda Prentice dancing in her living room. Wanda's one of those whose mind has gone but her body is in tip-top shape. She'll be in memory care soon (probably when people discover she spends her nights dancing in her living room). Still, it's a beautiful thing to see. I can't hear what she's listening to, but her body moves with a fluid grace I've never seen before. That's one thing I'll miss when I'm gone. Dancing. I didn't do enough of it as I got older and I don't know why. I loved how my body responded to music, but I always thought I needed a partner. Why couldn't I be more like Wanda and just dance whenever the feeling struck me, even if it struck me at 2:00 A.M. on a Monday. Falling feels a little like dancing actually, with my body twisting and turning in response to the air whistling around me.

And then my life *does* flash before my eyes. I'm at a party. My girlfriends and I have just graduated from nursing school and we're all dancing ecstatically to “Stuck on You” by Elvis Presley. Nothing mattered in that moment except being with my friends as we shook our bodies with abandon. I live in this moment of freedom and celebration and joy for what feels like an eternity.

Then I hit the ground.

1

May 6

First day of water aerobics and I have to ask myself, *Am I in hell?*

2

May 7

Day two and I've got another theory: Whoever invented water aerobics for seniors was a brilliant sociopath enacting revenge on the mother who abandoned him. I can't imagine a more humiliating torture than forcing eighty-year-old women to do leg lifts in a public pool that doubles as a giant toilet for children learning to swim.

3

May 8

The elder abuse continues. This time with knee swings to the tune of Benny Goodman. When does Lina, our "instructor," think we were all born? I grew up with the Rolling Stones for fuck's sake. And I still say fuck. I've been saying it quite a lot lately as a matter of fact.

4

May 9

Today I meet Ginny, who LOVES water aerobics. She's always smiling as she does her walk and squats, like all this bobbing up and down isn't a total humiliation.

"I'm Ginny," she says as we hoist ourselves out of the pool. She's a large woman shaped like a pear, which I've always thought was the most unfortunate of body types. It's like she's two different people above and below the waterline. It looks like she's swimming in a black slip, the kind I used to wear to bed when I dressed up for things like that. "Don't you just love Lina?" she says, dabbing her face with her faded pink terry cloth towel. I don't love Lina. I think Lina is a psychopath. She's one of those women who spouts a lot of nonsense about "being your best self" while standing in front of us with bleach blond hair and a bikini. If this exercise is so good for us, why isn't she in the pool doing it instead of standing on the pool deck so that all the male lifeguards can ogle her every time she shows us how to do cross-country sea legs.

"She's lovely," I say, and beat a hasty retreat to the locker room.

5

May 10

Ginny has latched onto me like a barnacle (and yes, I'm the whale in this metaphor). Now that we know most of the water aerobics routine (Lina is too lazy to change it or her big band swing soundtrack) we can chat as our arms and legs pump in the water. I learn that Ginny lives at Xanadu, an expensive senior home that my daughter Meg tried to get me into before she realized my meager pension wouldn't cover the $12,000 a month rent for a tiny studio apartment. Ginny's there because her husband was a doctor and the two of them sold their Palo Alto home to a couple of tech millionaires. After only six months in their new apartment, her husband died of an aggressive cancer. "It was a blessing," Ginny says. I notice she uses that word a lot when she's talking about life's horrors, whether it's her husband's agonizing death or this water aerobics class. When she learns that I live with my under-employed daughter and her juvenile delinquent son, she describes my living situation as a blessing too. Lucky for her I'm so exhausted from our workout, or I'd wrap my towel around her neck and strangle her.

6

May 11

Meg either forgets to pick me up from the YMCA or forgets to tell me she can't pick me up from the YMCA, so Ginny offers to drive me home. She's got a nice, new Subaru that's clean, roomy, and comes with heated seats, which feel great after getting out of the pool. When she turns the car on, John Denver's fluttery voice fills the confined space, singing about mountains in the springtime. In a flash, I'm transported back to a camping trip Greg and I took back when we were still married. It was in the seventies when Meg was five. The memory jars me with its emotional impact. Most of the time when I think back to my early days as a wife and mother, it's like watching a movie of someone else. But fucking John Denver makes me feel all the gratitude and hope I had back then. Greg's sales job was going great, and Meg was curious and playful, always asking us questions we couldn't answer. She was going to be so much better than me, with my high school diploma and dead-end job.

"You okay, Poppy?" Ginny asks, placing a hand on my knee.

I wipe away a tear and shake my head. "It's this song," I say. "It makes me think of my family."

"They're a blessing, aren't they?"

7

May 12

Ginny and I go out to lunch after water aerobics. Her treat. We go to a fancy place with an outdoor patio, ivy-covered walls, and white tablecloths. The waiter is tall and handsome and a little rude, which I like. Honestly, I get tired of people being so nice to me all the time just because of my gray hair. The other day a man beat me to the pharmacy door and walked right in ahead of me. I almost thanked him.

Ginny orders a fancy salad and I follow her lead, even though I'd be happy with a plate of French fries. She tells me her life story, which is one blessing after another. She and her husband were happily married for forty years. No children, but a rich life of work, travel, and pets. Ginny was a kindergarten teacher, which I probably could have guessed on the first try. She still dresses as if she's going to school, in large, brightly colored sweaters with bold patterns and designs. Today she's wearing a cardigan with decorative roses and a blue-and-white striped shirt. I feel my eyes crossing just looking at it.

My outfit is less bright and sunny, as is my life story. Married at nineteen, divorced at twenty-six, remarried at thirty-one, divorced again at forty-two. One daughter, one grandson, and no great-grandkids (a true blessing). A life spent refilling paper in Xerox machines at various office jobs.

"How'd you get into water aerobics?" Ginny asks.

"My daughter says I need more exercise."

"Don't we all."

"She's a former drug addict," I say, testing the limits of Ginny's sweet disposition. She reaches across the table and grabs my hand, which I suppose is better than her saying Meg's sobriety is a blessing.

"She's clean now," I say. "But it's a struggle. She comes to the YMCA to work out and thought it would be something that might help me too. She says I'm prone to depression."

"Are you?" Ginny asks.

"I think so. There's lots to be depressed about."

"Exercise can help with that, you know."

"That's what Meg says," I say. "I come for her mostly. If she has to take me to water aerobics, then she has to come to the gym too."

"What happened the other day?"

"She said she had to run some errands," I say.

"And is that true?"

I shrug. "I hope so. I'm too old to parent her anymore. She turned fifty-three this year."

"And her kids?"

"She's just got the one. Jeremy. Dad's not in the picture. Kid just stays in his room all day playing video games. I wouldn't be surprised if he's a porn addict."

"Oh dear," Ginny says, shaking her head.

We sit in silence for a minute until Ginny starts complimenting her quinoa salad. That's it, I think. In one short lunch I've frightened away Little Miss Sunshine with my life story. She will leave me alone after this.

Despite my hunger, I push my salad away. The thin slices of pear are not enough to balance the bitterness of the chicory. I grab another breadstick and bite down hard. "You can't fix me," I say silently to the fruits and vegetables on my plate. When I get home, I'll make myself a grilled cheese and eat it in front of the TV. Maybe top it off with some ice cream, if Jeremy hasn't finished the pint for breakfast.

8

May 12

That night, Xanadu is all over the local news.

> **TRAGEDY STRIKES XANADU RETIREMENT COMMUNITY AS RESIDENT FALLS TO HER DEATH**
>
> Xanadu Retirement Community is mourning the loss of one of its longtime residents, Cynthia Rhodes, 83, who tragically fell to her death from her tenth-floor balcony on Wednesday. Authorities have launched an investigation into the incident, though no details have been released yet.
>
> Cynthia Rhodes, known affectionately as "Belcher" to her friends, had been a vibrant member of the community. Her unexpected death has left many residents in shock and sorrow.
>
> While an investigation is ongoing, some residents have expressed concerns over Cynthia's recent mental state. Friends reported that she had been noticeably depressed following some unsettling medical news. "She wasn't

herself lately," remarked Barbara Vosovic, a close friend of Cynthia's. "She seemed really down, but she always put on a brave face for us."

However, Cynthia was also known for her spirited personality and resilience. Despite her struggles, she had recently found a new lease on life through a dating site. "Cynthia was a ball of energy," said neighbor Bernard Kelly. "She'd just met someone special online and was excited about the future. It's hard to believe she's gone."

Xanadu representatives have refused to comment on the incident, citing the ongoing investigation. "Our primary concern is the well-being of our residents," a spokesperson stated briefly.

As the community grapples with this sudden loss, many residents are left with questions and memories of a woman who touched their lives with her energy and spunk. The investigation is expected to provide more clarity on the circumstances surrounding Cynthia's tragic fall. In the meantime, the community has planned a memorial service to honor her memory and support those who knew her best.

The story only confirms my feelings that retirement homes are the depressing layovers to our final destination. When Meg first floated the idea of me moving into one, all I pictured was a sad place that reeked of piss and disinfectant, filled with lonely people who wandered the halls with vacant stares and rolling IV stands. This woman Cynthia probably couldn't take it anymore and saw a ten-story plunge as her only way out.

But then I remember that Ginny lives at Xanadu and my feelings about the story change. Something about Cynthia's death seems wrong to me. A vibrant robust woman throws herself off a tenth-story balcony? There's something they're not telling us here. I wonder how Ginny's going to see the bright side of this story.

So, of course, I ask her about it the next day.

9

May 13

"It's such a tragedy," she says, once we've taken our positions in the pool. We bob in place waiting for Lina to arrive. "She was such a lovely woman."

I want to ask how such a lovely woman gets "Belcher" as a nickname but that seems less important than finding out why she leaped from her tenth-floor balcony. "Do they know why she did it?" I ask instead.

Ginny shakes her head. "I heard she had advanced stage pancreatic cancer. Maybe she didn't want to suffer through the last few months she had."

"Did she have family?"

"Yes, a wonderful family. I'd see them eating dinner with her all the time."

"And she was dating someone?"

"Yes. Steven, I think his name was. They were making plans to take a cruise."

"Does he live at Xanadu?"

Ginny shakes her head. "I think they met online."

"Did Cynthia have a lot of money?"

"I think she was comfortable."

"Did she leave a note?"

"I don't know," Ginny says. "Listen to you. You sound like a regular police officer."

"My father was a police officer," I say, turning away.

"Maybe you get your inquisitive nature from him."

I resist the urge to dunk my head below water. I've spent my whole life trying to escape my father. I don't like being reminded that he might be hiding in my DNA somewhere.

I stop asking questions and busy myself adjusting a strap on my swimsuit. Where the hell is Lina, anyway? Does she think we have all day to sit in this ice bath? The water temperature is starting to give me the chills. Or maybe it's Cynthia's story. Why would a woman with Cynthia's money, education, and close family ties end her life this way? California has legalized assisted suicide. Why not opt for a more ceremonial passing? Why go out alone by flinging yourself over the balcony in the middle of the night? People with the nickname Belcher don't strike me as depressive loners. I know depressive loners. I see one every time I look in the mirror.

My thinking is interrupted by a new arrival. She walks onto the pool deck in a tight fitting, black swimsuit that showcases her nice hourglass figure. She's wearing a black swim cap, noseclip, and blue-tinted goggles, which she pulls down from her forehead before hopping in. I think she's going to join the swimmers at the other end, but she pushes her way into the front row of our group. When Lina finally shows up and starts class, the woman immediately puts us to shame with her strength and balance. She reminds me of one of those Russian swimmers we tried to ban from the Olympics for steroid use. I feel like we should start a similar campaign here as she is operating at a higher level than all the other bodies bobbing in the shallow end. Afterward I see her talking to Lina and wonder if they're related. They have the same broad shoulders and strong thighs. The woman bosses our instructor around like a mother, too, giving her unwelcome advice, which Lina listens to, nodding politely.

Of course, the woman complains to everyone in the locker room.

"I thought this was supposed to be a workout," she says, removing her swim cap and shaking out her dyed brown hair. Why women our age bother with colors and tints is a mystery to me. You can't hide a wrinkled bit of fruit by dipping it in chocolate.

No one says anything, which makes Ginny feel bad, I'm sure.

"You're in such good shape," Ginny says. "I wish I had your stamina."

"I was a competitive swimmer."

"Maybe you should start an advanced water aerobics class," I say, to which the woman nods. I don't think she gets that I'm joking. "Advanced water aerobics" is about the best example of an oxymoron that I can think of.

"That's a great idea," Ginny says. "You could whip some of those new moms into shape."

The woman grunts. "I'm too busy for that," she says, grabbing her towel and walking into the shower. Ginny and I look at each other in mild surprise. We've been put in the same category as our workout—not worth this woman's time or energy.

10

May 14

The woman returns the following day, this time with weights strapped on her ankles. They look like the monitor Meg had to wear after the judge granted her a compassionate release to take care of her newborn. She hops in the pool and marches to the front again, probably so she can intimidate Lina. I've got to say, this little drama has made these thirty minutes of torture more tolerable. It's fun watching Lina try to maintain her enthusiasm in the face of this woman's defiance. She follows Lina's instructions, but at a pace that's nearly double what the rest of us are doing. At the end of the session, she's up in Lina's face again sharing her feedback.

"You came back!" Ginny says, stating the obvious. We're in the locker room changing.

"The time of the class works best with my husband's physical therapy."

"I'm Ginny."

"Max," the woman says.

Both women look at me. "Poppy," I say.

"What kind of name is Poppy?" Max says.

"My mother loved flowers," I say. "And Max?"

"My mother wanted a boy."

"My mother named me after Queen Guinevere," Ginny says. "But I've always been Ginny. Guess I can't pull off that regal manner."

"Not in that swimsuit," Max says.

The room goes silent.

"That was a joke," Max says.

"You're funny," I say, and I mean it but only in the strange and unusual sense. Max joking is like me stripping. We may want to please an audience, but our ineptitude creates the opposite effect of what's intended.

Max leaves to shower and I stay with Ginny, who's busying herself by rummaging through her gym bag. There's really nothing I can say to make Ginny feel better. If I compliment her suit it will come across as pity. If I call Max a bitch it will come across as mean. So I ask her if she'd like to go to lunch.

"I'd love that," she says. We skip the shower and leave before Max exits from her stall.

11

May 14

We meet Meg in the lobby. Her newly blond shag looks untouched, which doesn't say a lot for her workout, and she's talking to some mustached and muscle-bound man in a tank top with the words *Boost a Move* written in cartoonish script. The *B* and *M* letters are big and bold, making him look like a walking advertisement for pooping.

I introduce Meg and Ginny. The man doesn't take his cue to leave. Meg doesn't introduce us so we stand around awkwardly until Ginny says, "Don't I know you?"

"Could be," Mr. Mustache says. "I provide customized bodywork to many seniors in this area." The man digs into his short shorts and pulls out a slightly damp business card and passes it to Ginny. *Craig Bagatelos, Miracle Worker.*

"You came to Xanadu and led us through some exercises."

"I did," Craig says. "Fancy place, Xanadu."

"I like it," Ginny says.

"Well, if you're ever interested in some one-on-one personal training designed to build strength and balance while simultaneously improving your cardiovascular endurance, let me know."

"Ginny and I are going out to lunch," I say, putting an end to this sales pitch.

Meg sighs like this is some huge inconvenience. I don't know if it's just me, but it's been very hard to see Meg as anything but a petulant teen. Those years were so difficult, they embedded in my brain, which seems a cruel punishment to inflict on a parent. If I could only think of Meg as a little girl with her giggles and squeals of delight, I'd probably be nicer. Part of me can never forgive her for becoming her own person though. That person being an asshole.

"Mom, I've been waiting," she whines. She zips up her HSN jacket to just under her ample bosom, drawing Mr. Mustache's attention just where she wants it.

"You have not," I say. "My class ended five minutes ago."

She looks at Craig and does an eye roll. *Parents, am I right?* they silently communicate to each other.

"Can Ginny drive you home?" Meg asks me.

"Ginny is standing right here," I say. "You can ask her."

"Sorry, Ginny," Meg says. "Mom got a DUI last month so I worry."

"I did not get a DUI," I say, infuriated that she would bring this up in the lobby of the YMCA. "It was a wet reckless and it wasn't my fault."

Meg did this all the time as a young woman—try to make herself look better by making fun of me. At the time, I thought it was a phase she'd grow out of, like her sneaking the occasional cigarette out of my purse. But the habit, like her smoking, became a permanent part of her personality. I endured her mockery because, again like her smoking, I felt responsible. Somehow, I'd broken something in my daughter that made her need this crutch to feel better about herself.

I pull Ginny away to save her from any more embarrassment.

"Bring me back some leftovers!" Meg says as we walk out the double doors.

Ginny and I don't say anything as we buckle in and pull out of the parking lot.

"Where do you want to go?" she asks.

I'm too upset to come up with a nice restaurant so I recommend a nearby Subway. Ginny drives to the mall where the sandwich store is located and circles the lot until she finds an open space. We walk in and get in line. Ginny is overwhelmed by the options and ends up taking forever. It's embarrassing because she's acting like a classic old person and I can feel the impatience of everyone in line behind us. She debates almost every single topping on display and rules them out for various gastrointestinal reasons. Finally, she decides on a turkey sandwich with mayo and lettuce. I want to pound my head against the cash register.

"I haven't been to a Subway in ages," she says as we sit down at a table near the window with a view of the parking lot. Back when I could drive, I'd sit here for hours and watch people fight over spaces.

"I'm sorry, I couldn't think of someplace nicer," I say. "My daughter rattles my brain."

"She seems lovely," Ginny says.

"She's terrible," I say. "Just like Max. Don't you hate bullies?"

Ginny doesn't respond.

"I want to hear you say something bad about one of them," I say, placing my sandwich down and folding my arms across my chest. I want her to know I mean business.

"Oh, I don't know."

"I can't be your friend unless I know who annoys you."

"I try to look on the bright side of things," Ginny says. "Life's too short."

"Exactly. That's why I don't put up with assholes. Unless I have to. Meg's an asshole, but she's my daughter so there's not much I can do. I'm the one who probably turned her into an asshole."

"I'm sure that's not true," Ginny says.

"It is. I accept responsibility. I should have been more patient and nurturing. But that's not in my nature. When she was little, I thought she'd turn me into a better person. I did all the things good mothers are supposed to do, became a regular Mary Poppins. But the thing about Mary Poppins is, once you take away her music and magic, she's just a bossy bitch. Once Meg realized I couldn't fly or talk to animals, she turned on me. After that, I became her sparring partner."

Ginny gives me a sad, pitying look.

"Your turn," I say. "Tell me who you hate."

Ginny picks at her sandwich. "No one. I've been very blessed."

"You were upset over what Max said. I saw it."

"She touched a nerve, yes. But that's my problem. I'm insecure about my weight."

"Who cares?"

"I still care what I look like."

"Why? Who do you have to impress?"

She leans forward and whispers, "I've started dating someone."

"Really?" I say surprised. I've heard people my age date. Some even have sex. But I've never met one of them.

"We met on Senior Moments," she says, adding, "It's a dating site," when she sees my blank expression. "That's the reason I'm taking this class. I want to lose ten pounds before we meet in person."

"How can you date someone you've never met in person?"

"It's what everyone does these days," she says.

It's what Cynthia did, I want to say, but keep my mouth shut. I don't want Ginny to think I'm obsessing over her neighbor's death, but I haven't been able to stop thinking about it since we last spoke. There have been no follow-up stories on the news, which I assume means the police aren't opening an investigation. Still, I expected to see something about a lawsuit from the family. If an eighty-three-year-old woman can crawl over a balcony railing unassisted, doesn't that indicate a safety violation?

"Poppy?" Ginny says, waving her hand in front of my face.

"Sorry," I say, snapping back to our conversation. "What's your boyfriend's name?"

"Cristóbal."

"Do you have a photo?"

Ginny scrolls through her phone and then hands it over so I can see. On the screen is a photo of Ricardo Montalbán, the original host of *Fantasy Island*. I don't have my glasses on, but that's what I see—a silver fox with dark, sexy eyes and a warm smile. The photo looks professional, not like the kind of selfies people my age take where there's a thumbprint obscuring half the face. I swipe right and there's a photo of Ginny on her bed in a voluminous nightgown, the kind Jane Austen probably slept in.

"Sexy," I say, showing her the photo.

"Give it back," she says, grabbing the phone and turning the same shade of pink as her tracksuit.

"You look great," I say.

"You're sweet," Ginny says. "But you're a liar."

And that's when I knew who Ginny hated: Ginny hated herself, which made me like her just a little more.

"He hasn't asked you for money, has he?" I had a scammer contact me during COVID, claiming he was Jeremy and needed $5,000 to cover his medical expenses. The loser had hacked into some site that told him I had a grandson. What the site didn't tell him was that my grandson lived in my basement and only made human contact when he needed more cereal.

"It's nothing like that," Ginny says. "He's a wealthy restaurateur in Miami."

"And he's on a dating site?" Seems like a wealthy restaurateur would have his pick of sexy diners if he lived in Miami.

Ginny nods. "There are lots of wealthy people on Senior Moments," she says. I catch a glimpse of Ginny's purse and picture it loaded with expensive lotions and candies.

I pick up my sandwich and take a bite to stop my interrogation. Here's the thing Ginny doesn't know about me and that I'm not yet ready to reveal: My experience with bullies (father, husbands, bosses) has made me pretty good at sniffing them out. Max is clearly a bully and this boyfriend feels like one too. I don't like that both Cynthia and Ginny met their boyfriends online, but that's probably my paranoia talking. My father used to spin wild conspiracy theories from random coincidences all the time, mostly involving my mother. If she served him steak two nights in a row, it was because she had fallen in love with our butcher. If she wore jewelry to church, it was because she wanted to seduce a deacon. She couldn't do anything without rousing his suspicion. I don't want to repeat the same mistake with Ginny. Without more proof that Cristóbal is a lowlife, I decide to focus on the more immediate threat.

"I think we should pull a prank on Max," I say. "Knock her off that pedestal she stands on."

12

May 15

The next day, Max shows up with her swim cap, noseclip, goggles, and ankle weights. This time, she's carrying tiny barbells as well. Why doesn't this woman just go to the gym with all the other weight lifters and leave us alone? She could join Meg's friend and spot him on the bench press, I'm sure.

After class, Max stays in the pool to swim laps. Ginny and I watch her while we towel ourselves dry. She's got a nice stroke and glides through the water barely making a splash. When an older gentleman in swim trunks joins her lane, she laps him in no time. When she bumps up against his feet again, she sinks under the lane line and joins a faster swimmer next door.

Ginny and I head to the locker room. Before going into the showers, I pause at Max's locker and point it out. "This is hers," I say, fingering the lock.

"Poppy," Ginny says in the admonishing tone she probably used with her kindergartners. "Leave her alone."

"It's a key lock," I say. "I bet her memory is going."

We shower in our bathing suits and emerge from our stalls toweled dry. Ginny has already changed into her clothes because she's either modest, embarrassed, or efficient. We're not like these Russian women who parade about the dressing rooms fully naked, their bodies like vanilla soft serve. Part of me respects their devil-may-care attitude and part of me resents it. Their personal freedom impacts my own, after all, as I'm forced to look away to maintain a neutral expression.

We pass Max on our way back to the locker room. She's got a pinkish glow from her extended workout and smiles as she walks into the shower but doesn't say anything. I notice that she's left her locker open so I call Ginny over to have a peek inside. There's a tracksuit, which she's hung on the hooks inside. On the bottom is a fanny pack that I'm tempted to zip open to examine its contents. I pull out one of Max's ankle weights and test its heft.

"These aren't that heavy," I say. "One or two pounds tops." The weights are bright red with a Sporti label written in slanted script across the top. The soft fabric is filled with something synthetic and squishy.

"Put that back," Ginny says, rushing over. She pulls me away before I can pry much further, which is a good thing because seconds later Max returns in a towel.

"Getting in an extra workout?" Ginny asks.

"I'm using water aerobics as my warm-up," Max says, whipping off her towel to show us her body, which is impressively strong. I'm happy to see she sags in all the places her corset of a bathing suit covers. Still, I turn around when it's my time to change. I pull on my clothes as quick as I can, feeling awkward and clumsy. Not for the first time do I wish we adopted the dress of a strict Islamic state.

When I turn around, Max is dressed in her tracksuit, cinching her fanny pack around her waist. She glances at an expensive-looking watch on her wrist and leaves without saying goodbye.

Meg isn't in the lobby when we enter and Ginny offers to wait just in case she's forgotten me again. I offer to buy Ginny something from the vending machine because I know she's hungry after our workout.

"I don't know how Max does it," Ginny says, eyeing the selection before choosing a bag of chips. "I'm exhausted after our class."

"She's just showing off," I say.

"If I was in that good of a shape, I'd show off too."

Ginny rips the bag open just as Max emerges from the elevator down the hallway. She's pushing a man in a wheelchair and I assume him to be her husband. Even sitting down, he's an imposing figure with a thick neck and barrel chest. He's dressed in a flannel shirt and cardigan. As she wheels him closer, I notice his hands shaking. Poor man must have Parkinson's.

Just as I'm about to have my first sympathetic feeling for Max, she says to Ginny in passing, "If you want to lose weight, I'd stay away from those."

"Who asked you?" I fire back.

Max stops and turns. "I was just trying to help," she says.

Before either of us can respond, she gives her husband a shove and continues her way down the hallway and out the door.

"She's right," Ginny says, tossing the bag into the trash. "I need to eat better."

"That woman can suck it, as my grandson is fond of saying."

Suddenly an idea forms in my mind. Before Ginny can talk me out of it, I stomp over to the receptionist's desk and ask to speak to the manager. A boy my grandson's age comes out in full customer service mode. He's got muscles bulging from his tight-fitting YMCA polo, but his eyes are kind and when he smiles he reveals a mouth of braces.

"How can I help you, ma'am?" he asks politely, his voice two octaves higher than I was anticipating.

"I don't want to cause a fuss," I say in my meekest old lady voice. "But there's something I need to bring to your attention. Can we speak in private?"

I wave goodbye to Ginny, who's standing in the lobby, wringing her hands. I'm not quite ready to bring her into my scheme yet. I'm not even sure it is a scheme to be honest. I'm running on pure malevolent instinct. I have enough self-awareness to know this isn't healthy, but like any addict, I'm powerless to control myself. It feels too good to be in control of things for a change.

The boy leads me into his office and offers me a seat, which I don't take.

"This won't take a minute," I say.

"What can I help you with?" he asks, leaning against his desk. I see a copy of *Middlemarch* sprouting sticky notes next to his fitness shake, which throws me. Everything would be so much easier if people just picked a personality lane and stayed in it.

"It's kind of a delicate situation," I say. "But I believe one of the girls in my water aerobics class has a bladder control problem."

13

May 15

After my meeting with the manager, I sit on the uncomfortable chairs in the lobby (an intentional purchase, I assume, for a gym that wants to discourage sitting) and wait for Meg to arrive. She's ten minutes late, probably to get back at me for yesterday. She emerges from the women's dressing room, stops to take a long sip from the water fountain, and then strolls leisurely toward me.

"What's wrong with you?" she asks.

"Nothing," I say.

"Why are you smiling like that?"

"Like what?"

"Like you're reading granddad's obituary."

"Don't be silly," I say. "Let's go."

We walk out together into the blinding light. Summer is right around the corner and I'm already dreading the heat and the longer days. Meg whips out a pair of sunglasses I've never seen before, forcing me to wonder if she's been on another shopping spree. She gets in the car and cranks the air-conditioning and music. A rapper belts out some nonsense about getting jiggy with it and Meg bounces in her seat all the way home.

❖

Home for us is a single-story tract house built in the fifties with a one-car garage and front porch. It was perfect when Greg and I were starting out, cozy in its small rooms and fenced-in backyard. But the place closed in on us as our family grew and intimacy turned into intrusion. We all had our places to escape the crowded chaos of the place: Meg would seal herself off in her room, I would smoke in the back garden, and Greg would hang out in bars and, eventually, other women's apartments.

The house still feels cramped with Meg, Jeremy, and me, but at least we're all adults and know how to give each other space. That doesn't mean we don't annoy each other. Meg and Jeremy say I watch TV at ear-splitting volumes. I complain about Meg making a mess in the kitchen for me to clean up. Neither Meg nor I know what the hell Jeremy does in the basement all day, but whatever it is involves a lot of pot smoking. Either he thinks we can't tell or he's too stoned to care. I'm not sure which is worse.

When we get home from the gym, he's got his head in the refrigerator searching for leftovers.

"Close the door, Jeremy," Meg says. "You're letting all the cold air out."

I walk over to the cupboard, grab the last clean glass, and fill it with water.

"Where are those chicken cutlets you made for dinner last night?" he asks, head buried in the crisper drawer. The sweet aroma of cannabis emanates off his body like he's been seasoned with herbs and spices. If I were the witch from Hansel and Gretel, I'd take this opportunity to push him in the oven.

"That was three nights ago and they're all gone," Meg answers, shoving him out of the way.

Jeremy straightens and as usual I'm amazed that someone so tall and skinny is related to me. I can see his mother's freckled cheekbones and close-set blue eyes, but the rest of him comes from his father, a man I met only a few times before he joined the circus. That's what I call it anyway. Meg always corrects me that he's a roadie for a rock band that had a string of hits in the nineties and now plays country fairs and carnivals. It doesn't really matter where the man is. All that matters is he's gone.

Jeremy runs a hand through his mop of black hair and grabs a box of Triscuits (*my* Triscuits). Without saying another word, he heads back to his dungeon.

"Jeremy," I say before he disappears. "I have a friend who just struck up a relationship with a man online. I'm worried the guy might not be on the up-and-up."

Jeremy turns away and looks down the staircase that leads to his hovel. I can tell he's fighting every instinct not to run down there and hide under the covers. "That's a pretty safe bet," he says.

"Why do you say that?"

"Because everyone lies on those dating sites."

And with that he disappears.

I stare at Meg hoping she'll call out his rudeness. When she doesn't, I finish my water and place the empty glass in the sink.

"If anyone needs to get to the gym, it's that boy," I say. "He's skin and bones."

"Give him a break. He's finding himself," Meg says.

"In the basement? Seems like he should look elsewhere."

"Everything you used to do in person, we do online now, Mom," Meg reminds me. "Work, dating, even exercise."

"I don't think I'd count what he does down there as exercise," I say. "Unless they're now handing out gold medals for masturbation marathons."

"Stop it," Meg says.

"You don't worry about him?" I ask.

"Of course I worry about him. I'm his mother. But he's twenty-four years old. It's not like I can tell him he's grounded."

Well, I'm not having any of it. I open the door and descend into the first circle of hell, which I believe is Limbo. The stairs creak so I grip the handrail to make sure I don't tumble down into the darkness. The wood is smooth and I take some comfort in its solidity. This was a mighty oak once, I remind myself, happy in a forest before it was reduced to this meager existence.

The basement is dark, lit now by computer monitors. Jeremy sits at his desk at the other end of the room, adjusting a headset on his mop of hair. The place smells of dirty laundry, spilled soda, and something funky and sour. I don't want to investigate or think about what it could be. There's one window that looks out on our weedy backyard that I could open to provide some much-needed ventilation, but know that if I do, Jeremy will forget to close it and he'll be consumed by raccoons.

When I reach the bottom, I flick on the light. Jeremy recoils, like I've just electrocuted him. And maybe I have. There are so many wires down here, snaking along the floor, each plugged into different power strips.

"Grandma!" Jeremy yells, spinning around in his office chair.

The room is a concrete bunker with a computer station, bed, and mini fridge. All my efforts to make the space more cozy, with carpets, posters, and—what was I thinking?—plants, have been rebuffed by Jeremy, who claims to be a brutalist, whatever that means.

"I need to talk to you," I say.

"I'm busy," he says, spinning back to his screens.

I walk over to the breaker box and fling open the metal door.

"Stop!" he says when he sees what I'm about to do. He removes his headset, closes his eyes, and takes a deep breath. "What do you want?"

I want you to treat me like a person. Someone deserving of attention. I want you to take an interest in my life. I may not have much of it left, you know, which is why you should get to know me. When I die, it will be too late and I'll just exist as a set of pixels for you. We are connected, Jeremy! I want to scream. *More than the people you interact with through that machine. I'm your flesh and blood and it should matter to you who I am because that's how you'll figure out who you are. Like it or not, you've got some of me in you. Isn't that reason enough to want to care about me? Just a little?*

I don't say any of this of course. I also don't fall back on my usual complaint that he could show a smidgen of respect toward the person who allows him to live rent free in her home. That's a broken record he doesn't listen to anymore.

"I want to know if my friend's boyfriend is real," I say.

"Do you have a photo?"

I shake my head.

Jeremy stares at me like he's in the process of rebooting. Maybe he is part robot now. Maybe these machines have taken over his body like those aliens did in that movie.

"I know his first name, will that help?" I say. "It's Cristóbal. He lives in Miami. He says he's a restaurateur."

Jeremy spins around and starts typing. I'm amazed at the swiftness and dexterity of his fingers as they move across the keyboard. He could have been a concert pianist, I think.

"What site did your friend meet him on?" Jeremy asks.

"Senior Moments," I say, happy I remember this detail, although it's hard to forget, it's so stupid.

"He seems legit," Jeremy says. "By that I mean, there's a profile of a Cristóbal Rios who lives in Miami and owns a restaurant."

"Well, that's a relief," I say. That's when I notice Jeremy looking at me with the same pitying look I gave him earlier when I thought about him dying a virgin in my basement.

"Grandma," he says. "Just because this checks out, doesn't mean it checks out."

"Speak English, Jeremy."

My grandson sighs. "If I wanted to, I could create a dating profile with your name and photo and scam some poor geezer into giving me all his money."

"You wouldn't do something like that, would you?"

"Of course not. I'm not a low-life asshole. But if I were, I could do it and the guy would never know he's being catfished because all your info would check out."

"Catfished?"

"When someone impersonates you online," Jeremy says.

"But wouldn't I get an alert or something saying I had created an account on a dating site?"

Jeremy sighs again and starts speaking as if I were a slow, dull child. "Only if I were dumb enough to use your real email, which I wouldn't do because that would defeat the whole purpose of the scam."

"So there's no way of knowing?"

"Has he asked her for money?"

"No."

"Has he asked for her social security number?"

"No."

"Then he might be legit," he says, and swivels back to computer monitors.

"You think so?" I say.

"No," he says. "He's definitely a scumbag. I mean, look at this guy. No one this good-looking, rich, and successful needs help finding women on a stupid dating site."

I grip the rail and slowly move back upstairs, taking one step at a time. How do I tell this to Ginny? She'll be devastated. If she even believes me. I need to find a way to confirm this before I do anything. There's a slim chance Cristóbal is real. What does Jeremy know about human relationships after all? I remind myself. He's been living in this hole for so long, his vision becoming more and more myopic. Maybe all he can see now is the bad in people, although something tells me he's inherited my ability to detect liars and cheats. I guess we'll just have to wait and see. In the meantime, I can work on phase two of my plan to get rid of Max. Once I'm back upstairs in the land of the living, I go on Amazon and buy the same ankle weights Max uses. They should be here tomorrow. Now all I need to do is persuade Ginny to participate.

14

May 16

"I think I know how to get back at Max," I say to Ginny before class. We're bobbing in the water, waiting for Lina to show up. I'm surprised by my newfound comfort level in the pool. I actually enjoy the smell of chemical vapors rising off the surface and the warm hold of the water, enveloping me. I feel protected here, unlike outside where I'm vulnerable to attack on all sides.

"Get back at her for what?" Ginny says.

"For being such a know-it-all," I say.

"I don't think we need to get back at her for that."

"Sure we do. She needs some humility."

Just then Max shows up in her matching black suit and cap, like she's attending somebody's funeral. She straps on her ankle weights before hopping into the pool.

"Where's Lina?" she asks, looking around.

No one answers. I wonder if the other ladies in our class resent Max as much as I do. Most of them are Russian or Chinese and have probably had their fill of obnoxious dictators.

"This is ridiculous," Max says after we've stood in the water for five minutes. She swims over to the ladder and pulls herself out. After she removes her ankle weights, I figure she's going to dive into one of the swimming lanes, but instead she walks over to where Lina usually stands and claps her hands loudly.

"Okay, ladies. Looks like I'm your substitute teacher for today. Who's ready for a real workout?"

We all look around, thinking for some reason that someone will raise her hand but no one does. This doesn't deter Max though. She starts in on some leg lifts at nearly three times Lina's usual pace. "Let's show everyone what we can do," she says.

We follow her lead because it would be rude not to. I feel like I've suddenly been conscripted into the Navy SEALs. Lina, being in her forties, probably feels sorry for her little ducklings bobbing in the water and takes it easy on us. Max, being our age, feels no such sympathy. If she can do this, we can do it, which is patently untrue. At one point, I look over at Ginny, whose head is barely floating above water.

"We can stop at any time, you know," I lean over and say.

"I'm fine," Ginny says, huffing.

"Ginny!" Max bellows. "Lift those legs higher. Kick, and kick, and kick."

Max demonstrates her side kick with some Rockette style agility.

"I think I'm having a heart attack," Ginny says.

I look over and see that she's nearly purple from fatigue. I stop the exercise and help her over to the ladder, where we rest. Max has barely broken a sweat.

"What was that you were saying about teaching Max some humility?" Ginny asks.

15

May 16

Ginny and I work on our plan at her place. It's the first time I've been to Xanadu and I have to say the place is not the hospital ward I'd imagined it to be.

Ginny pulls up to the front of an eleven-story building that feels like a monument of the past, a historic reminder of what happens when you don't have restrictive zoning laws protecting the views of wealthy homeowners. A valet helps us out of the car and then drives it away like we've just arrived at a five-star restaurant. When we enter the lobby, the receptionist, a cheerful Indian woman with a charming British accent, greets Ginny by name and calls me "Luv" as she hands over my guest pass. The lobby is bright and cheery with comfy couches and orchids dripping with flowers. Four women sit by the wall of windows playing bridge. There's a grand piano in the corner where a resident performs for a small audience.

"Can you give me a minute?" Ginny asks. "I just want to get my mail."

Ginny disappears into a room behind the receptionist area and I wander over to the shrine built for the woman who recently passed (*Passed nine floors on her way down to the sidewalk*, I think, incapable of turning off my dark sense of humor). I remind myself to stop being such an asshole, which just turns my inner critic against me. *Who's going to hold a memorial for you when you go?* she asks. I'll be lucky if Meg posts an obituary in the paper. When I die, people will most likely only know about it when my family starts selling my stuff on eBay.

I tell myself to shut up and try to connect with the photo of the woman pinned on the corkboard. She looks a little like Julie Andrews, with short gray hair, blue eyes, and a lovely smile. I can picture her being the spokesperson for a fancy brand of protein shake. Surrounding her portrait are testimonials to Cynthia's warmth and generosity. One says, "Nobody made me laugh like Belcher."

Why would this woman throw herself off her balcony? It seems even more preposterous now that I'm standing in her former lobby.

"Did you know Cynthia?" a voice with a slight Irish accent asks from behind me.

I turn around and see an elfish man with a white, neatly trimmed goatee, dressed in a wool button-down vest and holding a cane.

I shake my head. "I just read about her . . ."

"Suicide?" the man finishes for me. He leans closer. "That's the story they're telling us, but . . ." Now it's his turn to trail off. It's like neither of us has the stamina to get to the end of a sentence.

"You don't believe it?"

The man shrugs. "Are you a new resident?"

"No, I'm just here visiting a friend," I say. "I'm Poppy."

"Bernard," the man says extending a hand for me to shake. His skin is soft but his grip firm. "I didn't want to scare you in case you just moved in, but I think something's afoot."

"Really?" I say, intrigued.

"A woman like Belcher," he whispers. "She doesn't take the easy way out."

"I have to ask, how did she get the nickname Belcher?"

Bernard laughs, which makes his whole body shake, like he's being lightly tickled. "It was at one of our New Year's parties. We celebrate on the eleventh floor. Great views of the fireworks from up there. Anyway, Cynthia had just taken her first sip of champagne and as everything in the room went quiet, there's this enormous burp. Turns out she can't drink anything bubbly without belching. Well, you can imagine the uproar it caused. Cynthia laughed harder than anyone else. She kept us amused all night and her nickname was born."

"She sounds like a hoot," I say.

"Exactly," Bernard says. "A woman like that laughs in the face of death. If she were given a few months to live, she'd spend it planning and attending her own memorial just so she could hear all the nice things people had to say about her. She wouldn't leave without saying goodbye."

Bernard leans in and whispers. There's a faint trace of something medicinal on his breath that could be booze or some fancy cough syrup. "You know, she was on that dating site that's all the rage here."

"Senior Moments?"

"Senior Torments, more like," he says, chuckling.

"Why do you call it that?" I say, grabbing Bernard by the arm. I see him wince and relax my grip. "Do you think Cynthia was murdered by her online boyfriend?"

Bernard takes a step back. I can see him reevaluating me, trying to weigh my crazy against his crazy. "You've got a dark and twisted mind," he says, stroking his beard. "I like that."

"My friend," I say, surprised at how easily the words slip out of my mouth, "she's on the site. Could she be in danger?"

Bernard looks surprised at my worry and grips my hand to calm me down. "I didn't mean to frighten you, dear," he says. "Xanadu has strict protocols for allowing visitors in the building. If Cynthia's 'boyfriend' had come, there'd be some record of it. Plus, we have all this surveillance equipment."

Bernard points to the cameras that are positioned behind the receptionist's desk and in the corners of the lobby.

"The only way Cynthia would have thrown herself off the balcony is if she felt such shame that she saw it as her only way out."

"But I thought you didn't believe the suicide story," I say.

"I don't believe she killed herself *because she was sick*," Bernard says. "But I can see her 'boyfriend' luring her into something sordid and incriminating and giving her two options: Either pay up or be exposed. Belcher chose a third option."

Ginny suddenly appears to my right, holding an armful of letters and magazines. "Oh, I see you've met Bernard," she says, leaning in to kiss him on the cheek.

"I didn't know you were Ginny's friend," Bernard says. "Now I like you even more."

"Be careful with this one," Ginny says to me. "Half the women here are in love with him."

"The odds are in my favor," Bernard says. "There's ten women for every man in this place. No wonder they're all looking for love online."

The mention of this must make Ginny uncomfortable because she pulls me toward the elevators.

"Nice to meet you," I say as I'm led away.

"Hope to see you again, Poppy," Bernard says, waving.

We enter the elevator and Ginny pushes the button for nine. "He's a charmer," I say. "Why don't you date him?"

"Bernard's gay, dear," Ginny says. "And a terrible gossip. If you ask me, the man listens to too many true crime podcasts. Did he tell you his theory about Cynthia?"

"About her being lured into something shameful and degrading?" I say.

Ginny nods. "Can you imagine letting someone trick you into doing something illegal?"

Like how I convinced you to help me get even with Max? I think but don't say. I note Ginny's inability to notice when she's being manipulated by people she trusts.

As we ascend, I read over a posted list of activities happening in the building today: A guest lecture on Patagonia. A book club discussing some Noble laureate's latest. A class on journaling. Nothing suggests a criminal element.

We get out of the elevator and walk down the carpeted hallway to Ginny's room. The residents on this floor decorate the walls with their own prints so the place looks like an Impressionist museum. The quiet is interrupted when a woman bolts out of one of the rooms in tears.

"Sharon!" a voice says from inside. Sharon hits the opposite wall and then staggers toward us like a pinball trapped between bumpers. Ginny reaches out to steady her and pulls her into a tight embrace.

"Sharon, dear," she coos. "What's wrong?"

The woman is bleary eyed from drink. I recognize that panicked stare from when Meg was using, someone trying to keep two steps ahead of oblivion. Sharon clings to Ginny like she's a buoy, the only thing saving her from drowning. She sobs onto her shoulder, smearing her tracksuit with mascara.

And then she laughs.

I've got to say, it's a pretty quick one-eighty, emotions-wise. Her cackling is wild and deranged, in response to some sick joke neither Ginny nor I hear or understand.

An older couple rush out the open door and stand on either side of us. The woman, a tall, thin, elegant lady-of-the-manor type, peels Sharon off Ginny and holds her tight, whispering, "There, there." The man, also tall with sharp cheekbones and a white goatee, balances his martini while removing a handkerchief from his shirt pocket and handing it to Sharon.

Is she okay? Ginny mouths.

"She's still upset over Cynthia," the man says in a deep voice. He has a small black mole on his earlobe that concerns me. Then I notice it's a stud earring, which concerns me even more.

"We were having a tiny wake," the woman says, still cradling Sharon. "You know how close we all were."

Ginny doesn't respond to this with her usual bestowal of blessings. Instead, she stands there awkwardly trying to figure out whether to make introductions or a quick exit.

"You should dab that with cold water," I suggest, pointing at the stain on Ginny's shoulder.

"Alfonse, will you take Sharon back to her apartment?" the woman asks, swapping Sharon for the man's martini. "And pick up some more ice while you're at it."

Alfonse takes off down the hallway almost dragging Sharon alongside him, her bare feet bent at the ankles.

"You ladies care for a drink?"

"Thanks, Barbara, but we're busy," Ginny says. "This is my friend, Poppy."

"Nice to meet you, Poppy," she says. "Sorry, for all that. We don't usually have our nervous breakdowns until we see the dinner menu."

I look at Barbara's martini a little enviously. It's been awhile since I had a cocktail and hers looks delicious with its thin ice floes and stuffed olives. "Well, it must be a hard time for everyone," I say. "Such a tragedy."

"She left on her own terms," Barbara says. "I admire her courage."

I want to ask her for more details, but Ginny pulls me toward her door.

Once we're inside, she breathes out a sigh of relief. Ginny's apartment is bright and sunny, framed by a wall of windows on the east side that look out across the city and surrounding mountains. The living room is spacious, decorated in sagy greens and soft beige. Flowers in vases sit atop every table and I instinctively reach out to touch a sunflower to see if it's real, knowing from the scent that it's unnecessary to do so. Ginny ushers me over to the couch in the living room and brings me a glass of wine without asking. I notice she's poured herself a healthy glass of chardonnay as well.

"Nice neighbors," I say.

"Not really," Ginny says. "Barbara's kind of the mean girl on my block. She's always pleasant when we run into each other, but then she'll organize these parties and not invite me."

"What about Alfonsc?" I ask.

"That's her boyfriend. They met on Senior Moments."

"Really?" I say.

Ginny nods. "He moved to Xanadu after things got serious. Now they rule the school, as we used to say."

"Sounds like eighth grade all over again."

"Sometimes it feels that way," Ginny says, taking a sip. "You'd think we'd grow out of wanting to be liked."

"I have," I say.

"You're stronger than me," she says. "How do you do it?"

"You don't take shit from anyone. After we get even with Max, we'll work on your bitchy neighbor." *And your boyfriend*, I think.

Ginny stares at her glass, looking for her future in its crystal ball. "What did you have in mind?"

16

May 17

The next day, I take the bus to Ginny's in the morning so we can continue to plot our revenge. I tell Meg that I'm running some errands and will meet her at the gym. She barely acknowledges my change in routine and continues to swipe left and right on her phone. I'm sure she'll berate me later for not telling her about the change in plans and wonder aloud if I should see a neurologist.

Ginny and I work on the ankle weight all morning. It takes much longer than I anticipated, mostly because Ginny wants to back out of the plan. She really isn't cut out for this kind of sabotage and second-guesses all my ideas. What Ginny lacks in motivation, she more than makes up in craftsmanship, which is not surprising given her years as a kindergarten teacher. After refilling the ankle weight pouch, she stitches it up with just enough thread to hold the seam in place until we need it to rupture.

Before we leave, I open Ginny's sliding glass doors and step out onto her balcony. The space is long and narrow, with more than enough room for two patio chairs, an end table, and a small garden of potted plants. I walk up to the railing and place my hands on the cold metal. Even if this bar came loose, there's nearly four feet of concrete preventing someone from tipping over. I don't see how Cynthia's fall could be an accident, which means she either climbed over the barrier or she was thrown. I'm not ready to rule out the idea that someone pushed her. This place may have security guards and cameras, but that wouldn't keep out someone disguised as a nurse or electrician. For God's sake, didn't Ginny say Craig had led some fitness workshops here? If they let a guy like that in, why wouldn't they admit someone dressed as a UPS driver? Once you're past reception, it's just a few steps to get to an empty stairwell.

"We should go now or we're going to be late," Ginny says from inside.

By the time we're back in Ginny's car, there's only thirty minutes to get to the gym. If we don't arrive in the locker room before Max, none of our work will pay off. I make Ginny drive two miles over the speed limit because I'm so nervous.

Ginny pulls into the YMCA's parking lot while I scan the area for Max's car. It's not here. We rush inside and change in the locker room. By this point, Ginny's a mess and I'm about to slap her across the face to help her pull herself together. "I can't do it," she whispers when we're standing in front of our lockers.

"All you need to do is distract her for thirty seconds," I say. "I'll take care of everything else."

By the time Max enters, Ginny is sweating like she's already done a full cardio workout. She stands there, frozen in panic as Max opens her locker and starts changing into her suit. I have to literally push her toward Max to get her moving. "Max, dear," Ginny says. "Would you mind looking at a mole on my back?"

Max pulls up the straps of her swimsuit and says, "I am not a doctor," without turning around.

"You're not?" Ginny says. "I thought . . . well, you're so knowledgeable about so many things. I thought . . . I mean . . . Poppy looked at it and swears it's cancer . . . I just wanted a second opinion."

"You should go to a doctor for that," she says.

"Jesus, Max. Would it kill you to do her this simple favor?" I say.

I kick myself for jumping in but it bugs me that Max is being so stubborn. I mean, I know there's no mole and that we've staged this whole "medical emergency" as a way to distract her, but Max doesn't know that. She should look at the fucking mole!

Max sighs and walks with Ginny around the corner to the more brightly lit shower area. As soon as they turn the corner, I grab one of Max's ankle weights and replace it with the one I bought. I throw Max's into my locker and slam the door just as the two of them come back into the room.

"That's such a relief," Ginny is saying. "Thank you."

Max puts on her swimming gear and then straps on the ankle weights. My heart's pounding as I wait for her to notice the difference, but her goggles and noseclip have deprived her of the two senses she'd need to notice our switcheroo. When she grabs her hand weights and marches out to the pool deck, Ginny and I collapse on the wooden bench in front of the lockers.

"I think I'm going to be sick," Ginny says.

"It's all over," I say. "Let's go to class."

Lina returns full of apologies for missing class. Her cat was hit by a car and had to be rushed to the hospital. Thankfully, Conan O'Brien is going to make it, for which we all express gratitude.

Max is disappointed to see Lina standing in front of us again. Her brief stint of being in control must have stoked a fire in her that had long been doused. She sits on the bench and straps on her weights with exaggerated vigor. Hopefully, this will be the last time we have to put up with her superior attitude.

I look over at Ginny, who's staring straight ahead, like she's just spotted a fin circling in the water.

Max takes up her position in front of us, as usual. Her slick black helmet head a bobbing submarine missile waiting to be detonated. She turns around and says to the ladies lined up behind her, "You can follow me if you want a better workout."

Lina presses play on her boom box and the room fills with Billy Joel's "Uptown Girl," a slight improvement from her swing era soundtrack from previous classes. She begins with a warm-up that has us do some arm crosses and gentle leg lifts. Ginny and I follow the routine, keeping an eye on the water in front of us.

When Lina moves onto leg lifts, we know the time has come. I look at Ginny, who's whimpering like a sad puppy. I try to frighten her into silence with a cold stare but it only makes things worse. She starts to moan, which draws the attention of the Chinese ladies to our left. I try to telepathically split the seam of Max's ankle weight so that it releases the hidden treasure inside. But the seam doesn't need my mental powers to do its work. All it needs is Max's vigorous kicking. The more she lifts and kicks, the murkier the water around her becomes.

When the water tints a light brown, I release a startled cry and say loud enough for everyone to hear, "Max, dear. Are you okay?"

Lina stops her leg lifting and peers into the darkening water behind Max, who hasn't yet broken stride. "Oh my goodness," she says. Two small, brown lumps float up to the surface of the pool. "Everyone out of the pool!" she yells. "Now!"

There's a mad scramble to evacuate. Max is the only one who stays still, unclear about why everyone is panicking. When she turns around and sees the floating turd, she grunts and bats it away, which only hastens its dissolution into water. She swims to the edge and pulls herself out with the help of Lina.

After the lifeguards get everyone to safety, we all stand around and gaze at the floating cloud of chocolate frosting we froze and packed into Max's ankle weights. It's now become part of our pool's ecosystem. There's a mad scramble for showers. While we're waiting our turn, Lina comes in and touches Max gently on the shoulder.

"It's nothing to be ashamed of," she says, clearly relishing shaming her least favorite student in front of everyone. "It happens to everyone at a certain age."

17

May 17

I thought I'd take great pleasure in watching Max defend herself against the charge of incontinence, but she's strangely silent as she waits in line for the shower, not making eye contact with anyone who might cast a look of pity her way. We'd broken her but for some reason this doesn't feel like the victory I thought it would be. All we've done is turn our victimizer into a victim.

Ginny and I leave the shower and join Max and the others in the locker room, which is quiet as a doctor's waiting room. I turn to get dressed and all I hear is Max zipping up her tracksuit. Just as I pull up my sweatpants, I feel a bony claw grip me on the shoulder.

"I know it was you," Max whispers in my ear.

I freeze, not wanting to turn, knowing my guilt will be written all over my face. Of course, not turning around is also a confession, but it's an easier one to make than looking my victim in the eye. There's a reason the church builds those booths with the screen separating the priest from the sinner. I lean into my locker as far as I can, hoping it will shield me from the blows I'm about to receive from one of Max's dumbbells. But nothing happens. I turn around and she's gone. Ginny stands there, eyes bulging, clutching her purse like she's a witness to a mugging.

18

May 17

I tell Meg I'm going out to lunch with Ginny, which does not go over well. She tears out of the parking lot blasting some song about everybody working for the weekend.

Part of me wonders if my daughter's a little jealous that I've made a friend and all she has is Mr. Mustache. Did his BM tank top plant the seed for my scheme to get rid of Max? I wonder. Now that it's blown up in our faces, it gives me one more reason to dislike him.

"We have to apologize," Ginny says, as we sit in her parked car.

"Or—and hear me out—we could just move to another state."

"I can't live with the guilt."

"Max was awful. She got what was coming to her." The words make me sound like one of those single middle-aged women Disney cartoons used to villainize. "We could get in a lot of trouble. They're going to have to drain that pool and probably sterilize it."

Ginny groans. "What if we said we were confused? I've got early onset dementia."

"You do?" I ask.

"No, but I could say I do."

"No one would believe you. What we did required careful planning and execution. It was pretty flawless if I do say so myself."

"I can't believe we pulled it off, actually," Ginny says with a sly smile. "But that's not the point. The point is we did something cruel and we need to atone for it."

"Fine," I say.

Just then Max emerges through the gym's front door, pushing her husband in his wheelchair. Ginny and I duck down so she can't see us. We watch as Max helps her husband into the passenger seat of her SUV, folds and places his wheelchair in the back, and then hops in the driver's seat. She really is in enviously good shape, and I hate that I admire her.

"Let's follow her," I say, eager to flee the scene of the crime. "If we're going to apologize, it should be at her home."

Ginny nods and starts her car.

Ginny needs constant reminding that following someone does not mean attaching yourself to their bumper.

"You're supposed to stay invisible," I say. "We don't want her seeing us in her rearview mirror."

"Who looks in their rearview mirror?"

"People who don't get in accidents."

"I haven't gotten in an accident in years," Ginny says, which I believe. She drives like every street has a school with blind children playing outside. Luckily, Max is also a slow driver so it's easy to track her.

We drive for about fifteen minutes until Max pulls into the garage of a single-story cottage home with a white picket fence surrounding a manicured lawn and impressive garden. It's not hard to imagine

Max beating this patch of land into shape. Every blade of grass is standing at attention and her hydrangeas burst with red and blue flowers.

Ginny parks across the street but doesn't turn off the car because we still need the air-conditioning to think.

"We should have picked up a gift."

"What gift says, 'I'm sorry I told people you shit in the pool'?"

Ginny actually thinks about this one. "A nice chardonnay, maybe?"

"Let's get this over with," I say, opening the passenger door and marching across the street. I wait on the doorstep for Ginny before ringing the bell. Max has one of those doormats that welcomes you with its tough, resilient fibers.

We wait for a minute before Max answers the door. If she's surprised to see us, she doesn't show it.

"We're here to apologize," I say, getting right to the point. The faster we rip off this Band-Aid, the better.

Max narrows her eyes and stares at us with a look of hatred normally reserved for people who cut in line at the supermarket. I wait for her to slam the door in our faces but she doesn't move. I wonder suddenly if she's a robot, unable to process complex human emotions. That would explain her ability to plank at least.

"We feel so bad," Ginny says, wiping a tear away with the back of her hand. I'm lucky she's here with me. Her sincerity warms my cold delivery and makes it a bit more palatable.

"Come in," Max says, stepping aside and ushering us in.

Glancing at Ginny, I see she's torn between wanting to be polite and wanting to live another day. I don't see any way out of accepting Max's invitation, so I take a step forward. Before I walk through the open door,

I step aside to let Ginny enter ahead of me, just in case Max has a pair of hungry Dobermans waiting.

Max's house is as clean and well organized as her garden. In the foyer, Max asks us to remove our shoes, which we do. We place them with other sneakers under the coatrack, making sure to line them up in the neat row that's already established. Past the foyer is a comfy living room lined with bookshelves and landscapes painted in thick acrylic. Decorative throw pillows are carefully arranged on the tan sofa. On the coffee table is a book on some architect I've never heard of.

Max escorts us down the hardwood hallway to the kitchen in the back. The room is bright from all the windows that look out on the back garden. Ginny and I squeeze into a corner, unsure if we're being invited to sit down at the wooden table nestled in a nook with cushioned benches on either side. My backside bumps up against a counter that has a bowl of fruit, none of which is browning or shriveled.

"We don't want to intrude," Ginny says. "We just feel so bad."

Max pulls out a long blade from her knife block and approaches us. This is it, I tell myself. She's going to chop us up and compost us for those hydrangeas out front. She leans toward us and grabs a lemon from the bowl behind me. I breathe a sigh of relief as she walks it back to the cutting board and slices it down the middle with a dramatic chop. Then she opens the refrigerator door and pours herself a tall glass of iced tea.

"I'm curious," she says. "What is it you feel bad about?" She squeezes the lemon with her fist so that its juices drain into her glass. Sweet Jesus this woman is strong.

"You know," I say.

"I want to hear you say it," she says, taking a sip. Her steely calm unnerves me. If I were her, I'd be hurling cutlery at us right now.

"We were tired of you bullying us," I say.

"Is that what I was doing?" Max says. "Bullying you?"

"You said mean things to Ginny about her weight."

"I don't mind," Ginny says. "I need to lose a few pounds."

"And you took over the class, like it was your own. Which it's not. Not everyone wants to follow your exercise regimen, you know. We're happy with the way Lina runs the class."

Max nods, taking in my criticism like she's drinking a cool glass of water. "So you made it seem like I defecated in the pool," she says, finishing my story.

"It was Poppy's idea," Ginny says.

"Ginny!" I say.

"I'm sorry, but it was," Ginny says. "I went along with it, so I'm just as guilty."

"Maybe more so," Max says. "You knew what you were doing was wrong. I'm not so sure about this one." Max nods in my direction.

"You're right," Ginny says through tears. "I'm the worst!"

"I knew it was wrong," I say. "But I didn't care."

"Really?" Max says. "Why not?"

"Because I'm tired of being bossed around. My daughter bosses me around. My grandson bosses me around. The judge who took away my license bosses me around. People I don't even know tell me what I should eat, drink, or do just because I'm old. Well, I'm tired of it! When you started bossing me around, I couldn't take it anymore. I needed to strike back and since I don't have to live with you, you made a more convenient target."

Max takes a sip of iced tea. There's half a lemon in that glass and she doesn't even flinch at its sourness. "I can appreciate that," she says after some consideration. "Would either of you like some tea?"

Ginny accepts a glass to be polite. "Do you have any Sweet'N Low?" she asks.

"That stuff will kill you," Max says.

"For fuck's sake," I say, failing my attempt to match Max's composure. "You can't help yourself, can you?"

"Can't help myself doing what?" Max asks.

"Lecturing people," I say. "Talking down to them. All you have to say is 'No, I don't have any Sweet'N Low. Sorry.' That's it."

"No, I don't have any Sweet'N Low. Sorry," Max says. She looks at me to see if she's gotten it right, which only makes me feel like more of an asshole. Who am I to berate this woman after what I did to her? And why isn't she getting mad like me? Could it be that she's as desperate for companionship as Ginny and I? Are we the only guests she's had in her neat and tidy home? Who is she doing all this cleaning for if she doesn't have people coming over?

"Would you like some date syrup?" Max says. "It's a healthy alternative to refined sugar."

I try to refrain from rolling my eyes. Baby steps, I think. Baby steps.

Ginny accepts the date syrup and extols its restorative powers, which only encourages Max to place the bottle in her hands and tell her where she can get it, which is at a supermarket I've never heard of.

"I've decided what you two can do to make up for the damage you've done to my reputation."

"Have you?" I say. "Because I kind of thought this apology would be it."

"Unless you're ready to make a full confession to everyone at the gym, you've made it impossible for me to return there," Max says.

"I'll confess," Ginny states. "I'm sure they'll kick us out but we could find a new gym, right, Poppy?"

I look at Ginny. I know I recommended we do just that, but that was my dumb reptilian brain talking. "Meg," I say. "She needs this."

"Who's Meg?" Max asks.

"My daughter," I say. "She's in recovery. Again. The doctors think exercise will help keep her sober. The only reason I go to the YMCA is so she'll go. If I change gyms, I'm not sure she'll follow. Plus, I don't know if we can afford it."

"My husband's physical therapy is there too," Max says. "So I cannot leave. Which puts us in a difficult position."

"Isn't there anything we can do?" Ginny asks.

"There is," Max says. "You will join my walking club."

"You have a walking club?" I ask.

"I do now."

19

May 18

The first day of walking club requires a bit of subterfuge on my part. I have to pretend that I'm still going to water aerobics to get Meg to go to the gym. She suits up at home as usual. I notice she's spending more time in front of the mirror getting ready and wonder if things are heating up between her and Mr. Mustache. I'm pretty sure romantic relationships are discouraged while you're in recovery but I don't feel like it's my place to say anything.

When we arrive at the Y, Meg and I part ways at the entrance to the locker room. After she's gone to the weight room, I duck out and meet Ginny and Max around the corner. Max is already leading Ginny through some light stretching. Max is dressed in her light blue tracksuit and fanny pack. Ginny has paired a white button-down and cardigan with black tights. Her sneakers are pink and look brand new.

"I didn't bring my walking sticks," I say. "So no off-roading."

"I have to be back in an hour to pick up Harold," Max says.

"We're walking *for an hour*?" Ginny says, already breaking into a sweat.

"I've mapped out a forty-minute walk around the neighborhood," Max says. "Easy and flat for the most part."

"I told you she was going to kill us," I say to Ginny. "She just wants to make it look like an accident."

Max takes the lead and we set off at a brisk pace. I'd never tell Max this, but she does a good job keeping us on quieter, tree-lined streets that provide shade from the early morning sun. At one point, we cut through the middle of a public park where small children play with their mothers and nannies. Sometimes I forget what a nice town this is. I've lived here my entire adult life, but I've been such a recluse lately, I haven't noticed all the improvements that have sprung up around me. Have I been gentrified? I wonder. Is this why Meg keeps telling me I'm sitting on a gold mine? Everything seems better maintained than I remember. The lawns are greener, the park cleaner, more people are on bikes, and everyone has either a baby or a dog. Everything is blooming in the warmth of early summer, turning our walk into a kaleidoscope of colors.

Ginny and I don't talk much because we're working hard to keep up with Max, who's barely breaking a sweat. At one point, we beg for a water break, which Max allows, although she sets a timer for five minutes.

"How do you feel?" Max asks.

Ginny gives a thumbs-up while guzzling her water. Max eyes her plastic bottle and I know she wants to say something about Ginny single-handedly destroying the planet, but she refrains. Maybe she's not as annoying as I thought. I'm too quick to judge people. I need to give them time to reveal their multifaceted personalities.

"You really should get a reusable bottle," Max says after a minute.

Forget what I just said. I'm an insanely good judge of character.

Break time ends and we continue on our journey. I spend the rest of our walk wondering what Max gets out of punishing us this way. She could have just told Lina about our trick and gotten us kicked out of the class and the gym. It would have restored her reputation and sent us into exile forever. But instead, she chose to spend *more* time with us and despite what I said earlier, I don't think she wants to trigger a heart attack. I think she may actually like us, which is just mind-boggling. I mean, I can understand her liking Ginny. She is sweetness personified. But me? That's the real mystery. What could she see in an old, vindictive bitch like me? My own daughter doesn't even like me. But maybe Max is an old, vindictive bitch too. Maybe part of her respects what we did to her in the pool. As awful as the prank was, it was a little mischievous and mean, which are not adjectives most people associate with the elderly. We're supposed to be kind and wise, gentle and caring, despite the fact that we're speeding toward a cataclysmic end of our existence.

I guess it doesn't matter if Max likes us or is playing a long con where she builds trust only to walk us off a cliff; she's an interesting person to be with for an hour a day. I can tolerate people who don't pretend to be something they're not. Both Max and Ginny are authentically themselves. The question is, why are they tolerating me? I'm not nice, like Ginny, or capable like Max. I've failed at most things in my life and am probably a depressed misanthrope. Who would want to spend forty minutes walking with someone like that?

20

May 19

The following day, we walk the same route. I don't know if we're getting in better shape or we're just familiar with the path, but Ginny and I manage to keep pace with Max, even while we talk about our sleep patterns. Max sleeps in two-hour intervals, timed to when her husband needs to get up to use the bathroom. Ginny gets a solid seven hours plus a nap after lunch. I'm the only one who uses nighttime cold medicine to put me down.

"I don't need you to tell me it's bad, Max," I say preemptively. "I know it's bad and I don't care."

Max suggests a list of herbal remedies anyway.

"What is Harold's condition, if you don't mind me asking?" I shift the focus away from my health care and onto Max's husband's.

"He's old," Max says. "That's his condition."

"I mean, why does he need a physical therapist?" I ask.

"He falls a lot," Max says. "The doctor thinks it's a cognitive issue."

"Then why not cognitive therapy?" Ginny asks.

"He does that too," Max says. "You can't improve in one without the other. Healthy mind, healthy body."

"What would you count as improvement?" I ask.

"I'd be happy if he could make it to the toilet without my help," Max says.

It's hard to argue with having this as an end-of-life goal.

"I don't see my daughter walking me to the toilet in the middle of the night," I say.

"Come live in Xanadu!" Ginny says, her enthusiasm creating a bounce in her step.

"Can't afford it," I say. *Plus, the murders*, I think but don't say.

"You could if you sold your house," Max says.

"I can't do that to Meg and Jeremy," I say. "I doubt either of them could rent in this area on their salaries."

"What do they do?" Ginny asks.

"I don't really know." Gone are the days when jobs were simple and easy to define—doctor, lawyer, teacher. "Meg has her own business where she curates picnic baskets."

"That's a business?" Max asks.

I shrug. "It's like catering but for couples. She's actually pretty talented. I'll show you her Instagram later."

"And Jeremy?" Ginny asks.

"All I know is he's on his computer all day," I say. "He could be selling body parts on the dark web for all I know. Honestly, I expect the FBI to come knocking on my door every minute of the day. You have kids, Max?"

"We have three. My two girls live in Germany with their families and my son is in Spain. He and his partner just retired and bought a vineyard in Almería."

Of course they did, I think. It bothers me that Max can show off without even trying. I make a mental note never to ask her a question ever again. Something as simple as "Do you like cupcakes?" will probably result in her answering, "Not since I won *The Great British Bake Off*."

"Ginny has a boyfriend," I say to switch topics. It feels a little gossipy, even though I'm saying it in front of her. She slaps my shoulder playfully, like I'm revealing a big secret, but I can tell she's secretly pleased to have this information out there. I am, too, although not for the same reasons as Ginny. I want to see if Max smells a rat.

"What's his name?" Max asks.

"Cristóbal Rios," she says. "He runs a Cuban restaurant in Florida."

"They met online," I say. "What's the site called?"

"Senior Moments," Ginny says.

"Good for you," Max says. I wonder if she'll leave it at that but of course she can't. "Have you been on an actual date?"

"We go on lots of dates."

"I mean a date in the traditional sense. Where he picks you up in his car, takes you to dinner, picks up the check, that kind of thing."

"Well, no."

"He lives in Florida, Max," I remind her.

"Why don't you fly out and see him?" Max asks.

"I'm not ready," Ginny says, her already pink cheeks blushing red.

"But you say he's your boyfriend."

"He is. It's my first long-distance relationship."

"That is not a relationship."

"Try phrasing your statements in the form of a question, Max," I say, trying to smooth her delivery. I feel like a sculptor chiseling a chunk of granite.

"Like on *Jeopardy!*?" Max says.

"Exactly," I say. "Instead of saying, 'That is not a relationship,' you can say something like, 'What's online dating like anyway?'"

"What's online dating like anyway?" Max says. I give her a friendly nod, which she barely acknowledges.

"It's nice," Ginny says. "There's none of the pressure to look good, which is a relief because I still need to lose ten pounds. Plus, I can really think about what I'm going to say before I say it so I don't make a fool of myself."

"I wish all of life was like that," I say. "It would be nice to have the time to create a better response to assholes. The other day, a woman brought her dog into the supermarket and I wanted to say the perfect thing to shame her in front of the other shoppers."

"What did you say?" Max asks.

"Nothing! I carried that resentment around with me all day. If I had confronted her with the perfect insult, I would have been much happier."

"You could just cite the city ordinance that prohibits animals in places that sell food," Max offers.

"Yes, but that's not as funny."

"Do you want to be funny or effective?" Max asks.

"Can't I be both?"

"You spend too much time trying to hurt people," Max says. "All you do is hurt yourself."

There she goes again, I think, and open my mouth to fire back. Why did I think this woman could change at her age? How capable are any of us of changing, really? After eighty years on this planet your reward should be that you don't have to worry about improving yourself anymore. Clearly, your flawed personality has gotten you this far. Something must be working.

I wouldn't say Max is wrong though. My reactive behavior has only hurt myself. If I can do water aerobics and walk two miles a day, maybe I can shut my pie hole every once in a while. I have to think of silence as a yoga pose, only for my mouth.

I try to do it and it works.

"I'm sorry," Max says, slowing her pace to come alongside with me. "I agree with you. I too would like to have more time to craft my thoughts into words."

"Thank you," I say, and I smile, which feels weird.

"Ginny, may I see a photo of your boyfriend?" Max asks.

"No dick pics, please," I say.

"I would never!" Ginny says. She fumbles with her phone until she lands on the image she showed me the other day.

Max says nothing, which means she's got a whole lot of opinions she's keeping to herself.

"I understand why the younger generation dates this way," I say. "It's so much easier than when we were young, where you had to do everything face-to-face. Do you remember the first time you were naked in front of your husband? I was so shy, I hid under the covers."

"Me too," Ginny says. "For two years!"

"The Internet's changed everything."

"Not for the better," Max says, adding, "in my opinion."

We finish our walk in silence. When we get back to the gym, we separate—Ginny and I into the locker rooms and Max to pick up her husband. Ginny and I don't really need to change, but I need Meg to think I'm still doing water aerobics, which requires me to emerge from the locker area freshly showered. Ginny is nice enough to go along with my ruse and shower too so Meg doesn't get suspicious.

When we return to the lobby, Meg is busy flirting with Craig. I tell Ginny she doesn't have to wait and she leaves. After she's gone, Max exits the elevator down the hall pushing Harold. When she passes, she asks if I wouldn't mind accompanying her out to the parking lot. I know she doesn't need my help getting her husband into the car, so I figure she has something important to say. I tell Meg I'll be right back and follow Max out the door.

Sure enough, as soon as Max has Harold buckled in, she turns to me and says, "I don't think Ginny's boyfriend is real."

"Because he looks like Ricardo Montalbán?"

"I think she's getting scammed."

"I do too. There's something funny happening at her retirement home," I say. "Did you read about the woman thrown off her balcony?"

"I read about the woman who *fell* off her balcony," Max corrects.

I explain to Max how it's impossible to fall over a four-foot barrier and it's incredibly satisfying.

"So, you're saying someone she met online murdered her?" she says. "Why?"

"I don't know. Maybe she was dating a serial killer?"

Max shakes her head. "The news didn't mention any sign of a struggle."

She's right. Even Max couldn't deadlift a hundred-pound woman over a four-foot railing without someone hearing it, unless Cynthia lived on the deaf floor, which seems unlikely.

"Still, you're right to be concerned," Max says. "Whoever sent Ginny that photo is grooming her."

"Like a pedophile? Bit late for that, I think."

"I was suspicious when she told his name was Cristóbal Rios. That's the name of a character on *Star Trek: Picard*."

"How do you know that?"

"Harold and I are big fans."

"You and Harold are Trekkies?"

"We don't go to conventions, but yes."

I try to envision Max dressed up as a Vulcan and the image is surprisingly not difficult to conjure.

"Ricardo Montalbán was in a *Star Trek* movie, wasn't he?"

"He was Khan, yes," Max says. "But that wasn't him. Just someone who looks like him."

"What should we do?"

"You should say something," Max says. "Make sure she doesn't share any personal information—date of birth, social security number. Things like that."

"You want me to destroy the fantasy," I say, stuck on the image of Ricardo Montalbán welcoming Ginny as she disembarks *da plane, da plane.* Max wants me to be the hurricane that evacuates everyone off the island.

"I want you to keep her from getting swindled," she says.

"Why don't you do it?"

"You know as well as I do that she won't listen to me."

She's right. If Max says something, Ginny will be polite but she'll treat her concerns like all of Max's unwelcome advice—as something to acknowledge but ignore. Max warning her off Cristóbal would be like my doctor warning me off salt. I know he's right, but there's no way I'm eliminating that staple from my diet.

"She seems pretty smitten. It's going to be hard to make her break up with him."

"It will be easier after he steals all her money. You want to wait for that to happen?"

She has me there. "Okay, I'll do it," I say, and walk back into the gym.

21

May 19

I interrupt some hilarity between Meg and Craig. (Oh my, I just heard what a ridiculous couple name they have! This should be enough for them never to see each other again.) They both look at me like I'm some prim schoolteacher separating them at a high school dance. "Make room for Jesus," the nuns always said when I was a teen, which somehow made slow dancing feel even dirtier. Like I had just invited the Son of God into a three-way.

"Craig's taking me out to lunch," Meg says.

"Is that okay with you, Mrs. Montgomery?" he asks with mock formality. He's wearing his usual BM tank top, which reminds me to pick up some prune juice next time I'm at Walgreens.

"We'll drop you off first," Meg says. "Unless you want to take the bus."

I tell them I do not and follow them out to the car.

"Do you mind sitting in the back, Mom?" Meg asks, opening the door for me.

I most certainly do mind, but don't say anything. This is my car, after all. Why should Craig get preferential treatment? He's only a few inches taller than me and better at leg squats. I open the window and try not to think of his sweaty body rubbing up against my car's interior.

"Do you take fish oil, Poppy?" Craig asks as we pull out of the parking lot.

I debate opening the car door and hurling myself out onto the concrete. Scrapes and bruises couldn't be as painful as listening to Craig's sales pitch.

"Fish oil is the best source for omega-3 fatty acids," he says. "For the brain." He taps his forehead in case I've forgotten where the brain is located.

"There's nothing wrong with my brain," I say.

"It's also good for depression."

"But I don't want depression."

"To cure it. Not cause it."

"Are you by any chance selling this amazing elixir?" I say, pointing to his T-shirt.

"It's one of many vitamin supplements I sell. If you want, I can give you some samples."

"Thank you, but no. I've got no interest in prolonging my life. In fact, I think I'm ready to try some of the bad stuff." I pause. "Like heroin. Got any samples of that?"

Craig does not like having his sales pitch derailed like this. His eyes squint and his mouth twitches. He runs his tiny hand over his facial hair, the modern equivalent of a campy villain twirling the ends of his mustache.

"That's not a nice thing to say to someone in recovery, ma'am," he says.

"I'm sorry," I say, less worried I've caused offense than I am of him murdering me. Craig has no sense of humor. The only time I see him smile is when Meg is making fun of me. Those are the only jokes he seems comfortable around. Anything else is a potential blow to his ego.

The two of them ignore me the entire ride home while they go on about how "fucked up" everything is. The gym equipment is "fucked up." This protein bar is "fucked up." That Tesla passing us is "fucked up."

"I had this client the other day who demanded vegan cookies," Meg said.

"That's fucked up," Craig says.

"Tell me about it. I had to go to Whole Foods to pick them up."

"Fuck Whole Foods," Craig says.

"They're fucked up."

And on and on it goes. As usual, I listen to this conversation and wonder how much of it I'm responsible for. It's not like I swore like a sailor while raising Meg, although she certainly gave me cause to curse a blue streak. It's the attitude behind the swearing that bothers me. The feeling that the world is a horrible place and it's our job to point out all its flaws to people. I've done that my whole life and I'm sure that bleak worldview infected my daughter's outlook. Every setback she's experienced is never her fault. Someone or something else has screwed her over. It wasn't until she started parroting me that I heard how miserable I'd become. But by then, it was too late.

"Whoa," Craig says when we pull up in front of my house. "Nice place."

I don't know why he'd say that. The house is in terrible shape. But maybe he's talking about one of the other homes on my block. After my neighbors moved to retirement communities in cheaper states, the street has come back to life like a restored painting. The houses on either side of me have fresh coats of paints, landscaping, and fancier cars. Meg is always begging me to put some money into a remodel before we become the Boo Radley house of the neighborhood. I don't think she remembers that Boo Radley stabbed one of his parents with a pair of scissors.

I get out of the car and walk to the front door, hoping I'm not followed by Meg and Craig. But of course they do. Craig insists, despite Meg's objections. I'm sure she doesn't want him to see what's inside, namely her son. Has she told him about our own Boo Radley? I wonder. Most likely, he won't make an appearance and Meg can pretend I'm her only living relative. That would probably suit Craig just fine, I think.

Craig gets an abbreviated tour of our two-bedroom Craftsman bungalow. He's got an annoying habit of whistling when he sees something he likes. He whistles when he sees Meg's wedding photo in the living room (she looks so pretty in that photo. So full of joy and optimism). He whistles when he sees my antique writing desk (a gift from my grandmother). He whistles when he sees the ham I'm defrosting on the counter for dinner tonight. When Jeremy enters the kitchen from the basement door, he does not whistle but lets out a low grunt.

"Whassup, man," he says, thrusting out his fist. Jeremy looks like this stranger has been brought in to punch him.

"Jeremy, this is my friend Craig," Meg says.

Jeremy taps his fist against Craig's and then looks back at the doorway he's just emerged from, hoping he can turn around and return to his basement lair until his mom's "friend" has left the premises.

"They keep you chained up down there?" Craig asks, peering down the open doorway. The light from Jeremy's computer monitors (he has two running all the time) casts an eerie glow. Looking into our basement is like staring down into the mouth of an active volcano.

"We should go," Meg says.

Craig walks over to the back door and casts a glance at our backyard, which is a weedy patch of lawn that no one maintains or even looks at anymore. The last time I was back there was to remove a crow that had fallen from the sky. It literally dropped dead. If that's not an omen of bad luck, I don't know what is.

Meg and Craig leave for their lunch date and Jeremy and I both sink into seats at the kitchen table.

"She's not supposed to date during recovery," he says.

"I know," I say.

"She's especially not supposed to date losers using Hulk Hogan as their fashion guru."

"I thought the gym would help keep her active. You know what they say about endorphins."

"You should remind her to see her sponsor."

"Why is it my job to tell her what to do?"

"You're her mother. That's literally your job."

I don't have any other comeback except to shake my head. How did I get put in charge of everybody's well-being? First Ginny and now Meg? Who's looking out for me? Who's trying to lift my burdens? They're too heavy even for steroidal Craig to bench-press.

"Jeremy, I want you to do me a favor," I ask.

He looks down at his feet, which are covered in a pair of extra thick socks. These were a Christmas gift I gave him to encourage some outdoor exploring. Now, they're covered in dust and thinning at the heel from Jeremy wearing them as house slippers.

"I want you to create a profile for me on Senior Moments," I say.

"You want to start dating too?" he asks. It's like I've punched him in the gut. He slumps in his chair and crosses his long, bony arms around his middle. I'm not sure if I should be flattered or offended by his reaction to my request. Does Jeremy really depend on me that much? Maybe he's worried that I'll follow in his mother's footsteps and bring home a bunch of losers who'll want to evict him.

"No," I say, placing a hand on his shoulder. "I want to see if I can seduce my friend's boyfriend."

22

May 19

Jeremy's much more enthusiastic about helping me when he learns I want to break up a relationship rather than start one. To be clear, I don't want to steal Ginny's boyfriend; I just want to be sure he isn't stringing her along, making her fall in love with him so he can blackmail her and then throw her off a balcony. My intentions are honorable. If I can show her Cristóbal's flirting with me, it will be much easier to convince Ginny to break up with him.

Jeremy and I decide the best approach is to create a fake profile, rather than post any of my real information. He suggests I use a porn star name, which we create by combining the name of my first pet with the name of the street I grew up on: Stella LaFayette. While he creates her profile, I go into Meg's closet to create my disguise. Her room is small like mine and crammed with furniture. There's a four-poster bed, bureau, and exercise bike in the small 15' × 15' space. Unlike Jeremy, she's done her best to fill the room with color. The bed is covered in decorative pillows and throw blankets. The paint on the walls is a dark plum, which contrasts nicely with the beige bedspread and curtains. Under the window are four Amazon boxes, new purchases that make me question if Meg's shopping addiction is under control.

I grab the loudest print I can find—a billowy button-down with a pattern of tropical flowers—and throw it on. Then I reach up and pull down the hatbox that contains the wigs Meg has worn over the years. There's a white blond bob that's perfect. Before I leave, I grab a pair of cat eye reading glasses off her bureau and head to the basement door.

"'Alright, Mr. DeMille, I'm ready for my close-up,'" I say, and start descending the stairs à la Norma Desmond in the final shot of *Sunset Boulevard*. Jeremy looks at me like I've finally sunken into full-blown dementia.

I tone down the act so Jeremy can snap a photo that doesn't make me look insane. I'm trying to attract suitors, not repel them, he reminds me. I look at the uploaded photo and don't recognize myself, which is a good thing for undercover work. I must say it's nice to shed my old skin and become someone new. Jeremy turns me into a woman from Boca Raton with interests in reading, yoga, and horse breeding. We feel like that's the right combination of hobbies to make it hard to pinpoint any political affiliation.

"Ready?" he says, once the profile's complete.

I nod and we make our debut on the site.

"Now what?" I ask.

Jeremy types on his keyboard and Cristóbal's profile pops up. I see the same photo I confused with Ricardo Montalbán's headshot and read his info.

"Let's send him a message," I say.

Jeremy clicks on the envelope icon and a text box appears. "What do you want to say?" he asks, ready to take dictation.

"Uh . . ." It's been so long since I've flirted with anyone, I've forgotten the language one uses in situations like this. Plus, it's hard playing Cyrano to Jeremy's Christian. Maybe if Ginny or Max were sitting at the keyboard, it would be easier to feed them the words to use for a seduction. I don't want to embarrass myself by sounding pervy in front of my grandson.

Jeremy grows impatient with my stammering and starts typing while I look over his shoulder.

Hello there, handsome. I saw your profile and think you're the cat's meow. Do you love walks on the beach? Because I do. Let's take a stroll into the sunset soon. Love, Stella.

"How's that?" Jeremy asks, finger poised above the send button.

"Delete that right now," I say. "First off, no one my age uses the term 'cat's meow.' When do you think I last dated? The Jazz Age? Also, no old person loves walking on the beach. You might as well ask if he wants to bounce on my trampoline. And 'strolling into the sunset' sounds like I want him to join me in a suicide pact."

"Fine," Jeremy says, bristling at my criticism. "What do you want to say?"

"Uh, how about . . . Dear Cristóbal . . . So nice to find a fellow Floridian on this site. I'd love to drive down and see your restaurant. Care to meet up for a café con leche?"

I'm pretty impressed with my geography and Spanish skills, but Jeremy just shakes his head.

"You can't say that," he says. "If this guy's an imposter, he's not going to be interested in someone who wants to meet in person. We should probably change your location to some place in California."

Jeremy taps on his keyboard and moves me to Atherton.

"Okay, how about this . . ." I try again. "Dear Cristóbal . . . I love Cuban food . . . Can you send me your recipe for arroz con leche?"

"Is that really how old people flirt?" Jeremy asks.

"No, it's not," I say. I start pacing the room, trying to get into character. I'm Florida floozy Stella LaFayette, goddamn it! I try to impersonate the models I've seen on TV but my basement doesn't accommodate a runway walk. Before I've taken three steps, I'm up against a tower of cardboard boxes stacked against a concrete wall.

"'Hello, Cristóbal,'" I start again. "'Has anyone ever told you you look like Ricardo Montalbán? I had such a crush on him when I was younger. I bet you'd look great in his *Wrath of Khan* costume' . . ." I pause and tap Jeremy on the shoulder. "Add an 'LOL' or wink emoji after that," I direct, then continue. "'I'd love to get to know you better . . . If you're interested, write back' . . . yada yada yada . . . How's that?"

Jeremy types on his computer and adds to what I've dictated. "Just included some details about how you're in the middle of breeding season and can't leave California."

"Ooh, that's good," I say. "Add something flirty, like 'Why should the mares have all the fun.' Wink emoji."

"Ew," Jeremy says, scrunching up his face.

"Too slutty?" I ask.

Jeremy shrugs. "We're trying to lead this whore to water."

"You mean 'horse'?"

Jeremy pauses, considers what I just said, and nods. "That makes more sense," he says and hits send.

We're off to the races.

23

May 20

The next day, Ginny shows up wearing a sleek new Apple Watch. When Max and I comment on it, she says it was a gift from Cristóbal. "He wanted me to have something special," she says. "And encourage this physical fitness kick I'm on."

And monitor your location, I think but don't say.

"This is not a 'kick,'" Max says. "It's a health maintenance routine."

"Exactly," Ginny says. "This will help me track my data."

"How so?" I ask.

A pause. "Well, I haven't figured that out yet."

"I can show you," Max says. She flashes Ginny her wristwatch, which is bigger with more digital displays, like something you might find on an explosive device.

"That was nice of him to buy you a gift," I say, more to Max than Ginny. "Looks expensive."

Max grunts and then tries to disguise it as a cough, which doesn't fool anyone.

"He's sweet," Ginny says.

We walk in silence for a while after that. I was fully prepared to share with Ginny our concerns about her new relationship but after my conversation with Meg I'm not so sure. Meg didn't come back from her "lunch" until this morning when I was having my coffee. When I suggested she talk to her sponsor about her new relationship, she lit into me.

"It's not a relationship, Mom," she said, using air quotes around both *relationship* and *mom*.

"You see Craig every time we go to the gym."

"It's fine. I can handle it."

"Just call your sponsor. That's all I'm saying."

"Jesus, Mom. Can't you let me enjoy feeling good about things for a change? Why do you always want to fuck things up?"

I didn't say anything more after that.

Now, I'm wary of repeating the same conversation with Ginny. What's that saying? No good deed goes unpunished? Look at what we did to Max when she tried to help us get in better shape. We released a fake turd in the pool and told everyone it came from her.

But what's the alternative?

"A friend of mine just had her identity stolen," I say apropos of nothing. I think Ginny and Max were commenting on the dahlias we just passed.

"Oh no!" Ginny says. "The poor dear."

"What happened?" Max says.

"She told someone she met online her date of birth and social security number," I say. "That's all it took."

"Really?" Ginny says. "What's her name?"

"Who?"

"Your friend."

"Jennifer."

"Jennifer who?"

"Jennifer . . . Lopez," I say. Fuck, I was never good at thinking on my feet and I've only gotten worse since coming out the other end of menopause.

"Your friend's name is Jennifer Lopez," Ginny says.

"It is," I say. "She's not the singer though, if that's what you're wondering."

"That's not what I was wondering," Ginny says.

"Oh, Jesus, Poppy," Max says, shaking her head. "Ginny, we're worried your boyfriend is scamming you. You haven't given him any personal information, have you?"

"Would a fake boyfriend give me a watch like this?" Ginny says, holding up her wrist.

"Did he buy you that watch or did you buy it?" Max asks. "Because the band perfectly matches your walking shoes."

Ginny lowers her wrist and starts pumping her arms like she's pounding a drum, or our heads, in steady rhythmic fashion. "I bought it with money Cristóbal gave me," she says. "He's never asked me for anything, except my love."

Max and I share a glance.

"Why not use that money to go on a trip with Cristóbal?" Max asks. "Or visit him in Florida?"

"I want to lose ten pounds first."

"Does Cristóbal care about that?" I ask.

"No, he says I'm beautiful. It's something I want to do."

"We're just worried about you, Ginny," I say. "People take advantage of women our age."

"That is so sweet," Ginny says, laying a hand on my arm. "But trust me, I know what I'm doing. Cristóbal is planning to come visit me in the fall. He's opening a restaurant out here."

"That's great," I say.

"The second he asks you to be an investor, walk away," Max says.

"He's already got investors," Ginny says. "They've been giving him all the money he needs for the building and the equipment."

"I trust you've Googled him," Max asks.

"Of course. You can too if you don't believe me."

We're a few blocks away from the Y when an ambulance races past with its sirens on. We pick up our pace, either out of dread or curiosity. There's nothing more nerve-racking than seeing the paramedics race down your street and wondering if they're finally coming for you but they're ahead of schedule.

Sure enough, when we enter the gym's parking lot, the ambulance is parked at the entrance, its back doors open waiting to swallow up someone from the gym. *Please let it be Craig*, I find myself thinking, which is horrible, I know. I don't wish for a massive cardiac arrest or anything, just a concussion, maybe, or a sprained ankle.

But it's not Craig they wheel past us on the stretcher. It's Harold. Max flies to his side, pushing aside a young EMT to lean over her husband's body. Harold doesn't respond to Max's cries, just stares blankly off to the side. Before everything fully registers, the ambulance closes its doors and disappears out the parking lot.

"Oh no," Ginny says. "Poor Max."

We race inside to find out what happened. It takes us awhile to find someone willing to talk to us. The whole staff is running around, trying to manage the chaos and calm the other patrons. The young woman who works at the receptionist's desk tells us they think Harold might have had a stroke. "Luckily he was with his physical therapist," she says, probably to minimize the gym's liability. "Or things could have been a lot worse."

Ginny and I drive to the hospital and wait in the lobby. We want to help Max with her car and bring anything she needs from home. It's torture waiting with all the other distraught friends and families. The dread and terror in the room is palpable, made somehow worse by the *People* magazine covers of celebrity comeback stories. This week's issue features an actress I've never heard of discussing finding love in her forties.

"This is a horrible place to die," Ginny says. The comment surprises me and I look over to see her hands gripping the arms of her chair, like she's at the dentist.

"We don't know if Harold's going to die," I say. "We don't know anything."

"You're right," Ginny says, smiling weakly. "I think I'm having a bit of PTSD sitting here."

"You can go if you need to," I say. "Max will understand."

"I'm fine," she says, shaking her head. She picks up a *People* magazine and flips through its pages.

"I'm going to get us something to eat," I say, and leave the waiting area.

I find a vending machine tucked away near the elevators. There's a woman Meg's age pacing in front, mid-conversation. Her bedhead and makeup-free face tell me she's been here awhile. She's talking in hushed tones, but the cavernous hallway amplifies the stress in her voice.

"She should have just let him take it . . . I know . . . It's only because it was a gift from Kirk that . . . No, they say it's a compound fracture . . . Yeah, the police are with her now . . ."

I pretend to be absorbed in my chip selection.

A young man who looks like a middle schooler in scrubs comes out and stands in front of her. The woman ends her call and asks the doctor how her mom is doing.

"She's going to be fine. We're setting the arm and bandaging the abrasions. You should be able to take her home in a few hours. She'll need full-time care at home for at least six weeks."

"She lives in a retirement home. I've got her a room on their skilled nursing floor."

I can't keep standing in front of the vending machine without it becoming obvious I'm eavesdropping, so I purchase some chips and hope the bag gets stuck on the coil. It does not. So I feed another dollar in and look for an item more likely to snag. Unfortunately, nothing malfunctions, so I keep buying chips. If either of these two ask, I'll say I'm catering a party in the pediatric ward.

"Are the police still with her?" the woman asks.

"Yes, it sounds like she put up quite a fight."

"How could someone do that? Beat up an old lady for a piece of jewelry? She had it for less than twenty-four hours."

"I hope they catch the guy," the doctor says. "Your mom's lucky she was in bed or her injuries would be a lot worse."

"And here I was worried about her online dating."

"She's dating, is she?"

"She met someone online. The necklace was a one-month anniversary gift. She's distraught that it's gone."

"Necklaces are replaceable."

"I'm hoping her boyfriend is too."

They finish up and walk back through the doors that lead to the ER. I want to follow and conduct my own investigation: *What retirement home does your mom live in? How did she meet her boyfriend? How long has he been sending her gifts? Is his name really Kirk? As in Captain Kirk?* Instead, I gather up my seven bags of chips and make my way back to Ginny, suddenly worried that her new Apple Watch will make her the thief's next target. Maybe Cristóbal isn't the villain here. Maybe it's someone who's hacked into Senior Moments in order to monitor the gift exchanges and steal them as soon as they arrive.

Ginny gives me a curious, but not unhappy, look when she sees my potato chip haul. I hand her a bag just as Max enters the room. Our friend looks tired, which is not an adjective I thought I'd ever use to describe her. Her body lists to the side, like someone walking with a sprained ankle. She doesn't say anything about the potato chips, which tells me the news about Harold isn't good.

Max says that Harold had a hemorrhagic stroke and needs emergency surgery. Of course she goes into way too much scientific detail and all I take away is they have to drill a hole in his head to drain the blood filling his brain. She's committed to staying in the hospital so we offer to pick up her car from the gym and bring her an overnight bag.

"You can't drive, can you?" Max asks me.

"This is an emergency," I say. "And it's just a few blocks to Ginny's. She'll take over from there."

We say our goodbyes and leave. When we're buckled in, I turn to Ginny and ask if she's okay. She takes a few deep breaths before responding.

"I spent a lot of time in this hospital when Colin was dying," she says. She digs in her purse and pulls out a tissue to dab her eyes. "I'd hoped to never set foot in that place again."

"I'm sorry," I say. "I guess that's one benefit of divorce. I wouldn't mind seeing either of my exes in the hospital."

Ginny laughs. "You don't mean that."

"I don't," I say. But I do. The main reason I still subscribe to the newspaper is so I can scan the obituary pages looking for news of their deaths.

"Do you think it's a good idea to wear that expensive watch out in public?" I ask.

"Where else am I going to wear it?" she asks.

"Maybe keep it hidden," I say, pulling the cuff of her sleeve over the device. "I hear those things are magnets for street criminals."

24

May 20

Ginny and I drive back to the gym and pick up Max's car. I follow Ginny to Max's house, being careful to obey all the traffic laws I remember. I wonder what the judge would do to me if I were caught driving with a suspended license. People my age don't really get arrested and thrown in jail. It's bad optics to cuff someone's grandmother and force her into the back seat of a squad car. It's one of the perks of being old: No one thinks we're a threat to anyone but ourselves. You have to be Bernie Madoff to provoke the kind of hate that sends you away for what's left of your life.

When we arrive at Max's house, both Ginny and I are hesitant to enter. Max has given us a very detailed list of items to pack for her (including lavender-scented hand cream) but it still feels strange to walk into her home without her being there. We've only known Max for a few weeks, and one of those weeks we were actively trying to ruin her reputation. But now we're friends I guess, and this is what friends do for each other. I walk up to the front door, insert the key, and go inside.

Ginny and I make a concerted effort not to snoop but it's hard not letting some details filter into our consciousness. Each room contains information about different aspects of Max and Harold's lives. We learn about their health from the bathroom. The medicine cabinet is filled with prescription bottles, almost all for Harold, making us realize he's sicker than Max has let on.

We see whom they love in the bedroom. Their dresser is crowded with photos of their children and grandchildren, all beautiful and happy. The photos are the kind people send out around the holidays, generic smiles enhanced with soft lighting. If it wasn't for the shared olive complexions, dark hair, and triangular faces, you might mistake the photos as the ones that come with the purchase of a new frame. The only image with any personality is a school photo of a little girl who scowls with her dark, intense eyes, as if blaming the viewer for her bad pageboy haircut. My guess is that Max likes this grandchild the best.

The office is where we learn about the family finances. There's a printout of an article that Max has highlighted about how to sell your home without a realtor. When I point it out to Ginny, her eyes go wide in surprise. All the clues we've gathered going from room to room start to fit together then: Harold's medical bills have bankrupted Max and she's too proud to ask her children for help. The only way out of this financial mess is to sell the house. Harold's current hospital stay has only made things worse, I imagine.

The house starts feeling a little claustrophobic so Ginny and I pack up the rest of the items on Max's list and get out of there. After we lock the front door, we walk to our cars and drive back to the hospital. The whole way there, I think about the heavy lifting Max has been doing, maintaining her better-than-you persona. I try to figure out if knowing the truth about her makes me like her more or less. Either she's a determined go-getter, unwilling to let the vagaries of life beat her down, or she's a pathological liar who only pretends to know the secret of a healthy, happy life, when really she's as clueless as the rest of us.

Given her current life crisis, I decide to withhold judgment for now.

We figure Max will need her car so I follow Ginny back to the hospital. Before dropping off the overnight bag, we stop by the gift shop and pick up some expensive flowers. It feels strange to give Max another thing she'll have to watch slowly die, but Ginny insists the bouquet will provide necessary color to the sterile room. Max appreciates the gesture. At least I think she does. She's too busy bossing the nurses around to pay us much attention.

By the time we leave, we're both exhausted and starving. Ginny invites me to dine with her at Xanadu and I happily accept. I'm ready for someone else to cook and clean and refill my wineglass.

"Do you mind if we eat in my room?" she asks as we pull into the lot. "I don't think I have the energy for our cafeteria."

"Is it the mile long buffet?"

"It's the communal dining. Xanadu promotes relationship building through family style seating. Normally, I love the camaraderie but tonight I don't feel like chitchatting."

"I never feel like chitchatting."

"We can place an order to go and take it up to my room. I've got a nice bottle of chardonnay chilling in the fridge."

Xanadu has a station at the front entrance of the cafeteria where you select your food from a touch screen display. While we wait for our meals to arrive, I scan the room, which is packed for dinner at 5:30 P.M. . . . An elegantly dressed woman stands up in the middle of the room and screams "You idiot!" at her waiter. The young man jerks back in surprise and bumps into the tray he's placed on a stand, upending it and sending the remaining plates crashing to the carpeted floor.

The poor boy doesn't know which mess he should attend to first. He opts for the screaming woman, which is probably a mistake as nothing he can say or do will calm her down. "This is vintage couture!" she says, pointing at the red sauce that's splattered on her white silk blouse.

The other waitstaff rush over to help their coworker. They scramble to pick up the food and broken plates, while the boy begs for forgiveness.

The woman's tablemates gather around, sprinkling her with salt and dabbing the stain with wet napkins. The woman has no patience for their help and pushes them away. "Just leave me alone!" she screams. "Will you all just leave me alone!"

Her reaction is extreme, which only draws more attention to her. She throws her napkin on the ground and stomps away from her table.

"Someone's going to pay for this!" she says.

The waiter looks down at the floor. No one comes to comfort him, I notice. He stands alone like Frankenstein's monster suddenly made aware of his own clumsy strength. Even his coworkers scatter after they've cleaned up his mess. My heart goes out to the boy until I see him glaring at his accuser. This isn't their first run-in, I think, and instinctively pull Ginny close.

The woman doesn't break stride or make eye contact as she passes us.

"Was that . . . ?" I whisper.

"Sharon," Ginny says.

The drunk woman I met in the hall on my last visit.

"She certainly has a flair for dramatic exits," I say.

Just then our food arrives. Sharon is still waiting for the elevator to arrive so we linger by the cafeteria entrance, examining our Styrofoam containers. When we hear the ping of doors opening, we wait for her to disappear before we grab the next car to take us to Ginny's floor.

Second Victim

My whole life, I've always known when it's time to leave.

With my first husband, it was after his first million and before his first indictment.

With my second husband, it was after his first cancer diagnosis and before his second.

With my third husband, it was after his affair and before I shot him.

I've always drawn the line at murder, but with Fred, my third and final husband, I was too close to pulling the trigger and becoming a cliché: Jilted wife kills cheating husband. I would have been the laughingstock at the golf club—a fate worse than prison time.

But I didn't need to shoot him. I already had enough money from my first two marriages to convince Fred we didn't need a prenup. Divorcing him set me up in Dior and Cartier for the rest of my life. Now I can sit back and enjoy ruining the man's reputation by posting embarrassing photos of him dining with disgraced celebrities and military despots.

Such a good track record, which is why I'm surprised I messed up the timing of my departure now. The optimal exit strategy would have been before Cynthia's death. If anyone at Xanadu were to find out I was complicit in that, if word ever reached my daughter Dana, I don't think I could live with the shame. I'd been so careful my whole life and one mistake was going to label me a monster forever.

Leaving now though . . . I don't know. It feels like I'm exiting midscene, forcing the rest of the actors to improvise on stage. Not that I care what happens to any of those losers at Xanadu. The retired professors and well-connected philanthropists never treated me with anything but condescension. Like their inherited wealth and privilege was somehow better than my earned wealth and privilege. Thank God for Barbara, who came in and put all those snobs in their place with her looks and glamour and casual cruelty. I didn't always agree with her, but I loved being in her inner circle. She'll be angry with me over my little disappearance, but I don't see any way I can stay without her turning against me too. I slipped a note under her door on my way out saying I would be gone for a few weeks to visit Dana and asking her to take care of my plants. She'll kill them all, I'm sure, but that's the least of my problems right now. I've got other deaths I need to avoid, namely mine.

I pack an overnight bag with a change of clothes and my expensive jewelry. Everything else stays in the apartment. I say goodbye to my Manolos, Ferragamos, and Prada sandals, all of which will probably end up on eBay given Dana's Sasquatchian proportions. The only item in my closet that's easy to leave is my now-ruined silk blouse. Why I wore that on Meatloaf Monday is something I'll never understand. I blame the two martinis Alfonse encouraged me to drink at Barbara's before dinner. And that idiot waiter. If there's any justice in the world, he'll be fired by daybreak.

When it's quiet, I sneak out my door and enter the staircase. It's going to cripple me taking the stairs nine stories down, but I don't want to risk the trapped box of the elevator. Also, the elevators open into the front lobby, which is always brightly lit with surveillance cameras and a night watchman. Say one thing for Xanadu: They know how to make their residents feel safe. Unfortunately, all those precautions can be used against me now, so it's better to exit the stairwell on the second floor, take the walkway over to the skilled nursing wing, and then use their exit to the parking lot behind the building. From there I can call an Uber and have someone drive me to the airport.

Where I go next is anyone's guess. All I know is it needs to be far away, in a country that doesn't have an extradition treaty with the US. Singapore, maybe? The mystery of my disappearance will make me the center of attention, for once, instead of Barbara, who, despite her many charms, always had to make everything about her. I actually like this idea.

I do feel a little bad leaving Dana without saying goodbye, but she deserves to suffer after her attempts at conservatorship. She tried to convince a judge my excessive drinking and spending habits were evidence of mental decline but I had the receipts to prove these were habits I'd had since my thirties. That put an end to that.

Dana's a smart girl. She'll find me eventually. I'm not good at hiding my digital footprint. The first time I withdraw money from a bank, she'll know my location.

Of course, that means he will too.

My only hope is that he'll leave me alone, rather than travel across time zones to shut me up. My exit should tell him that I just want out.

By the time I reach the second floor, my knees are screaming. I don't know if I'll be able to make it. I consider sneaking into one of the apartments (no one locks their doors at Xanadu. Why would they? It's so safe!) and commandeering a walker or wheelchair. But that would just slow me down. I place my faith in all the yoga I've been doing since I moved here and keep going, using the handrails attached to the walls for support.

The street is quiet. I should keep walking and have the car pick me up farther away but I can't take another step. I call the Uber and see that it will take ten minutes for it to arrive. I should have brought a heavier sweater. I rub my arms to stay warm, but can't rid myself of the chill that's seeping in.

Xanadu hovers over me like some giant tsunami wave about to crash down and engulf me in water and debris. I won't miss this place and wonder how I lasted as long as I did. It was because of him, of course. He made me feel special. Smart. Important. I hadn't felt that way in so long, it was like a drug I didn't know I was addicted to. Now I realize I was just another old fool, like Cynthia and the rest of them.

A light pops on in a tenth-floor apartment, illuminating a dark figure standing by the window. Is it him? I wonder. It's too far away to tell but my instincts tell me to run. Of course, I can't run. I can barely stand. My knees feel like they're on fire. I'm a sitting duck so I do the only thing I can do, which is wave. The person waves back and I smile, despite the circumstances.

I'll never know who my last friendly contact was that evening because just then my Uber arrived. Only it wasn't my Uber. It was him. And he didn't slow down, even after he ran over me.

25

June 8

"Don't let the perfect be the enemy of the good," I say on our daily walk around Max's neighborhood.

Harold needs round-the-clock care, which proves too difficult even for someone like Max. The first nurse is a lovely Filipino woman named Jasmine. She quits after Max berates her about her perfume. Then comes the Salvadoran, who Max fires after catching him on his phone during Harold's nap. After that it's a stream of people I don't even bother keeping track of because I know they'll be gone when they don't cool Harold's soup or tuck in a bedsheet correctly.

An intervention becomes necessary.

"Easy for you to say," Max says, pumping her arms like a drum major.

"You think these nurses can bring Harold back?" I ask. "Because they can't. No one can."

Harold's stroke hasn't totally incapacitated him, but it's left him dependent on others for most basic functions. He's become a baby who needs to be fed, bathed, and changed. Ginny and I have been helping out with the shopping and cleaning, and even those small contributions exhaust us.

"I'm not an idiot," Max says. "I just want him to be comfortable."

I look to Ginny for support, but she's struggling to keep up with us. The summer heat has arrived and I see she's already sweating through her pink T-shirt. With shaking hands she unscrews the top of her water bottle and takes a deep sip. I stop to adjust my Velcro shoe straps to give her time to catch her breath. Ginny mouths me a *thank you*.

This is the only time Max leaves the house. She sets a grueling pace for us in order to get back before the nurse burns the house down.

"What makes you think Harold's not comfortable?" I ask on bended knee.

Max continues to walk in place. "I know what he likes." Then adds, "That last woman fell asleep during *Jeopardy!*"

"What's wrong with that?"

"What if Harold had to use the restroom?"

"He's in a diaper, isn't he?"

"That's not the point," she says, turning and walking away from us. Ginny and I exchange glances and race to catch up.

"Are *you* getting enough sleep?" Ginny asks. Finally.

"I get enough."

"Because, forgive me for saying this, dear, you look exhausted."

Well played, Ginny, I think to myself. Attack where Max is most vulnerable—her invulnerability.

"I'm fine," Max says.

"Prove it."

"What are you talking about?" Max says. We're at the busiest intersection of our walk—a four-way stop near the elementary school. We can hear kids being released for lunch at whatever camp they're attending. A tiny stampede of feet against concrete.

"Come have lunch with us," Ginny says. "There's a Panera two blocks from here."

"I can't," Max says.

"You can," I say. "Harold will be fine. That new one you have, she's Russian, isn't she? She's a tough cookie."

"I think she smokes when I'm not home."

"C'mon," Ginny says. "It will do you good."

Max looks left then right, like she's checking for traffic. She's at a crossroads, for sure. Should she follow her duty as a wife or her duty to herself? In the end, she answers in the only way Max can. "I'll give you twenty minutes," she says. "But I'm doubling our pace afterward."

At lunch, we try to distract Max with stories of our own. I talk about Meg, who is now spending half the week at her new boyfriend's apartment, leaving me alone with Jeremy, who only emerges from his basement lair when he needs to eat or shower, neither of which he does with great regularity. I don't tell them about our efforts to seduce Cristóbal, which have so far been unsuccessful. He hasn't responded to my flirty message, which oddly disappoints me. Shouldn't I want him to be the good guy Ginny thinks he is?

"What about you, Ginny?" I ask, changing the subject. "How are things going with your boyfriend?"

Ginny stabs a tomato with her fork. Max shamed us into getting salads when we both really wanted the sausage and scrambled egg on an Asiago bagel.

"Good," she says, taking a long sip of her iced tea. She's stalling, I can tell. No way she's that thirsty with all the water she drinks on our walk. She's already used the restroom twice since we sat down.

We wait for her to say more but she focuses her energy on slicing her hard-boiled egg in half. "He sent me the cutest text for my birthday," she says, whipping out her phone.

"When was your birthday?" I ask.

"Last Thursday," Max answers.

"How did you know?" I ask. I spend more time with Ginny than Max. How did she get this information ahead of me?

"It's on her Facebook page," Max says.

"You're on Facebook?" I ask.

"Of course," Max says. "It's how I stay in touch with my children and grandchildren, although the kids don't post as much as they do on Instagram and TikTok."

"Jesus, I really am an asshole," I say, looking at Ginny for confirmation.

"You are not," Ginny says. "I think it's admirable you're not on social media."

"Admirable?" I say.

"Yes," Ginny says. "I never feel better about myself after spending time online. All those happy families make me feel so lonely. Plus, Barbara and the other popular ladies at Xanadu post photos of parties and day trips they've taken without me and then ask why I didn't like their posts when I see them in the dining hall. So, then I have to like things I don't like, which only makes me feel worse about myself."

"So delete your account," Max says.

"I know, I should," Ginny says. "But former students reach out to me on Facebook and I want to hear from them."

I take a sip of my iced tea. I was never tempted by social media. Just as I was never tempted to visit Thailand. Everyone talks about the beautiful beaches and kindhearted people, but you have to navigate through the crowded, seedy streets of Bangkok in order to find them. It just doesn't seem worth the hassle.

"I'm sorry I missed your birthday," I say.

Ginny waves my concern away.

"I'll text you a reminder next year," Max says, taking out her phone and tapping on her screen. It's moments like this when I think death will come as a welcome relief.

"What did Cristóbal send you?" I ask.

Ginny scrolls through her messages and finds the birthday greeting. I don't have my glasses so I have to bring the screen close to make out the image. It's a picture of a dog wearing a pointy hat with the caption **Let's Paw-ty!**

I hold on to the phone so I can glimpse part of their conversation. Ginny's been kind of tight lipped about her relationship, so this is a window into what geriatric flirting looks like. I'm imagining a lot of pillow talk on the firmness of mattress beds.

That is adorable, Ginny writes and adds a heart emoji.

I put something extra in the bank for you, Cristóbal responds.

That is so sweet.

Buy yourself something special. Send me a photo. Make it sexy.

I have to scroll down to see the image. It's a picture of Ginny wrapped in a weighted blanket.

Ginny snatches the phone out of my hands.

"I hope you were naked under that blanket," I say with a wink.

"I most certainly was not," Ginny says, blushing pink. I've never met someone easier to embarrass. She's like a chameleon changing color every time it nears the thought of genitalia.

"Never send a naked photo online," Max says. "Unless you want to be the centerfold on some fetishistic website."

The color drains from Ginny's face, leaving her as pale as the hard-boiled egg she just consumed.

"What's that about him putting something extra in the bank for you?" I ask. "You haven't given him access to your checking account, have you?"

"Ginny!" Max says, with surprising force. She slams her fork down on the table, causing the plates to jump. The teens wolfing down their sandwiches next to us look up from their phones at the commotion.

Ginny puts a calming hand on Max and squeezes. "Cristóbal hasn't asked me for a penny. He's the one giving me money."

This mollifies Max. She leans back and uses the napkin in her lap to dab at the spittle that's moistened her lips.

"So, he's given you access to his bank account?" I ask.

"Well, no," Ginny says. She tears off the bread roll, which she's been saving as dessert. She butters it generously and plops it in her mouth, closing her eyes in an ecstasy of chewing. "I've given him permission to transfer money into my account so I can help him purchase things for his new restaurant."

Max and I exchange glances. This doesn't feel right, but neither of us knows why.

"There are a lot of expenses to cover. Every week he's having me drive up to Oakland or San Francisco to look at possible locations. He wants to take over an industrial site and make it all fancy and posh. The money he gives me is for gas and the occasional appliance I purchase for his kitchen."

"Why doesn't he come out and manage these business transactions?" Max asks.

"Because he's busy managing two restaurants already," Ginny says. "Plus, he trusts me."

"When is the restaurant going to open?" I ask.

"Oh, not for another year. Maybe two."

"He must be rich."

"He does very well."

"And yet, he still hasn't come out to visit," Max says.

"Like I said, he's busy," Ginny makes a big production of looking at her watch and then showing it to Max. "Twenty minutes are up. Should we get going?"

Max keeps her promises and practically races back home. The accelerated pace feels even more punishing after our meal, but we keep up, mostly by keeping our conversation to a minimum. Ginny doesn't want to talk about her relationship and Max and I don't want to upset her by asking any more probing questions. When I get home, I'll see if there's anything Jeremy can do to make me more attractive to Cristóbal so I can put a stop to this nonsense once and for all.

26

June 8

That evening I lure Jeremy up from his hovel with his favorite meal—cheesy pasta, which is just noodles, marinara sauce, and Parmesan cheese. It's the easiest meal to make but he acts like I'm building a pyramid every time I try to walk him through the process.

Jeremy's a good kid so it pains me to think of him spending the bulk of his life in a basement. When he finally emerges I'm struck, not for the first time, how little he appears to be aging. He still looks like a scrawny teenager to me, even though he's twenty-four. It probably helps that he rarely sees the sun and doesn't drink or have sex. Maybe the marijuana relaxes the wrinkles away too. Is this how humans are evolving? I wonder.

"Hungry?" I ask, filling a plate.

He grunts in response. Sweet Jesus, has he lost the ability to speak now? It wouldn't surprise me if he and his online friends only communicate through tapping on their keyboards. I hand him the steaming plate of boiled noodles.

When he turns to leave I clear my throat to remind him of our one rule: We eat dinner together. It's the only way I can maintain the illusion that we're still a family and not a bunch of roommates thrown together by chance, although now that I think about it, that describes most families too.

"Where's Mom?" Jeremy asks, sitting down.

"Out with her boyfriend," I say, filling a glass of wine and sitting down next to him. The wooden chair creaks as I ease into it. I think I've had these things since my first marriage. Strange to think what's durable and what isn't.

Jeremy shoves a fork of pasta in his mouth and grunts again.

"What?" I ask. "Do young people even use terms like 'boyfriend' or 'girlfriend' anymore with all the gender fluidity? Not that Meg and her whatever-you-call-him are young. When I was her age, I was already twice divorced and transitioning into sweatpants."

Jeremy chews, swallows, and takes a drink of water.

"Speaking of dating," I say. "Any response from Cristóbal?"

Jeremy shakes his head. "Lots of other assholes are interested in you though," he says with a mouth full of noodles.

"Really?" I say. I don't know why I'm flattered. A cut of raw meat doesn't think it's special when a pack of wolves fights over it. "Can I see?"

Jeremy uses his fork like a broom and scrapes the remains of his food into the dustpan of his mouth. He then stands up and walks out of the room, not even bothering to clear his plate or thank me. I clear my throat loud enough for him to get the message. He returns sheepishly and moves his dish to the sink. "Come on," he says and grabs a kitchen chair so I'll have somewhere to sit once we're at his workstation.

I follow him down into the darkness, which feels oddly comforting, like being trapped inside on a rainy day. For a second, I get why Jeremy might prefer this habitat to the one upstairs. He can shut out the world down here and only see the things he wants to see.

He offers me his chair and I ease myself into it, wary of its wheeled feet. Instinctively, I grip the armrests, thinking the thing might swivel out from under me, dumping me on the concrete floor. Jeremy sits next to me and starts typing furiously on his keyboard. One by one, boxes start to appear on his screen. Jeremy moves them around like a magician doing a card trick.

"Okay, here's asshole number one," he says.

A handsome man appears on the screen. He looks a little like an actor from that soap opera I watched years ago. He's got swept back silver hair and a tanned face. His features are birdlike, thin and beady. I bet he's a cyclist. He seems like he'd have more than one set of spandex leggings.

"He's definitely a troll," Jeremy says. "I found this profile photo on three different websites, which tells me this guy's an amateur. Here's asshole number two."

Another good-looking man appears, this one Black. He's older and more in my league, by which I mean he looks prediabetic. He's got the jolly smile of a guy who dresses up as Santa Claus every Christmas.

"He's a little smarter and didn't use a photo that could be found doing a simple reverse image search," Jeremy says. "But he's clearly a scam artist."

"How do you know?"

"Check out our chat," Jeremy says.

"You're *chatting* with him?" I ask.

Jeremy pauses. "Yeah, is that okay?"

"I mean, sure. I guess."

I look at Jeremy and worry I've created a monster. If this monster limits his attacks to online predators, I guess I'm okay with that. Still, I'd rather be responsible for turning him on to pickleball.

Jeremy moves his cursor to the other monitor and pulls up the Senior Moments dating site. Another chat box opens and he enlarges it so I can see. Even though it takes up the entire screen, I need the glasses I wear as a necklace to read.

You are a beautiful woman

You're not so bad yourself. Do you like rollerblading?

I am a big fan

Where do you blade?

All over. The beach. The park.

I like the park too but I don't like ducks

I too am not a fan

I shot one the other day.

He probably deserved it.

The police warned me not to do it again. It scares the children.

Children are a blessing.

I'm glad you feel that way. I have eight.

Eight children?

Yes, but it's okay because I'm rich.

Your children are lucky.

I tell that to my conjoined twins but they don't listen.

You are a good mother.

If I could get pregnant again, I would

I would like to make a baby with you.

"Hilarious, right?" Jeremy says. "The guy doesn't even realize I'm messing with him. On to asshole number three."

Jeremy pulls up another face, this one of a man who looks like a college professor. He's got a long face, like Lincoln, a gray beard, and rimless glasses.

"This one's already scammed two women," he says. "I copied his texts and found he'd repeated the same lines on multiple dating sites. One woman I reached out to claimed he conned her out of $5,000."

I sit back amazed. "You did all this in the time I was gone?" I say.

"It was easy," Jeremy says. "And I gotta admit, kind of fun."

"Any legitimate guys interested in me?" I ask.

"Oh sure," Jeremy says. "But I don't want to mess with them."

"Show me a nice guy," I say, scooting forward.

"Why?" he asks.

"I'm curious."

Jeremy shows me one gentleman from Maine with kind eyes and a scraggly beard, a guy from Texas in a cowboy hat with dentures, and a grandfather from Oregon with thick glasses and gray Afro.

The last profile he pulls up is an elderly man named Bao Duong. "I like this guy the best," Jeremy says. He's very dapper and handsome, like an Asian Obama. He has the kind of face that makes you trust him immediately. Is it the big ears that do it? I wonder. If he didn't have those appendages sticking out of the side of his head, he'd be too good looking, even with his lined face and receding hairline. Those ears make him seem like a good listener.

"He's local," Jeremy says. "Lives over in Oakland. I want him to be my new grandfather."

"I think you've lost sight of our mission here, dear," I say.

Jeremy sighs and closes the window.

"I guess it's good that Cristóbal isn't one of those assholes," I say.

"We don't know that yet," Jeremy says.

I shake my head. "He's giving Ginny all this money," I say.

"What's this now?"

"He's opening a restaurant in San Francisco and Ginny has been helping him, purchasing kitchen equipment and stuff."

"Sounds like she's a money mule," Jeremy says.

"Jeremy, stop using language I don't understand."

"A money mule is someone who unknowingly launders money for criminals," Jeremy says.

"How is this money laundering?"

"Let's say Cristóbal is a drug dealer. He needs to find a way to clean his dirty money so he gives it to your friend. She then writes checks to bogus entities and voila! Money cleaned."

Jeremy must see the look of horror on my face because he turns away and starts typing. That kind of raw human emotion is too much for him to handle so he retreats into the pixelated world where he controls everything.

He pulls up story after story of elderly women becoming unwitting accomplices in money laundering operations. A woman in Utah was arrested by the Feds after her Ghanian "boyfriend" tricked her into cashing his checks and sending him the money in Bitcoin. A woman in Kirkland thought she was building an orphanage in Honduras only to learn she was cleaning money for a drug cartel. A woman in Cambridge (Cambridge! Where all the smart people live!) washed the profits from a sex trafficking ring in what she thought were legitimate money transfers between her boss and his employees.

The more I read, the more infuriated I become. How can people take advantage of lonely, vulnerable women like this? Was Ginny even capable of making such complicated financial transactions? If Cristóbal's new restaurant were bogus, wouldn't the bank or some federal agent put a stop to these deposits and withdrawals? Something didn't add up. Maybe Ginny wasn't telling us the whole story out of fear or embarrassment. She was too trusting. Too easily manipulated. Hadn't I been able to convince her to stuff an ankle weight with cake frosting? Imagine what a professional con artist could do with such a mark.

Then the fear that's always lingering in the back of my mind steps forward: What if Cynthia's death is somehow connected to this? What if she was a money mule too and got tired of washing Cristóbal's dirty laundry? There's the motive I've been searching for! I feel a strange kind of satisfaction in having my suspicions justified, but that feeling is quickly replaced with dread. If I'm right, then Ginny is in even more danger than I realized.

27

June 9

Meg stumbles in at daybreak. I'm sitting at the kitchen table doing my crossword. It's my quiet time. Jeremy usually doesn't crawl out of bed until the afternoon and Meg, well, her schedule varies depending on who she's been out with the night before. If she's coming home at this hour, things can't have gone well with Craig.

The first thing I notice is her annoyance at seeing me. Like I'm the one invading her space. Then I see she's barely put together. She hasn't brushed her hair and her blondish waves look brittle and dry. Her face, free of makeup, is pink and puffy, the result of some crying jag. Her black dress is twisted and bunched up around the top and she's holding her high-heeled shoes in her left hand. This is a walk of shame if I've ever seen one. I brace myself for her to projectile vomit all her anger and disappointment on me.

Instead, she collapses into the chair opposite and starts sobbing. I'm on my feet in an instant and cradling her in my arms. Say what you will about me as a mother, but I never could stand to see my child suffer. Even when I was the cause of their suffering, I would do my best to comfort them, which probably sent some very weird mixed signals.

Meg smells of perfume and cigarettes. Not a good sign. If Meg was smoking last night, that meant she was probably drinking, too, those two habits following each other like thunder and lightning. I hope that's all she got into. I can't take another round of rehab, emotionally or financially.

"Can I get you a cup of coffee?" I ask.

Meg nods and I go to pour her a cup. I've always thought our coffee preferences speak to our different ways of dealing with the world. I take mine black, having developed a taste for dark and bitter blends. Meg, on the other hand, cuts hers with whipping cream and teaspoons of sugar until it hardly seems like coffee anymore.

"What happened?" I ask, handing her the cup.

Meg takes a sip and grimaces. It's her way of thanking me for screwing up her order. Again.

"Craig wants me to move in," Meg says.

I take my time walking back to my chair, sensing a trap. Years of living with Meg has trained me to maintain a poker face until Meg lays all her cards on the table.

"How do you feel about that?" I ask cautiously. Even that tepid response is enough to set her off.

"How do I feel about it? I feel fucking great, Mom. That's why I'm back here at the butt crack of dawn with you and your crossword puzzle."

Meg takes a sip of coffee and starts to cry again. I don't get up to comfort her this time.

"It's just . . . things are moving so fast, you know?" she says. "We've only been dating a month. I don't want to rush into things. But he's pretty insistent. He got really mad when I hesitated. Said I thought I was too good for him."

"But you stayed the night?" I ask, which is the wrong thing to say. This is my problem with Meg. I get hung up on details instead of addressing the bigger picture.

"Jesus, Mom. We had the fight this morning."

I look at the clock. It's 6:30 A.M. How do you have a fight like this so early? I wonder. But then, I realize that's what Meg and I are doing right now so it kind of makes sense. "What are you going to do?"

"I don't know," Meg says. "I don't want to lose him, but I'm not ready to move in with him either. His place is pretty shitty. He lives in one of those apartment complexes on El Camino. The people living on the floor below him have chickens as pets."

I have so many things I want to say. *That's your biggest objection to his offer? That you'd have to live with chickens? What about the fact that this guy is a total loser? He's not looking for a romantic life partner. He probably needs someone to help him do his laundry and unload all those vitamin supplements he got conned into buying. If you move in with him, it will be the worst decision you ever make. Well, maybe not the worst. There are some spectacular screwups I could list here from the time you assaulted that pizza delivery man to your most recent fiasco of sleeping with your boss's twenty-two-year-old son.* "Chickens, huh," I say instead.

"I don't know. Maybe I should just do it," Meg says. "It can't be any worse than where I'm living now."

"Thanks," I say.

"You know what I mean," Meg says. "What fifty-year-old woman still lives with her mother?"

Fifty-three-year-old woman, I silently correct.

"Sounds like you've got a lot to think about," I say.

Meg pushes her chair away and stands up with such force she nearly tips over her coffee. "Thanks, Mom. You've been a huge help as always."

And with that she leaves the room.

I sit and stare at my crossword. A six-letter word for poisonous fish. *Puffer*, I think but don't write it down. Instead, I clear the coffee cups and wash them in the sink. It takes every ounce of strength I have not to throw the cups on the kitchen tile and watch them shatter into tiny shards. Ten years ago, I would have done it. My anger erupting, just like Meg's, over the smallest of things. As much as she drives me crazy, I see that Meg is my daughter through and through. It's weird to see a version of yourself making all the same mistakes you did. I look at Meg and see my past. I'm sure she looks at me and sees her future. What a frightening mirror. No wonder she's contemplating moving in with a guy she hardly knows.

28

June 9

Ginny picks me up for our walking date in such a gay mood that I almost feel bad for all the scheming I've been doing behind her back. When I get in her car, she's dressed in new mauve sweats and a matching bandana. It suits her coloring and I tell her.

"Thank you," she says. "Cristóbal got it for me, along with this." She pulls on a gold chain around her neck until it reveals a heart tag pendant. I can't read the engraving but I'm sure it uses their initials in some romantic way.

"He's a generous man," I say.

"Oh, Poppy, you have no idea. Last night we were talking and I told him about Max's financial woes and he offered to send her $5,000 to help her through this rough time. It won't cover her medical bills, obviously, but isn't that sweet? He doesn't even know her."

"That's very sweet," I say.

I can't share my suspicions of her being a money mule. Not when she's this happy. Besides what kind of scam involves sending your victim tracksuits and jewelry? None that I've read about, that's for sure.

"Let's call him," I say.

Ginny looks over at me and the momentary distraction makes her veer into the bike lane where she nearly knocks over a guy keeping pace with us on his e-bike. The guy slams his hand against my window and shouts something in Chinese.

"Maybe when we get to Max's," I say, waving an apology to the man.

When we're safely parked in front of Max's house, I demand Ginny take out her phone and call Cristóbal. "Let's FaceTime him," I say. "I want to see that handsome face of his."

Ginny fumbles with her phone, clearly excited and apprehensive about introducing me to her boyfriend. It's kind of cute, actually, seeing her get all nervous like a schoolgirl. I try to remember the last time someone made me feel this giddy. The UPS driver maybe? But that was only because he was delivering some much-needed bunion pads.

Ginny checks her reflection in the rearview mirror and doesn't like what she sees. "Let's get out of the car," she says. "I think the lighting will be better."

We get out and I follow Ginny up and down the block before she finds the perfect spot of shade with a nice backdrop of bougainvillea. She takes a few deep breaths and dials. As soon as we hear the phone ringing, Ginny positions the phone in front of her face and waits for Cristóbal to pick up. I see her face twitching in anticipation. She's trying to relax but it's almost impossible with the amount of nervous energy flooding her system right now. I wonder if Cristóbal will think she's having a stroke when he picks up.

"I've never FaceTimed him before," Ginny says, almost conspiratorially.

I fight the urge to slap the phone out of her outstretched hand. I suddenly don't want to witness this first contact. It's too intimate for an audience. Now I'm as nervous and giddy as she is listening to the ringtone.

He doesn't pick up.

"He's probably busy with a lunch rush," she says, pocketing her phone.

I add three hours to our time: 2:30 P.M. Doesn't seem like time for a lunch rush but I keep my mouth shut and walk with Ginny to Max's house.

❖

"Ginny, how much money has Cristóbal deposited into your account?" Max asks, picking up the thread of the conversation from yesterday. I try to make eye contact with her to warn her that now is not the time. Ginny is too much in love. She wants Max to notice her new tracksuit and necklace, to bask in Ginny's new romance, not to question it. If I've learned anything raising Meg, it's that there's a time and place for critical inquiry. You have to wait for the first sign of rain before you forecast a storm. You can't do it on a sunny day without the person thinking you're crazy.

"Oh, I don't know. Maybe $200,000."

I want to stay out of this conversation but this stops me in my tracks. "Two hundred thousand dollars!"

"Opening a restaurant is expensive," Ginny says.

"And your bank hasn't raised any red flags with all that money?" Max asks.

Ginny shakes her head. "Why would they?" Ginny asks. "I transfer money all the time from one account to another."

"Cristóbal can't transfer money *out* of your account, can he?" I ask.

"Oh no," she says. "He won't have that kind of permission until we're married."

"Have you heard about money mules?" I ask.

Ginny laughs. "Oh goodness, is that what you think I am?"

"Well, yes," I say. "Cristóbal's giving you money and you're writing the checks."

"I've written very few checks," Ginny says. "Cristóbal handles most of the finances."

"And you've never met Cristóbal face-to-face?" Max asks.

"Can we talk about something else please?" Ginny says, quickening her pace. It's the first time since we started walking together that she's pulled ahead of us. Her backside looks slimmer from this vantage point and I wonder if it's the result of our walking or her new tracksuit. Either way, she's moving forward with a lot more confidence.

"We're just worried about you," I say.

"I'm surprised the FBI hasn't come knocking on your door," Max says. "You know this is illegal, right? You could go to jail."

"It's not illegal," Ginny says. "I'm just helping a friend with a legitimate business."

"A friend you've never met," Max says.

"Will you two please stop," Ginny says, stopping mid-step and turning around to face us, her round face pink and shiny. "I know you mean well but I'm getting tired of defending my relationship every time we get together."

"Let's try FaceTiming him again," I offer. "If Max and I could meet him, I'm sure we'd feel less worried about this situation."

"Fine," Ginny says, pulling the phone out of her fanny pack. Before she dials, she dabs her face with Kleenex, fluffs her hair, and uses the phone's camera to find the best lighting for her face. She hits the dial button and we all wait as the phone rings and rings.

"He didn't pick up last time," I say to Max.

"Ginny, I think you have to accept the fact that . . ." Max begins, but she's cut off when the phone stops ringing and we see what looks like the inside of a hairy cave.

"Hello? Ginny?" a confused voice answers.

"Cristóbal!" Ginny squeals. "You're on FaceTime. Pull the phone away from your ear."

"What?" the voice says. "Sorry, it's hard to hear you. I'm in the restaurant and things are kind of busy right now."

"I've got some friends I'd like you to meet," Ginny says.

Max and I take up positions on either side of Ginny, peering into the phone. Ginny's positioned us so that the sun is in our faces, probably to avoid uncomplimentary shadows, but it makes it hard to see the image on the screen. The picture shifts from a close-up of an ear to a close-up of a bearded chin. On the way down, I think I catch a glimpse of a diamond stud earring.

"Further away," Ginny instructs. "Like me. See how you can see my whole face?"

"I'm sorry, dear, I can barely hear you," the man says. "Is something wrong? Were we supposed to chat now?"

The man has a slight accent, but it's hard to place. I don't know if I've ever heard a Cuban accent besides Ricky Ricardo.

"No, I just wanted my friends to meet you. This is Max and Poppy," she says, panning her phone from left to right in a futile gesture to make us visible to her gentleman caller. The man still has the phone too close to his face so all we're catching now is nostril hair.

"Nice to meet you," he says.

Max and I mumble our greeting, more for Ginny's sake than for Cristóbal.

"They don't believe you're real," Ginny says.

"Oh, I'm real alright," he says, laughing. "I'm the real deal."

Oh jeez.

"Listen honey, I've got to go," Cristóbal says. "I just lost my maître d' for tonight and we're scrambling. I'll call you later, okay?"

"Okay. Sorry to bother you," Ginny says. "Thanks for picking up."

The phone disconnects and Ginny spins around to face us. "Satisfied?"

Max and I nod our heads and follow Ginny as she leads us down the block. All I can think about is that Ricardo Montalbán would be better groomed.

29

June 9

Ginny invites me to dine with her at Xanadu after I complain about my fridge being empty. Having a suspended license has made food shopping a real chore and I refuse to become one of those little old ladies who wheels her food items down the sidewalk in a folding shopping cart. Jeremy has set something up online to get his food delivered, but unless the app lets me squeeze my own cantaloupe, I refuse to use it.

Ginny leaves me in the lobby while she goes to retrieve a bottle of wine from her room. I could go with her, I suppose, but I'm tired from the day's walk and welcome a few minutes to people watch. The sliding glass doors are closed, blocking the residents' access to the dining hall. They linger in the lobby like farm animals waiting to be fed. The women and men aren't dressed up exactly, but they all look like they've ironed their clothes and combed their hair. Meals must be the time to see and be seen at Xanadu and I wonder if that gets tiresome after a while. One of the nice things about living with Jeremy is that neither of us is embarrassed to be seen eating dinner in our pajamas.

When Ginny returns, she's accompanied by Barbara and her entourage. I don't see Sharon anywhere and wonder if she's still upset about her stained blouse. Maybe she's embarrassed about all the fuss she made. A lot of crying over spilled spaghetti sauce if you ask me.

Ginny looks uncomfortable surrounded by these ladies in their cashmere sweaters and wide-leg pants, their hair done in elaborate updos. The women are all Popsicle stick thin, like those actresses who star in movies about women who find love on vacation with their book club. Barbara is clearly the queen bee, effortlessly regal, like Scandinavian royalty. Her boyfriend, Alfonse, stands by her side carrying two bottles of wine in plastic tote bags filled with ice.

"Look who I ran into," Ginny says, gripping her wine bottle and shielding its label from view.

"I'm Barbara," Barbara says, extending a soft, lotioned hand for me to shake. The woman either doesn't remember meeting me or this is early onset Alzheimer's. At my age, it's impossible to tell if you're being intentionally snubbed or not.

"Poppy," I say.

"I'd invite you two to join us but unfortunately our table is full," Barbara says, motioning to the crowd surrounding her.

"Oh, we already have plans," I say, feeling bold.

"Who are you dining with tonight?" Barbara asks Ginny.

I see Bernard emerge from the elevators, dressed smartly in some corduroy trousers and suspenders. He's carrying a cane but he doesn't walk like he needs it. I wonder if it's more a fashion accessory than a tool to balance his thin frame. "Bernard!" I say waving him over.

He smiles when he sees me but his mood changes abruptly when he catches sight of Barbara. The smile spasms on his face and turns into a sneer, the kind I've trained myself to catch the moment it snakes across my own face. Meg says I broadcast my dislike for people, so I've practiced maintaining a more neutral expression when in conversations with neighbors, dog walkers, and anyone in retail.

"Poppy," he says, lightly touching my arm. "So nice to see you again. Glad our little house of horrors didn't frighten you away."

Barbara grunts in response.

"Have you all heard the latest?" he asks. "Sharon's gone missing."

He turns to Barbara with a look of malevolent glee I haven't seen since I stopped watching *The Real Housewives.*

"She hasn't gone missing," Barbara says, rolling her eyes. "She's visiting her daughter, Bernard."

"So you say."

"I can show you the letter she left me again if it will help your memory."

"My memory's just fine, thank you," Bernard says. "I remember the last time she visited her daughter, she stayed only a few days because of her allergies."

"Oh, that's terrible," Ginny chimes in. "What's she allergic to?"

"Her grandchildren," Bernard says, chuckling. "Hates the little buggers."

"Oh, you're impossible," Barbara huffs. She turns on her heels and leads her companions into the cafeteria.

I've never desired the company of another human being more in my life.

"Please join us for dinner," I beg.

"I'd love to," he says, crooking his elbow so we can link arms. I'm in love with this man. I don't care that he's gay. What does it matter now, anyway? He likes to gossip, and I like to wallow in misery. We're made for each other.

The dining hall is large, divided into four distinct dining sections—two near the entrance and two in the back. A wall of windows looks out onto a shaded courtyard. Ginny leads us to an open table in the corner set for four.

"Fancy," I say, removing the napkin from my water glass and placing it in my lap.

The young man who ruined Sharon's top is our waiter. I'm happy to see he hasn't been fired, but not convinced he's chosen the right profession. He lists slightly as he stands and takes our order. Ginny and Bernard get the fish, which I consider a brave choice. I order the Caesar salad.

"What kind of dressing would you like on that?" he asks. He doesn't look me in the eye, so focused is he on scribbling on his pad of paper.

"What kind of dressing?" I ask.

"Yes, ma'am."

I look at Ginny for confirmation that my hearing isn't failing me. She just shrugs and uncorks the bottle of wine we've brought down from her room.

"The Caesar dressing," I say.

The boy nods. He's got a faint wisp of a mustache that looks like a beaded lip curtain.

"Can you bring us three wineglasses, Alfredo?" Ginny asks.

The boy looks at the bottle of wine like it's an explosive Ginny's just activated. When he starts to remove our water glasses, Ginny stops him with a gentle hand on his arm. "We'll keep the water."

Alfredo nods and doesn't return. After five minutes, we drink our water and refill our glasses with chardonnay.

"Is my Caesar salad going to come with ranch dressing?" I ask.

"Help's been hard to find," Bernard says. "Alfredo's doing his best, but he's got this whole section to manage."

I take a sip of wine and wonder what will happen to all the retirement homes that can no longer afford to pay their workers a livable wage. If Xanadu, with its million dollar move-in fee, can't hire waiters who know what dressing goes on a Caesar salad, what hope do other care facilities have? Where will all the caretakers come from? As an old person, I'm not sure I want to be revered the way the elderly are in Japan, but I'd also like not to be warehoused and forgotten either. If Meg and Jeremy ever leave, God forbid, I won't have anyone to help me manage the most basic tasks, unless Silicon Valley starts mass-producing cheap robots to cook, clean, and play Scrabble with me. And who wants to play Scrabble against an AI robot with access to every word ever created since the dawn of time anyway?

"You ever been married, Bernard?" I ask, hoping the answer is no so he doesn't have any expectations going into our union.

Bernard leans over and smiles in a playfully devilish way. "Why, you interested?"

I feel my face flush. Ginny and Bernard smile at my discomfort. "Bernard's a widower," Ginny says. "His husband died three years ago. Just before he moved in here."

"They don't allow same-sex couples here at Xanadu so he had to go," Bernard says, drawing a finger across his throat.

"That's not true, is it?" Ginny says.

"It's not stated anywhere explicitly," Bernard says. "But do you see any gay or lesbian couples here?"

"Oh my word," I say. "Who cares about that stuff at our age?"

"Apparently, Barbara and her cronies do," Bernard says. "We were on the waiting list for years while Robert was sick. They said he didn't meet the requirements for independent living or some such nonsense."

"You have to be able to walk through the door unassisted," Ginny says.

"I'm surprised you wanted to live here after they put you through all that."

"This was the only place where I could perform my cabaret act. All the other nightclubs kicked me out."

"Bernard is our resident musician," Ginny says. "He plays the piano in the lobby every Thursday night."

"Lucky for me most of the residents are hard of hearing," he says.

"Don't be so modest," Ginny says. "He's a beautiful player."

"Then how come I never see you in the audience, Ginny?"

"Poppy and I will go tonight," she says, looking at me for confirmation.

"I wouldn't miss it for the world," I say.

Alfredo arrives with our food and fills our water glasses. I place a hand over mine to keep him from diluting my wine and he gives me a nice washing. He apologizes and rushes off in a panic.

I pat my hand dry, while Bernard lightly chuckles. "That boy," he says, shaking his head. "Like watching a puppy in a room full of squirrels."

We spend the rest of dinner swapping stories. I forgot what it's like to be interested in someone else's life and have them be interested in mine. Bernard tells us about bouncing between apartments in Buenos Aires and Paris, playing music, hanging out with artists, falling in love. It's a highlight reel, of course. We'll need a few more dinners to get to the more tragic parts of Bernard's story.

When the Popsicle ladies saunter past they're careful not to look in our direction.

"Tell me more about what you think happened to Sharon," I say leaning in. "She was on the Senior Torments dating site too, wasn't she?"

"Oh, stop it, you two," Ginny says.

"She was," Bernard says.

"How would you know that?" Ginny asks.

"I'm the building's tech support, remember?" Bernard says. "Sharon needed help syncing her devices so I got to peek at some of her apps. Senior Moments was on the homepage."

"And you think someone on Senior Moments killed these women?" I say, happy for once to have a co-conspiracist at the table.

"It's what Cynthia and Sharon had in common," Bernard says.

"Oh, please," Ginny says. "They had much more in common than that. And Sharon isn't dead, Bernard. She's visiting her daughter."

"So Barbara says."

"Why would she lie?"

Bernard shrugs. "Maybe because she doesn't want to be queen bee of a dying hive. If Xanadu gets a reputation as a murder palace, everyone's going to flock to the other retirement homes."

"Barbara could do that too, couldn't she?" I ask. "She seems like she's loaded."

"Oh, you've noticed, have you?" Bernard says, laughing.

"She's not on a fixed income like the rest of us," Ginny says.

"The other day, she took her crew to Le Colonial for a tasting of Caymus Cabernets."

"Those are two hundred dollars a bottle!"

"They are," Bernard says. "How do you know that?"

"Cristóbal wanted me to buy a couple cases for his restaurant."

Bernard looks at me, but his expression is vague and shifting. Some combination of concern, interest, and glee. I'm reminded that with gossips, there is no such thing as bad news.

"Personally, I prefer a residence with a bit of scandal," he says. "Keeps things interesting. Without these murders, what would we have to talk about? Grandchildren? Our Wordle scores?" Bernard shudders at the thought.

"I got it in three today," Ginny says.

"I need to stretch these muscles," Bernard says, interlacing his fingers and bending them back, like a burglar loosening up before cracking a safe. "It was lovely seeing you again, Poppy."

"You too, Bernard," I say. "I'm looking forward to hearing you play."

We follow him to the piano and settle on some foldout chairs in the back. There are already a dozen or so people waiting for the musician to arrive. Bernard greets each of them personally and takes any request they have. When he starts to play, the music transforms the lobby into a concert hall. Most of Bernard's repertoire consists of showtunes I don't recognize. But the audience knows them and sings along in wobbly voices. I even hear Ginny humming along at one point. I look over at her and catch her smiling, the song clearly triggering some happy memory she luxuriates in. I grab her hand, feel her soft skin in mine, and squeeze, hoping some of her joy transfers over to me.

Another Xanadu resident has left the building and all I can think about is that Ginny will be next.

30

June 9

Ginny is annoyingly chipper about Cristóbal as she drives me home as if to punish me for encouraging Bernard's speculation that Cynthia and Sharon were killed by someone they met on Senior Moments. Did she tell me about their plans to cruise around the Cayman Islands? Cristóbal has a yacht with a staff of people who wait on you hand and foot. Of course, she's going to have to lose ten more pounds to be "swimsuit ready" but she's positive she can do it with Max's help. She can already notice a difference in her butt and asks me if I've noticed it too, to which I nod and say, "Sure have," and go back to staring out the window.

We pass the houses of people I've known. Or knew. People who managed to stay together, raise families, live happy and fulfilling lives. That Eichler with the bricked driveway is the Fosters' place. Greg and I used to go camping with Bill and Elaine when our kids were in elementary school. Elaine and I would volunteer for school events and then sneak in booze and complain about the other mothers. She was always saying that Bill worked too much, but they managed to stay together, raising their kids and going on vacations. They still decorate their house for

Halloween and pass out candy for God's sake. Who does that once your kids have moved out of the house? They do. The weirdos.

Ginny's yammering on about her diet and I try to pay attention, but I keep getting distracted by memory lane. There's Kim and Rob's place. They used to have the best dinner parties. Every time it was a different country's cuisine and they did all the cooking themselves. Was that why my marriages failed? Did I not find enough activities for my husbands and me to do together? Would things have been different if only I loved muscle cars or gun shows? Kim and Rob moved to a bigger house after they had their fourth child. Four children! They still send me holiday cards. Each year they add another baby or two. Not Kim and Rob. Their children. That would be pretty grotesque if Kim and Rob were still having babies. They must all get together every year to take the picture, maybe for Thanksgiving or summer vacation. That alone is impressive. When was the last time Meg, Jeremy, and I posed for anything? And we all live in the same house!

Maybe I'm suspicious of Ginny's relationship because it's another example of happiness eluding me. If I'm being honest, part of the reason I want to prove Ginny is getting scammed is because it fits my theory that all relationships are built on lies. If someone shows an interest in you, they probably want something besides your company. Often, it's someone to have sex with. At my age, it's someone to cook and clean for them. Or worse, someone whose income can make up for a life of poor planning and bad decisions. Just look at Meg and her new boyfriend. You think Mr. Mustache is so desperate to move in together because she's such a catch? That guy didn't take an interest in my daughter until he saw my zip code. Now all he's got to do is convince Meg to put me in a home so he can sell the house and start podcasting about his line of stool softeners.

"You okay, Poppy?" Ginny asks, pulling up in front of my house. It's such a sad, neglected thing compared to the others on my street, like that child who always came to school in mismatched, dirty clothes and scratched his head all day.

"Just tired," I say.

Ginny sighs. "I'm such a ninny, blathering on about Boost a Move so much."

"I'm sorry, what?"

"The vitamin supplement. Cristóbal's been taking it for years and says it's done wonders for his gut health."

"That's Craig's company, Ginny," I nearly scream. "The one he's always advertising on his tank tops."

"Maybe that's why it sounded so familiar."

"Don't you think that's strange?"

"Not really," Ginny says. "Craig's a personal trainer, isn't he? Seems like a product he might endorse."

"He's not endorsing the product. He's selling it."

"I'm sure a lot of people sell it, dear. It's very popular. Lots of people at Xanadu take it."

"It just seems like a big coincidence."

"Coincidence of what?" Ginny says, annoyed. "You think Cristóbal and Craig are working together to get me to buy vitamin supplements now?"

When she puts it like that, it does sound ridiculous. It also doesn't explain all the lavish gifts Cristóbal has given Ginny throughout their courtship. No way Craig could afford to be that generous.

"I don't know," I say. "Just promise me you won't take that supplement. If Craig works for the company, it's got to be snake oil. He tried to sell me a batch the other day. Said it would cure my depression."

"Maybe you *should* see someone about that," Ginny says. "You see the dark side in everything."

I'm about to spit out some venom, but I remember to plank my tongue. With my mouth closed, I'm forced to swallow my own poison, which leaves a bitter taste in my throat. Before my eyes well up, I thank Ginny for the ride and get out of the car.

"Poppy, I'm sorry," Ginny says before I can close the door. "I shouldn't have said that."

"No, you're right," I say. "I'll see you tomorrow."

I wave goodbye and enter my house. The place is quiet and I walk through the rooms adjusting and straightening things that don't need adjusting or straightening. Eventually, I end up in the kitchen where I fill a glass of water at the sink. I go online and look up Boost a Move. The website is a repository of stock photos and implausible testimonials. Beside every five-star review saying the product cured rheumatism, arthritis, ulcers, and cancer is a photo of a geriatric woman playing tennis, toweling off after a swim, and in one shot that must be AI generated, scaling Half Dome in Yosemite.

Is everyone scamming seniors now? I think, slamming my laptop shut. How did we become such easy targets? We're supposed to be the wise sages everyone turns to for advice. Instead, we're the dupes everyone thinks they can lie, cheat, and steal from. They make us fall in love to get our money. They sell us a magical elixir to get our money. What happened to the good old days when someone would just point a gun to your head and demand you hand over your purse? At least those criminals were honest. They didn't add insult to injury.

I'm so mad, I pound on Jeremy's door. There's no answer. It's seven o'clock so I know he's home. After waiting a few minutes, I open the door and flick on the light.

"Jeremy, I'm coming down," I warn him. I worry one day that I'll interrupt something truly disturbing, like some Satanic ritual involving candles and pig's blood, but so far it's just been a lot of farting.

"What?" he says from his computer station. He's got his headphones on and some kind of first-person shooter game on the screen in front of him.

"These scammers," I say, pointing at Jeremy's monitors. "How amateur are they?"

"Very," he says.

"How hard would it be to scam them?" I ask.

"Like shooting ducks in a barrel," he says.

"Fish, Jeremy," I say. "The expression is 'like shooting *fish* in a barrel.'" Unless of course he means ducks, which I don't think he does. Jeremy's not very good at idioms.

Jeremy waves me off, eager to get back to his game.

"Let's start with the professor, then," I say. "The one who's already conned two women."

"You sure?" Jeremy asks.

I nod. "What do we do?"

"We string him along until he asks for money."

"Then what?"

"That depends," Jeremy says. "How much do you want him to suffer?"

I don't have to think about this. Not even for a second. "I want him to suffer," I say. "I want him to suffer a lot."

31

June 9

In retrospect, I probably should have said something to Jeremy about the dangerous game we were playing. Here I was, inviting him to a treasure hunt without telling him about the sharks and pirates. I don't know why I didn't say anything. I want to think it's because I didn't think we were in danger. That's easier for me to accept than the alternative: that I let my hate of bullies supersede my love for my grandson.

I don't need therapy to tell me why I can't stand bullies. First off, it's not a psychological disorder to fight back when someone tries to hurt you. That's just self-preservation. It takes courage and strength to stand up to assholes. The thing I can't understand is why bullies have been a near constant in my life. I mean, if you hate something so much, wouldn't you do everything you could to avoid it? Bullies are like onions for me though—in every dish whether you want them there or not.

My father was my first bully. Growing up, he was always in a foul mood, despite having a depression-proof job on Bend, Oregon's, police force. Dad liked to brag about all the losers he put away but in my six-year-old imagination I saw him as bringing all those bad men home to us. Every night, at least every night that I remember, he'd come home drunk, scream, and break things, until he passed out on our couch. By the time I was ten, I started hoping some criminal would kidnap him and hold him for ransom just so we could have the pleasure of refusing to pay. But Bend wasn't a dangerous town, unfortunately. It didn't have bootleggers or mobsters who might help put us out of our misery. Dad was the biggest threat to law-abiding citizens there, which meant we were trapped.

Mom did her best to keep me safe. Women in those days didn't have many options if they wanted to leave their abusive husbands. They had fewer options if their abusive husband was a police officer. Her best defensive strategy was being an unimpeachable wife. She knew Dad's triggers and cleared those land mines every day before he got home. Our house was spotless, the fridge always full, her body always perfumed and presentable. Timing dinner so that it would be ready and warm was impossible though as Dad's arrival was totally unpredictable. It didn't matter if he stumbled in at five, eight, or ten o'clock, she'd have food on the table and a smile on her face. If we were lucky, Dad would pass out in his mashed potatoes. If we weren't, we'd have to sit and watch this human volcano grumble until he spewed hot lava over both of us.

I don't know who I hated more growing up. My father the asshole, or my mother who never fought back. I vowed never to be like either of them, but somehow I became a freakish hybrid of both, a suspicious and sneaky child who quietly tortured people she saw as threats.

Getting even with Dad was easy. I'd collect spiders and release them on his body after he passed out. I gathered bushels of poison oak and rubbed it all over his underwear. I spent whole afternoons rounding up feral cats just so I could release them in his car. These tiny ambushes sustained me until I got my ultimate revenge: running off with the boy my dad hated most in the world.

Greg was a troublemaker. Not a criminal who robbed banks or anything, but he wasn't averse to stealing a car when he needed one. He'd gotten into it with my dad on more than one occasion. After he "fell" while in police custody and got sent to the hospital with a broken collarbone, he started paying me more attention. I should have known then he was enacting his own form of revenge against my dad in carting me away.

I'd like to say our mutual loathing of my dad sustained our first years of marriage. Those were happy times as we travelled south to California, sending Dad photos of our Vegas wedding, my pregnancy, Meg's birth. We took such delight imagining Dad opening our letters, seeing all the evidence of a crime he was incapable of stopping. I'm sure Mom never let him see a single piece of our correspondence, preferring to keep him in the dark on the new life I had started. This too brought its own satisfaction, the knowledge that his only daughter had become a cold case, filed away and forgotten until someone at work or church made the mistake of asking about me.

I called Mom whenever I was sure Dad would be out of the house so we could talk. She was sorry I had to take such extreme measures to escape, but I assured her I was happy and that she could come join us anytime. Greg had gotten a job at an apricot orchard, first working in the fields then moving on to management after he impressed some computer geek by the name of David Packard. She declined my offer, predictably, saying she didn't want to be anyone's burden.

I vowed never to be like her, which I probably took to extremes. If you're constantly looking for bullies, you'll see them everywhere, even in your own children. That's Dad's ultimate revenge on me. He's the ghost that's haunted every relationship and why, even though I complain about my daughter and grandson all the time, I'm terrified of them abandoning me.

32

June 12

Three days later, I'm about to start my morning crossword when Jeremy surprises me by making an appearance. He's either just woken up or he hasn't been asleep—the two look almost indistinguishable from each other. "Ready to go to work?" he says, rubbing his eyes.

"Have you slept?" I ask, looking at his disheveled appearance.

"Some," he said. "I've been setting up our sting operation. C'mon, check it out."

He motions for me to follow him downstairs, which is at least ten degrees cooler than the kitchen. Before I descend too far I turn around and grab a sweater from my dresser. It's a Christmas gift from Meg. I think it's called *athleisure*, which sounds to me like an oxymoron, sportswear designed for the sedentary.

When I finally join Jeremy, he's sitting at his workstation, which now has an additional monitor. "Let's do some hacking," he says, spinning in his seat. I sit in the kitchen chair and put on my glasses. He's got a chat box from the dating site up and running and I can see he's been busy flirting with Bao, his would-be Vietnamese grandpa. When he sees me looking, he quickly minimizes the window so I can't eavesdrop.

"Before we do this," I say. "I want to establish some ground rules."

"No kinky sex talk. Got it."

"Not that," I say. "If we're going to hurt people, I want to make sure they deserve it. I want us to be more like Robin Hood and less like Bernie Madoff."

"All these guys are douchebags," Jeremy says. "Trust me."

"Yes, but some are worse than others," I say. "Take that guy from Nigeria, for example. What do you think his life is like? Do you think he has the same opportunities we have here?"

Jeremy opens another window and starts typing. "Nigeria is the twenty-seventh largest economy in the world," he reads. "Its GDP growth, especially in areas of industry and services, is incredibly high. Its unemployment rate is 6 percent. It has the highest number of universities of any country in Africa. I'd say they're doing pretty well."

"What about the history of colonialism and oppression?" I ask. I don't know that history myself, but I assume it's pretty bad. No one was a bigger bully than Great Britain in Africa. "Let's leave any country below the equator off our list."

"Nigeria is above the equator, Grandma," Jeremy says.

"You know what I mean," I say. "No African countries. Let's leave India out too."

"India's a gold mine of scammers," Jeremy whines.

"No India," I say. "Let's just target white people. Like in Russia."

"That sounds pretty racist," Jeremy says.

"Can't I be racist against my own race?" I ask.

Jeremy shrugs. "I've given up trying to keep track of all the ways I can be racist."

"That sounds pretty racist," I say, poking him in the shoulder.

"You're making this less fun, Grandma," Jeremy whines.

"Let's just target people in the US. I don't care what race they are. If they grew up here and know enough to set up fake identities to scam old people out of money, they deserve to be punished."

"Deal," Jeremy says and turns back to his chat box.

"Can I bring you something to eat?" I offer.

"A grilled cheese would be nice," Jeremy says.

"Coming right up."

I'm in the middle of making Jeremy his breakfast when Meg and Craig waltz in the front door. Meg doesn't announce she's got a visitor, which is kind of rude given the time of day. It's only 9:00 A.M. I could be in my pajamas. I'm suddenly grateful for my athleisure wear.

"Can I get one of those?" Craig says, nodding in the direction of the grilled cheese. Does he think he's charming me? He'd have better luck if he brought me a coffee and donut. But both of them are empty-handed.

"Sorry, out of cheese," I lie, hoping Meg doesn't poke her head into the fridge. I go back to watching the bread sizzle in the pan. Jeremy likes his grilled cheese only partially melted so I have to time this just right.

"Who's that for?" Meg asks. I notice both of them remain standing, which means they're not staying long.

"Your son," I say, sliding the sandwich onto a plate.

"He's awake?" Meg says.

I scoot past her and walk the sandwich down to Jeremy. "Your mom's here," I say, placing the plate next to his keyboard.

"Hmph," Jeremy says. He stuffs his mouth with sandwich and chews. I regret not bringing him a glass of milk. "Come back down after she leaves," he says. "I think our professor is about to pop the question."

"You mean propose?"

"I mean ask for money."

I walk back upstairs. I hope all this traveling between floors doesn't ruin my knees for walking club later. My joints are starting to protest loudly.

When I reenter the kitchen, Meg and Craig are gone, which means their visit wasn't driven by the need for breakfast. I find them in Meg's room. She's piling clothes into an open suitcase on her bed, while Craig looks at the base of a lamp on Meg's bedside table.

"You going somewhere?" I ask.

"I'm moving out," Meg says, opening her closet and lifting an armful of clothes off the rack. "We discussed this, Mom, remember?"

Meg's gaslighting me again. "We talked about the *possibility* of you moving out," I say.

Meg looks at Craig. *Here we go again*, her face seems to say. I'm half tempted to rebut this characterization of me having a senior moment with a very clear summary of our conversation. *You said things were moving too fast and that when you hesitated Craig acted like a baby and accused you of thinking you were better than him*, I want to say. But I don't. Meg has obviously made her decision and there's nothing I can do to stop her and I'm not even sure I want to. If Craig thinks he's taking that lamp though, he's got another thing coming.

"Leave your address so I can forward your mail," I say, and leave the room.

I go back to the kitchen and pour myself a fresh cup of coffee. For me, the hardest part of Meg's recovery was learning how to step away and I'm still not very good at it. At least now, I don't say the first thing that pops into my head. I've learned that I will lose every argument with her so it's better not to engage. When she was younger, I fought her over every stupid decision she made, thinking my anger could scare her straight. But all my screaming did was feed her desire to escape, not just me, but everything. So, I had to teach myself to see Meg less as my daughter and more like a tenant, someone who would come and go and whom I had no emotional attachment to. But this too had its own repercussions as Meg shared in therapy. "You abandoned me when I needed you the most," she said. "Well, you abandoned me first," I responded, which the therapist seized on immediately.

"You have to stop seeing Meg's addiction as a rebuke of your parenting," she said.

"Isn't it though?" I said, honestly confused about how to see it any other way.

"Your father was an alcoholic," the therapist kindly pointed out. "Meg has a genetic predisposition for addiction."

"So I'm the common denominator," I said. "Whether it's nature or nurture, I'm the one to blame."

While Meg is in the bathroom filling her toiletry bag with her pills, lotions, and makeup, Craig hauls her suitcase out to his truck. When he comes back, he lingers in the doorway, adjusting his black BM T-shirt. I've got to say, it's a better look than the tank tops he wears at the gym. At least in this T-shirt all I see is the silhouette of his muscles without all the moles and sprouting hairs. I wait for him to say something, but he's scanning the counter space, probably taking inventory of my appliances. I go back to doing my crossword puzzle.

"You want my address?" he asks finally, holding out a meaty hand for my pencil. I hand it over along with a strip of newspaper. He scribbles the address and I notice for the first time that he's left-handed. *The sign of the devil*, I think to myself, repeating mother's mantra from many years ago.

Meg comes back in holding two vinyl cases stuffed with all her essential beauty products. "Well, we're off," she says brightly. "We're just going to grab a few pieces of furniture."

"That furniture isn't yours," I say. "It stays in the house."

"What are you going to do with it?" Meg asks.

Save it for when you come back, I want to say. *Keep it from showing up on eBay. Protect it from being branded by Craig's carved initials.* "Maybe I'll rent the room out," I say.

"Seriously?" Meg says.

I shrug. "You never know."

"Mom, come on," Meg whines. "Craig lives in a bachelor pad. I want to make it more homey."

"Then buy your own stuff," I say.

"Can I at least take the coffee table?"

I shake my head. "That was my mother's. It's a family heirloom."

"But I'm family," Meg says.

"Then you're welcome to come visit it anytime."

Meg sighs and looks at Craig, another piece of nonverbal communication passing between them. Craig turns and walks out of the room without saying goodbye. When Meg follows him, I shout, "Aren't you going to say goodbye to your son?"

I see Meg hesitate. She takes a step toward the basement door, but Craig calls her from the front door. "Babe, I've got to get this truck back by ten."

"I'll text him later," Meg says and leaves the room.

I follow them out of the house. I'm curious to see the size of the truck Craig borrowed to haul Meg's suitcases. It's enormous. I'd need a hydraulic lift just to get into the passenger seat. Did this guy really think I was going to let him haul away my furniture? I brace myself for what's coming next, having lived through this before. The first time Meg left the house, she was only seventeen. She ran away with another loser boyfriend and I didn't hear from her for three months. One day I woke up and all my jewelry was gone. When she eventually returned, she confessed to having stolen it and begged me to send her to rehab, which I did. The next time, Meg was in her late twenties, just after she had Jeremy. She left with another addict but not before selling my mother's silver flatware. The only reason she didn't grab my furniture is because she didn't have someone with a U-Haul.

But now she does.

I make a mental note to call someone in to change the locks this week. It might be a good time to get Jeremy to help me install a video surveillance system while I'm at it.

I return to the basement lair and take a seat next to my grandson.

"Mom gone?" he asks.

"Yup."

"She moving in with that guy?"

"Looks like it."

Jeremy taps on his keyboard, flirting with a man who wants to retire to Lake Como with me.

"How are things going with what's-his-name?"

"Rufus Wellington?"

I laugh. "That name is almost aggressively English."

"His real name is Todd Blutch."

"How do you know?"

"I have access to his computer."

"How'd you do that?"

Jeremy explains the process to me in technical terms that are beyond my comprehension. When he sees my bewilderment, he starts talking to me like I'm a five-year-old.

"Imagine you're a little girl and I give you a doll you want more than anything. Only the doll has a tiny camera inside that lets me spy on you."

"That's a disturbing scenario," I say.

Jeremy nods, accepting my criticism. "Okay. You know the expression, 'You catch more bees with honey'?"

"It's flies," I say. "You catch flies with honey."

"I don't think that's right," Jeremy says. "But anyway, what I've created here is called a honeypot. First, I load the computer with lots of fake information about your net worth, making it seem like you're a millionaire. Then I let your suitors hack into the computer."

"How do you do that?"

"Usually, they send me a link to open that installs the malware. This guy Blutch sent you a link, claiming it was a funny video of two pandas in a hammock."

"Ooh, let me see," I say.

"It was a fake, Grandma," Jeremy says, exasperated. "Never open links like that. They're just ways for hackers to take control of your computer. Blutch got control of my computer, my honeypot computer. When he clicked on your fake bank statement, it gave me access to his computer."

Jeremy sees my disappointment about the pandas so he pulls up a panda video on TikTok for me to watch. They are adorable enough to distract me from the fact that we have nabbed our first victim.

"Now what?" I ask when the video ends.

"That's up to you. Now that I have control of his computer, I can steal his identity, hold his files hostage, blackmail him. It all depends on how low you want to go."

I want to go subterranean, I almost say. But this was my grandson. I have to set a better example than that, right? Jeremy has some dark power and I need him to harness it for good, not evil, otherwise he'll wind up as one of these scammers we're trying to fight. "How much flirting are you willing to do?" I ask.

Jeremy turns away from me and smiles at his screen. "This is going to sound strange, but I kind of don't mind the flirting."

"Really?" I say, surprised. "Is that what you were doing with Bao?"

I try to keep my voice judgment-free but Jeremy cringes in embarrassment.

"It's okay if you like him," I say. I've heard about men seeking "daddies" on the Internet, although Bao seems more like a granddaddy. Maybe these *Harold and Maude* relationships are common in gay culture? What do I know?

Jeremy scowls. "It's not like that," he says. "I just like talking with the guy. He knows a surprising amount about weed strains for an old dude. I think he grows it in his backyard. I've had to turn you into a heavy pot smoker to get him to share his gardening tips."

"He has a cannabis garden?" I say.

Jeremy nods with more enthusiasm than I've seen since . . . forever. "It doesn't feel right to catfish the guy," he says, "which means I'll have to kill you and take over as a grieving grandson to continue the relationship."

"I applaud your ethics, Jeremy, but don't kill me off until we get even with Rufus. Can you make him buy me something expensive?

Something I can sell so I can give the money to my friend? Her husband just had a stroke and she needs all the help she can get."

"I think I can do that," Jeremy says. "This guy already thinks you're loaded thanks to the phony bank records I put on your desktop. He might be willing to make a small investment if he thinks it's going to pay off later."

"Just don't get caught," I say.

"Don't worry about me," Jeremy says. "These guys are idiots."

33

June 12

Max is waiting for us when we pull up in front of her house. She's in her dark purple tracksuit and stretching on the sidewalk. Just seeing her dip into a hamstring stretch is enough to make my muscles sore. Ginny and I groan before stepping out of the air-conditioned car. Why am I putting myself through this agony? I ask myself for the thousandth time. It's either a way to stave off death or hurry it along.

Max seems distracted on our walk, letting muscle memory guide her rather than any conscious decision-making. When we pass the playground, she doesn't stop to do a pull-up on the jungle gym. It's been her life's mission to get Ginny and me to lift our bodies an inch off the ground, but now she passes the rusty torture device without comment.

"Six thousand one hundred and eight," Max mumbles under her breath. That's the cost of Harold's new bed, a mechanical crib that keeps him from falling out at night. I know this because Max can't stop repeating the number like it's her step count goal.

"Call your kids," I say.

Max shakes her head. "I can't."

"Why not?" I say. "They're all success stories. They owe you."

Max gives me the side-eye. We clearly have different beliefs when it comes to parental obligation. If I were drowning, I'd like my kids to try and save me. Max, on the other hand, would rather quietly go under and not interrupt their sunset cruise.

"How do you think they'll feel when they find out you lost all your savings to pay these home care bills?" I ask.

"Or had to sell your house?" Ginny chimes in.

"I'm not selling the house," Max says. "Not while Harold's still alive."

"All we're saying is this shouldn't be something you fight alone," I say.

Max picks up her pace and creates some distance between us. Why does her stubbornness bother me so much? I've only known her a little over a month and only tolerated her for half that time. Somehow, I've come to depend on her in ways that mystify me. What initially bothered me about her personality—her imperiousness, her condescension, her toned arms—are now the things I like best about her. I've never met someone as competent and capable as Max. Maybe that's why her fall from grace hurts so much. If the world can break her down, what chance do the rest of us have?

We return to Max's house huffing and puffing. Well, Ginny and I do. Max still has the energy to do some jumping jacks on her lawn. She's a bundle of pent-up energy. Or maybe she's just avoiding going back into the house, a place that smells of Harold's body slowly shutting down.

Eventually we go inside for some water. Max points Ginny and me in the direction of the kitchen while she goes to check on Harold and his nurse. It's not long before we hear Max barking commands like she's leading another water aerobics class.

"Honestly," she says storming into the kitchen. Ginny and I stare out the window, pretending to watch a hummingbird zip around the garden. "You'd think someone from Russia would be more sensitive to cold."

The house feels fine to me. I'm more concerned about the unwashed plate in the sink. If Max sees that she's going to lose it and fire this woman.

"We're just admiring your hydrangeas," Ginny says, directing Max's attention outside.

I use her diversion to stash the plate in the dishwasher.

"What are you doing?" Max asks.

"I made myself some toast," I say, wiping my mouth of invisible bread crumbs.

Max squints, trying to spot the lie. Ginny sits her down at the kitchen table. "Let me get you something to drink, dear," she says moving toward the refrigerator. "Want some iced tea?"

Max nods. While Ginny is filling her glass, I sit down. "You need help."

"I've got Svetlana."

"Not for long," I say. "You're driving her crazy."

"I'm not the one trying to create Siberian conditions in the home of an invalid."

"It's perfectly comfortable in here," I say, thankful for the air-conditioning. I never had it installed and have to sit in front of a fan when it gets this hot outside.

Max sighs. "Truth is, I don't know how much longer I can afford her. She's only here twenty hours a week as it is."

"Let us help you," Ginny says.

"You are helping me," Max says. "These walks are my only escape from this place."

"We want to do more," Ginny says. She looks at me and I nod, although to be honest I don't know what more I can do. I'm already dipping into my savings to bring Max meals twice a week. Ginny may have a rich boyfriend, but I do not.

"You're already doing too much," Max says. She gulps down her iced tea and stands up to put the glass in the dishwasher.

"Let me set up a GoFundMe account for you," Ginny says.

"What's that?" Max asks.

"It's an online fundraising site," Ginny says. "People use them to help pay medical bills."

"Why would strangers want to pay my medical bills?" Max asks.

"Not just strangers," Ginny says. "People in your social network."

"You're my social network," Max says.

"I can send the link out to the residents of Xanadu," Ginny says. "They're very generous."

"I don't know," Max says.

"If Harold needed a kidney, would you accept one from a stranger?" I ask.

"Of course," Max says.

"Well, this is the same thing."

"It is not the same thing," Max says. "One involves a lifesaving organ and the other is asking for a handout."

"It's not a handout," Ginny says. "It's a donation to a worthy cause."

"I'm sure there are more worthy causes," Max says.

"None for me," I say.

"Me neither," Ginny says. "Let me do this for you, please."

"Fine," Max says. "But I don't want to be involved."

"I won't say a word," Ginny says. "But I will need a photo of Harold. Preferably one that elicits sympathy."

"I can give you the one of him in the Peace Corps," Max says.

"Perfect," Ginny says.

Max disappears and comes back holding a large, leather-bound, photo album. She places it between us and flips through the plastic sheathed pages until she lands on a photo of a young, blond Harold sitting astride a horse while a bunch of African children work the fields around him.

"Uh," Ginny says. "Let's see what else you have."

We continue to flip through the pages until we find a picture of Harold standing behind a well, arm in arm with beaming local villagers. Harold is Lawrence of Arabia handsome, if Lawrence looked like the actor who played him in the movie. He's tanned, slim, and healthy, a different species of man from the one lying in bed down the hall. Time is the most devious of thieves, I think. It steals everything and then leaves us with a bill we can't afford to pay.

"Do you have any photos of you when you were younger?" I ask.

Max flips through the photo album until landing on a picture of her, standing on a train platform, suitcase in hand. The photo is grainy black and white, but I can tell Max was a fiery redhead with a knockout body that even an ugly khaki skirt can't hide.

"When was this taken?" I ask.

"When I left South Africa," Max says. "My parents had a farm there."

I stare at the photo, mesmerized by the young beauty staring back at me. It's easier to see the resemblance between past and present Max than past and present Harold. She's still got the same strong, assertive attitude. I picture her about to embark on some incredible adventure to far-off lands filled with exotic creatures and spicy foods.

"Where were you going?" Ginny asks.

"Houston," Max says.

"Houston?" I say.

"I got a swimming scholarship at the university there."

"Of course," I say.

"That's where I learned what was really happening in South Africa," she says. "I never went back."

"Is that where you met Harold?" Ginny asks.

Max shakes her head. "Graduate school. He had just come back from the Peace Corps and was getting his civil engineering degree. I was getting my PhD in epidemiology. Zena Stein was a hero of mine."

Ginny and I nod our heads. Neither of us knows who Zena Stein is. I'm pretty sure we don't know what epidemiology is either.

"Should we be calling you Doctor Schelling?" Ginny asks.

"I never finished my dissertation," Max says. "I got pregnant my second year of graduate school."

"Do you regret it?" I ask.

Max pauses, looks down at the girl about to board the train that will take her to the future. "Sometimes," she says. "I think I let my children be my excuse for not trying harder."

"I can't imagine you not trying harder," Ginny says, shaking her head.

"I worked in labs but always struggled with the lead researcher. I don't know if you've noticed, but I can be a bit bossy."

Ginny and I burst out laughing.

"Home was the only place I felt in charge. Everywhere else, I had to follow someone else's rules and systems. That's hard for me. But without my doctorate, I could never run a lab the way I wanted it run. So, I struggled professionally."

"But your kids all turned out great," I say.

"Yes," Max says. "They're all smart and capable. At this point, I just hope they're happy."

Harold moans from down the hallway and we take that as our cue to leave. When Ginny and I are heading back to my house, I ask her to explain to me the logistics of a GoFundMe site.

"What if no one contributes?" I ask.

"We'll contribute," she says.

"I don't have a lot of money, Ginny," I remind her.

"I'll contribute then," she says. "And Cristóbal."

Her mention of Cristóbal's name reminds me that I have my own online suitor I can use. Instead of asking Rufus Wellington for diamonds, maybe I can ask him to contribute to a worthy cause. I'm sure he'd give a little something if it meant getting in my good graces.

34

June 12

It's quiet in the house now that Meg's gone. I don't like it. As much as my daughter drives me nuts, being alone in the house is even worse. Of course, I'm not alone. I'm still living with my grandson, who I see at meals or when he wants to give me an update on how my cyber dating is going. Apparently, he's turned me into a regular Liz Taylor on the platform.

"How would you feel about moving upstairs?" I ask him at dinner.

"Into Mom's room?"

"Yes."

"I don't know," he says crunching down on a piece of toast. I cooked up two salmon steaks I got on sale at Grocery Outlet but forgot we were out of rice. I don't think Jeremy minds though. He's just happy I'm not forcing him to eat his vegetables. "I kind of like my setup downstairs."

"Why don't you use downstairs as an office and your upstairs as a living space?"

"My living space is my office."

"I don't like you sleeping down there," I say. "Don't the rats bother you?"

"The poison's got most of them," Jeremy says. "Have you thought more about getting a cat?"

Meg and Jeremy had begged me to get a cat, which I refused. I told them I didn't need another mouth to feed but really, I'm more of a dog person and don't trust felines ever since I caught one with the head of a blue jay in its mouth.

"If you move upstairs, we can get a cat," I say.

Jeremy thinks about it. "What happens when Mom comes back?" he asks.

"Then you can go back downstairs," I say. "Only this time with a cat."

Jeremy doesn't give me an answer, but after dinner, we go into Meg's room and start to redecorate. There's not much we can do about the furniture. The four-poster bed frame and mahogany bureau both came from my mom and are too bulky for us to move. When Jeremy starts removing the framed flower prints from the wall, I know he's accepted my offer. All of Meg's prints and faux antique mirrors go into the closet, along with her throw pillows and blankets. By the time Jeremy's done, the room is a blank slate, minus the picture-hanging hardware, which studs the walls like those ugly face piercings young people seem to like.

When Jeremy moves his things upstairs, I'm shocked to see how little space they require. He's got two sweatshirts, a jacket, one pair of shoes, two pairs of jeans, and an armful of T-shirts, socks, and underwear. "Jeremy, we need to take you clothes shopping," I say, watching him dump his wardrobe into one drawer of the bureau.

"After we get a cat," he says.

The next day, we drive to the SPCA with our newly purchased cat carrier to do our pet shopping. I'd prefer an older cat, one that's been abandoned by its family and already knows how to live with humans.

Jeremy wants a kitten though, and I'm so pleased to see him engaging with another living creature that I allow it. Watching him move from window to window, trying to make a connection with the kittens housed in the carpeted pens, I can't help but think of him scouring those dating sites for scammers, only here, all the profiles are adorable, with names like Jitterbug and Peanut. He's falling in love with all of them. If these kittens were smarter, they could scam Jeremy out of every cent he owns.

He eventually decides on a black cat with white spots named Scampers. Jeremy feels like his dark fur will make him a better rat trapper when he's ready to start hunting. Once we're home, he cradles him for hours, stroking his fur and whispering in his ear, which has a little chunk bitten out of it.

Before long, the house fills with life again. Jeremy doesn't want Scampers in the basement until he's ready to battle the rodents, so he keeps him upstairs. That means he's upstairs more than ever too. Every hour or so, he takes a break from his computer work and comes up to play with the kitten, who is a bundle of energy that even I find endearing. Jeremy takes on the job of potty training the animal, keeping the litter box in the back laundry room where I can't see it or smell it. He's also going out more for toys and treats, which he brings home to the cat's delight. "Look, Grandma, I'm catfishing," Jeremy says, dangling a feather on a string in front of the leaping kitten. I'm happy to say I get the joke.

We don't hear anything from Meg, which isn't unusual. I collect her mail, mostly junk, so that I can hand deliver it in a week or two. Until then, I try not to worry about how she's doing. Fifty-three-year-old women aren't known for their hell-raising. If Meg starts drinking again, she'll only hurt herself. But she's been down that path before and can navigate the steps to recovery with her eyes closed.

35

June 14

"Rufus wants to talk to you," Jeremy announces Thursday morning. I'm doing my crossword, trying to remember the lead singer for the Beach Boys.

"Excuse me?"

"Rufus, the professor," Jeremy says, looking around for Scampers, who usually comes skidding around the corner when Jeremy makes an appearance upstairs.

"I don't want to talk to him," I say. "Or any of them."

Jeremy opens the refrigerator and pulls out a tin of cat food. He only wants the best for Scampers and has been footing the bill for the expensive brand. I don't ask him where he's getting the money, worried that I've lured him into a life of crime—first by setting up this Internet scam and then by giving him more incentive to rip people off.

As soon as Jeremy opens the can, Scampers comes leaping into the kitchen from the front room where all the morning light is. The kitten still hasn't learned how to move on the linoleum surface and has to work twice as hard to reach his destination. As soon as he gets to his food bowl, he face-plants into the wet gunk and inhales it.

"You may have to, Grandma," Jeremy says. "I could deepfake your voice, but I'm worried I won't stay in character. If I say 'dude' or 'bruh' accidentally, he'll know something's up."

"You can fake my voice?"

Jeremy nods. "All the scammers are doing it."

"How?"

"If there's a recording of your voice online, like from a TikTok or Instagram post, they can copy it and make it say anything. Imagine getting a phone call in the middle of the night from a grandchild saying their car's broke down and they need money right away."

"This world is a terrible place," I say.

"Can you just flirt with Rufus a little?" Jeremy says. "You still remember how to do that, don't you?"

I don't. That's a muscle that's been inactive for a very long time and it was never fully developed to begin with. I'll have to channel Stella LaFayette again, maybe put on the outfit I wore for my profile photo to get into character. Like Ginny said, online dating is easier because you're never talking face-to-face. I'll be a lot looser knowing the person isn't watching my neck wattle.

"When does he want to talk?" I ask.

"Uh, now," Jeremy says. "He's waiting downstairs."

"Are you serious?"

"Yes, I said you had to go to the bathroom."

"You told my Internet boyfriend I had to go to the bathroom?"

"What?" Jeremy says. "People your age have to go all the time, don't they?"

I groan and follow Jeremy downstairs, making sure to shut the door behind me so Scampers doesn't follow us down. I can hear him clawing the door as I descend.

Jeremy sits me down and helps me position the headset. He puts one on too and promises to coach me in case I get into trouble.

"Don't forget. You're Stella LaFayette, originally from Boca Raton, now residing in Atherton," he says. "You lost your husband two years ago to a heart attack and now spend your days at the track with your racehorses."

"Do you have a piece of paper so I can write all this down?"

"Here, I'll pull up your profile," Jeremy says. He types on the keyboard and up pops my dating profile on the screen to my left. I like this flirtatious version of me. Somehow, I've become a woman who hasn't given up. Stella LaFayette is a bit ridiculous, sure, but I bet she's happy and has lots of friends to keep her company. I scan the other info on the page and see that she's got 4,023 hearts besides her name.

"What are those?" I say, pointing.

"Those are people who are interested in you."

"That's quite a lot, isn't it?"

"You're very popular thanks to your inheritance," Jeremy says.

It's so silly to take pleasure in this but I do. What a nice thing to know. In real life, you could spend your entire life unaware that this many people found you attractive. I wonder how many love connections I missed because I wasn't paying attention or misinterpreted someone's wink as a nervous tic. It would be nice if computers took all this guesswork away, but if this dating app is any indication, they've just added another layer of bullshit to sift through.

"So, 'Rufus' is a college professor, specializing in ancient Roman civilizations."

"And who is he really?" I ask.

"He's a white supremacist in Idaho who's been arrested twice for drunk driving."

"Oh dear," I say.

"But don't worry about that. All he talks about is whisking you away to Italy. He says he has a villa near where George Clooney lives."

"Well that sounds nice," I say. "And you're sure he can't trace any of this back to me."

"Positive," Jeremy says. "I have access to his computer and he's a total amateur. Once we're done with him, I'll lock him out so he has no way to find us. Of course, we'll have to delete your dating profile, which will disappoint a lot of your suitors."

"Won't be the first time," I say with a wink. "What if I want him to donate money to my friend's GoFundMe account?"

Jeremy shakes his head. "If it's a legit account, then it's a breadcrumb he can use to find us," he says. "Better to get something you can sell and then put the money in the account yourself. Ask for a gift card. That's the currency most of these guys use."

"Got it," I say. I take a couple of deep breaths. "Okay, put him on."

Jeremy types on the keyboard, chatting with Rufus I suppose. Then he points his finger at me to tell me that I'm on. I hear the sound of static followed by some heavy breathing. "Hello?" I say, in my frailest old lady voice.

"Stella?" a man says. His voice is deep and gravelly, like that actor on the show with all the stabbings. It's hard to pinpoint the age. If I were to guess, I'd say mid-fifties, but he could be one of those deepfakes Jeremy just told me about. Maybe he's really a ten-year-old girl, to which I say, *More power to you, sister.* "So good to hear your voice."

"You too," I say.

Jeremy pantomimes a smile like a pageant mom. He points to my profile photo on the screen, a woman with Carol Channing hair and infused with joie de vivre. I straighten up and do my best to channel Blanche DuBois.

"I'm sorry to keep you waiting while I performed my ablutions," I say, immediately regretting the Southern accent. Jeremy stares at me, wide-eyed in horror. There's a pause at the other end of the line, an almost dead silence, and I wonder if my suitor has hung up on me. I look at the screen and picture one heart being removed from my total.

"It was worth the wait," he finally says. "You sound as pretty as you look."

"That's sweet," I say, toning Blanche DuDois down a notch. I should have imitated Ginny instead of a doomed Southern belle. I need to be sweeter, more innocent. Someone easily duped into romance. "What's the weather like there?"

Jeremy rolls his eyes and pretends to pound his head against the desk. His play-by-play commentary is not helping so I turn around to shield myself from his critiques.

"It's hot and humid." he sighs. "I wish I were in Lake Como now. Summers there are heavenly."

"I've never been to that part of Italy," I say, pleased with the phrasing. I've never been to Italy or anywhere outside the country for that matter, but Stella would have travelled there at some point in her marriage. Isn't that what rich couples do? Rent a vineyard or coastal estate for the summer and have affairs with the hired help?

"It's beautiful. In summer, we take the boat to a small town with the most delightful piazza."

I have to choke back a laugh at the sound of this. My Southern accent is flawless compared to this man's attempt at sounding British. Like hearing a line of Shakespeare being read by Don Rickles. What a couple of liars we are. I'm suddenly transported back in time after my first divorce when I'd chat up strangers in bars and conveniently forget to mention that I had a kid who was spending the weekend with her father.

"Why aren't you in Italy now?" I ask.

"I have to teach a summer seminar on Plato. As soon as the session ends though, I'm hopping on the first plane. Care to join me?"

"Rufus," I say, attempting to giggle. "Buy a girl a drink first."

"I'm sorry," he says. "I just feel like I already know you."

"Me too," I say, wishing Jeremy had shown me a bit of this history. It would have been helpful to know what we've been talking about these past few days. I'm flying blind here. This feeling of uncertainty is familiar. It's how I always felt when a man showed any interest in me. On some level, I always knew I was being scammed. Men trade compliments or feign intimacy to get what they want (i.e., sex). But this attention vanished around the same time my butt disappeared. Now the only time a man chats me up is if he's trying to convince me to buy a pair of uncomfortable shoes. I decide right then to take control of this conversation and steer it more toward getting what I want.

"Of all my suitors, you're the one I feel a special connection to," I say.

"All your suitors?" Rufus says. "I didn't realize you were playing the field."

"Aren't you?"

"I only have eyes for you."

"Liar," I say, laughing. "A widower with a house in Lake Como has got to be very popular with the ladies. I bet you've got lots of hearts next to your name."

"I never said I was a widower," Rufus says.

I turn around and find Jeremy scanning our chat. He turns to me and shakes his head in a panic.

"I'm sorry. I must have confused you with someone else," I stammer. "My memory's not what it used to be, I'm afraid."

"How many men are you currently dating?"

"I'm not dating any of them. Currently."

"Have any of the others promised to whisk you away to Italy?"

"They give me more tangible things."

"Such as?"

"I'm partial to perfumes. I like to smell nice."

I tap Jeremy on the shoulder and point to the monitor. He opens Amazon and searches for women's perfumes, sorting the results from the highest price to the low. My eyes bulge at the some of the $2,000 and higher brands on display. What are these tinctures made of? Endangered species?

"Gucci's my favorite," I say, spotting a bottle for $999.

"I'll send you some," Rufus says. "What's your address?"

Jeremy shakes his head.

"I don't give out my address to people I meet online," I say. "My grandchildren have warned me. You know there are a lot of scammers that take advantage of the elderly."

"We'll just have to figure out another way then."

"Well, Francois just gave me an Amazon gift card," I say. "Sent the code through the dating app. It worked out just fine. He's coming from New Orleans to take me out next week."

"Gift card, huh?"

I look at Jeremy to see if I've overplayed my hand. He twirls his pointer finger in the air, which is a gesture I don't understand. He's either telling me to stir things up or wind things down.

"He picked out some earrings he wants me to wear for our first date. Isn't that sweet?"

Rufus is silent and I worry that I've lost him.

"Rufus?"

I look at Jeremy who shrugs. I've blown it. Somehow this guy has seen through my act. Maybe these scammers are more sophisticated than I realized. They spend their time online stealing from people, after all. They must recognize the signs of a con.

But then I remember how Ginny, a woman who spent her entire career listening to made-up stories, fell for Cristóbal's promises of opening a restaurant together: The trick to fooling people is to lie about something they want to believe is true.

"Rufus, I can't accept your invitation to Italy, unless I know you're serious."

"I am serious," Rufus says.

I exhale, relieved my fish is still squirming on the line. "We have a connection, don't we?"

"Yes."

"My late husband didn't care about beauty and art and culture. He only loved money. While I'm grateful for everything he provided me with, I missed having someone I could talk to about the finer things in life."

Jeremy stands up and does one of those dance moves football players do after scoring a touchdown. I turn away to hide my embarrassment and my shame. Jeremy doesn't realize it but I've just revealed a bit of truth about his grandfather. With barely a high school education, Greg fought hard to provide for me and Meg. He's the reason I have a house to live in today and for that I'm eternally grateful. But he wasn't much interested in anything besides making money. He scrimped and saved and lifted us up into the middle class. It wasn't until after he was successful that he decided to enjoy life. With someone else. Shirley, his second wife, got the trips to Italy, while Meg and I were trapped in a house that became our main (sometimes only) source of income.

"I need to go," I say. "I'm taking my grandson to our beach club so he can teach me pickleball. Can we talk later?"

We say our goodbyes and promise to talk again that evening. When the call ends, Jeremy stares at me in amazement.

"Holy shit, Grandma. You were amazing. I thought you were totally going to boff it at the start, but you played that guy like a friggin' shark."

"You mean fiddle?"

"Whatever, you were amazing."

"I was, wasn't I?"

"Your Southern accent kind of went in and out, but not enough to notice," Jeremy says. "I expect we'll see a gift card in our account within a few days."

"Good, because I don't want to waste my time with more conversations like that. I feel bad scamming this guy."

"Don't be," Jeremy says. "Remember, he's not Rufus Wellington, classics professor. He's a loser from Idaho trying to steal money from vulnerable people."

"It might help if you could show me a photo of him."

Jeremy turns to his computer and taps away. Within minutes he's pulled up a photo from the man's computer. He puts the image full screen and I see a middle-aged man who looks like a doughy version of Craig, Meg's boyfriend. He's got the shaved head and cold, dead eyes of someone who tortures dogs for a living. In the photo he smiles, revealing some brownish, misaligned teeth. Behind him are a lot of torches lighting up the night sky.

"Tell me when the gift card arrives," I say. "Then shut his computer down permanently."

36

June 17

A gift card for $500 comes a few days later. Jeremy finds someone online who buys the code from us, which allows me to deposit the money into Max's GoFundMe account. Jeremy then locks Rufus or Todd out of his computer and deletes my profile from the dating site.

"That's a lot of work for $500," I say. "Are you sure you don't want a cut?"

"I don't need the money, Grandma," Jeremy says.

"Why not?" I ask. "Do you have a job?"

"Not in the traditional sense."

"In what sense then?"

Jeremy sighs, which means he's going to have to use a lot of words to explain something to me. "I go after bug bounties."

I wait for him to continue.

"I help companies find bugs in their software that make them vulnerable to hackers."

"But aren't you a hacker?" I ask.

"I'm white hat," he says. "The good kind."

"And does that pay well?" I ask.

"It does," he says.

"Are we white hats?"

Jeremy shakes his head. "We're gray hats," he says. "People who do unethical things for ethical reasons."

"I can live with that," I say. "Can you?"

"That depends," he says. "How long do you see us scamming people?"

Tell him about Cynthia, I think. *And Sharon. And Ginny. Tell him you think your friend is in danger and you don't know how to keep her safe.*

"You want spaghetti?" I say instead.

Jeremy nods and I start busying myself with meal prep. Should I share my suspicions with him? What if it turns my gray hat into a tinfoil hat? Or worse, what if Jeremy offers to help and draws the attention of the Senior Moments Psycho? I couldn't live with myself if something bad happened to my grandson. Now that Meg's gone, I'm his only caretaker. I have to protect him, which means shielding him from my paranoia. There's no evidence any of these women were killed, I remind myself. And Cristóbal could be a legit boyfriend. Until I know different, there's no reason to put anyone else in danger.

I step away from the boiling water on the stovetop and look at Jeremy. Even though we live under the same roof, we don't know each other very well. I've always complained about being invisible to him, but I've never really seen him either. There are lots of ways life hasn't been kind to the boy. He never knew his father, except through the traits he inherited from him: a hyperactive mind, a thin and sickly physique, and a propensity toward misanthropy (well, that last one he may have gotten from me). He either never figured out how face-to-face relationships work, or he figured it out and decided it wasn't an arena in which he could compete and quietly withdrew. But he's not the failure I thought he was. He's just a little lost is all. Somewhere along the line, he turned left when everyone else turned right and got trapped in a basement and couldn't find his way out. I can't believe I'm saying this, but what he needs is a water aerobics class.

I scoop spaghetti onto a plate and cover it with marinara sauce and cheese. It's my way of saying thank you for all the time he's spent flirting with those old men.

"What about that Vietnamese fellow you liked?" I ask. "Bao."

"What about him?" Jeremy says, mouth full of noodles.

"Are you going to stay in touch?"

"How am I supposed to do that?"

"I thought you said you were going to reach out to him after you killed me off?"

"I was joking," Jeremy says.

"You should do it," I say, sitting down. I stick my fork into my spaghetti and twirl the noodles around in a circle. "Where does he live?"

"In Oakland."

"That's close. Why don't you visit? Here," I say, reaching over and picking up a colander. "Tell him I left him this in my will."

"That's stupid," Jeremy says.

I put down the colander and walk into the living room to look around. The place is littered with Mom's things; I'm sure I can find something that might appeal to an eighty-year-old Vietnamese man. I spy a hand-carved cigar box on the mantel and pick it up. Despite my best efforts, I can't for the life of me attach a memory to the thing. Was it my dad's? He had a lot of bad habits but I don't remember cigar smoking being one of them. Maybe something Meg picked up at the flea market and forgot to take with her. It's a beautiful piece of craftsmanship with the carving seamlessly integrated into the cedarwood surface. I dump out its contents on the coffee table, mostly receipts, paper clips, and loose change. I doubt whoever made this beauty wanted it filled with this kind of car detritus. I wipe it down with my sleeve and bring it back to the kitchen to present to Jeremy.

"Here," I say, placing the box on the table. "Give him this. It's an antique."

Jeremy picks up the box and examines it with his eyes and hands. "This is nice, Grandma. Why do you want to give it to a stranger?"

"I'm giving it to you," I say.

Jeremy places it in front of him and continues to trace the lines of curved wood with his finger.

"You really helped me, Jeremy," I say. "I think you like helping people. I think you could help Bao if you wanted to. He sounds like my friend, Ginny—alone and trying to find company through a stupid dating site. You made a connection with him and I think that connection is as good for you as it is for him. Take this box to him from me and see how he really lives. You'll know what to do after that."

Jeremy laughs. "I would like to see his garden. And his Ka-Bar knife collection."

"And then let's get to work on our next victim," I say. "I'm thinking we go bigger next time."

"How so?"

"What if we waited until we got a bunch of these gift cards before we killed me off? You think you could find more scumbags?"

"Like leading whores to water," he says, smiling so that I know he's making a clever pun.

Whore #1

A ruddy-faced Scotsman living in Albuquerque posing as Sean McGregor, descendent of the Viscount of Kirkcaldy. Real name Stuart Robertson, currently on unpaid leave from his IT job for sexual harassment. Looks like a man refusing to back down in a staring contest with a solar eclipse. When we finally talk, he sounds like Mrs. Doubtfire on a bender. He claims to own a castle near Perthshire which he visits every summer with his grandchildren ("wee bairns" he calls them). He offers to make me Lady of the Manor. I ask him if his place comes with a helipad. He sends me a $1,000 gift card.

Whores #2 and #3

Two overweight guys I call Tweedledum and Tweedledee due to their shaved heads and matching unibrows. (Jeremy has hacked into their video surveillance and turned the cameras on them.) They work together in a cramped office in Cheektowaga and take turns impersonating James Radcliff, a real estate mogul from Buffalo. When I tell "James" about the time I visited Kim and Terry Pegula on their yacht in Boca, the boys pump their fists in the air revealing shaved armpits. (Alopecia, maybe?) I embellish my story with details about the bathrooms on the lower deck that come equipped with fish tanks to remove the dead skin on your feet. The next day, I get a gift card for $2,000.

Whore #4

A middle-aged Pakistani American man impersonating an elderly Japanese man who sounds like Morgan Freeman if Morgan Freeman used his vocal powers to sell you car insurance. "Hiro" is very charming and tells me how he trains Olympic judo athletes at his studio in Park City. (This guy lives in a studio in Charlottesville.) I tell him that's a great coincidence because my nephew has a movie premiering at Sundance this year and would he like to join us for a cast party with Margot Robbie? Two days later I get a gift card for $2,000.

Whore #5

Forty-something guy who pops pills and curls weights while talking into a headset. Spends a lot of time in front of the mirror flexing muscles while talking about his rheumatism. He's the dumbest of all my suitors and doesn't pick up on any of the hints I give to send me money. Finally, I have to lay it on the line. "Sebastian," I say. "I'm old and don't have time to waste on people who aren't in my tax bracket. You need to show me that you're serious or we're through." Two days later I get a gift card for $50, which means he's either the dumbest mark or the smartest.

37

July 1

Two weeks later and I feel fit as a fiddle. Or fit as a trombone as my grandson would say. I'm sure some of it has to do with the walking. I have to give Max some credit. Regular amounts of exercise and a healthier diet have done wonders for my health. I'm sleeping better, have more energy, and don't moan as much going up and down the stairs to the basement. My outlook's changed too. I'm not waking up every morning looking for fresh evidence that the world's an overflowing shit-hole now that every day brings new opportunities to screw over another worthless bastard. Vengeance is a great tonic for old age.

The only downside is that my dating scam has distracted me from Ginny's problems and when she picks me up today, I realize my fun has come at her expense. If I'm the picture of health, then she's my negative image. She looks wan and listless, like she's already walked her 2.3 miles with ten-pound ankle weights. Her skin is the color of wet cement and her outfit is not color coordinated with the usual flair. Rather than do her hair, she's just pulled the greasy strands back with a headband. She smiles when I get in the car, but she's hiding most of her face behind a pair of oversized sunglasses I've never seen her wear before.

"Hello, Jackie O," I say, buckling in.

Ginny forces out a laugh and touches the frames. "It's so bright out today," she says, pulling away from the curb.

"You okay?" I ask, noting Ginny's nervous driving. She keeps adjusting her rearview mirror and tapping her steering wheel. We come to an intersection and Ginny stops, even though we don't have a stop sign, to allow a car with tinted windows and thumping music to cross. Someone behind us honks and Ginny curses—actually curses—before pressing down on the accelerator.

"Fiddlesticks!" she says.

She turns on the radio to an NPR story about a congresswoman's husband who's been bludgeoned by a home intruder and quickly switches stations until she finds some classical music. When the music crescendos into something that might accompany a shark attack, Ginny punches the off button and we sit in silence.

"How's our campaign going?" I ask, trying to distract her.

"Incredible," she says. "We've nearly raised $12,000."

I do the math. At least half that has come from me. Jeremy has a broker who buys our gift cards and deposits the money directly into the GoFundMe account. Not bad for two weeks' worth of work, I think. I try to feel more like Robin Hood than some high-class sex worker. Neither does honest work, but every nickel I take from these scumbags restores some karmic balance to the universe.

"Where's the money coming from?" I ask, all innocent.

"A lot of anonymous donors," Ginny says. "Max's story has really resonated with people."

I haven't told Ginny or Max what I'm up to because I know they'd disapprove. It's been hard keeping this a secret though. Imagine you had a superpower that allowed you to control the spinning wheels on slot machines. Not the kind of talent that would earn you a place with the Avengers, but it's powerful enough to keep to yourself. This is how I feel about my Internet scam. Somehow, I've tapped into a superpower I didn't know I had. If I want to keep sharing the wealth with my friends, they can never know how I come into my money.

We get to Max's house and park. On our way in, we take a moment to pull some weeds from her front yard. "These hydrangeas need water," Ginny says, patting one of the pink flowers like it's the head of a baby. It's a team effort to do any gardening for Max because she takes such pride in her landscaping skills. If we were to tell her to water her lawn, it would only give her another reason to beat herself up, and she's strong enough to make those blows hurt. What we've been doing is secretly watering, pruning, and clearing so Max won't have to. This requires me to distract Max with some made-up interest in stretching exercises while Ginny sneaks outside and does whatever upkeep needs doing.

Max opens her front door and scowls. "What's wrong with you two?" she asks, toggling her attention between us.

"What?" I say.

"You look like a cat that ate the canary." She turns to Ginny. "You look like the canary's sister."

I look at Ginny and notice she does look a little funereal today. She's paired the big sunglasses with a gray Stanford T-shirt and black sweatpants.

Max pulls the door closed behind her and sets off as if a starter pistol's just been fired. Ginny and I race to catch up with her.

We talk about the usual stuff, mostly news-related items relating to scandals, ineptitude, or crime. Max brings up the story about the neighbor whose topiary hedges were destroyed by a crazy person. Ginny reminds Max not to use the term *crazy* to describe the mentally ill, which Max says is crazy. "I'm not worried about offending the lunatics who set fire to a person's lawn just because they see a bunch of giant penises."

I think we're all on the same page on this.

Eventually, we get around to asking about Harold's health, which is polite but pointless as nothing's changed and nothing will change until he dies of natural causes. He's a body in a bed is how Max puts it. "It's not how he wanted to go," Max says. "Problem is, he can still breathe on his own, which makes ending his life impossible."

Ginny stops. At first we think she needs a break, so we circle back and wait for her to catch her breath. But Ginny isn't tired; she's angry. At least I think she's angry. I've never seen Ginny lose her cool. She's struggling with some powerful emotion though, because she looks around as if she's lost her car in a crowded parking lot.

"How can you talk like that?" she asks when we lean in to see if she's okay.

"Talk like what?" Max says.

"Talk about ending Harold's life," Ginny says. "I'd trade everything to have one more day with Colin."

"That's just selfish," Max says, retreating as if Ginny just coughed in her face.

Ginny looks like she's about to faint, so I grab her by the elbow and lead her over to a parked SUV so she can lean against something sturdy. "Have some water, Ginny," I say, wishing I had something stronger. If anyone needs a drink right now, it's her.

"Maybe it is selfish," Ginny says. "I just miss him so much."

"You think I don't miss Harold?" Max says. Now she's starting to get angry, only with Max her anger is easy to see. She might as well be waving a flag that says *Fuck You* in giant, flaming letters.

"That's not what she meant," I say.

"I envy you, Ginny," Max says. "Your husband left you with only sadness. You could grieve like a proper widow. Every day I look at Harold, I can feel him judging me for prolonging his suffering. By the time he dies, he could very well hate me. Imagine living with that for the rest of your life."

I'm torn between who to comfort: Ginny, who's wiping her snot on her sleeve, or Max, who looks like she's going to punch the next innocent bystander who walks by. I reach into my fanny pack and take out a pack of tissues and offer them to Ginny, who grabs a bunch and blows.

"Thank you," she says.

I offer some to Max, who waves them off like they're a pack of cigarettes. I want to say something consoling, the way Ginny would, but nothing comes. What Max is going through is hell and there's nothing anyone can say or do to make it better. All the pride I'd felt about raising $12,000 for Harold's care now seems meaningless compared to her suffering. We might as well use that money to hire a contract killer to euthanize Harold in his sleep.

"You should have gotten divorced years ago like me," I say. "Makes end-of-life care a lot easier."

My feeble joke does its trick and both women come back from their corners. I try not to think too much that it's my pathetic love life that's put their misery in perspective. The problem is, life screws you either way: Either you love someone and their death kills you, or you love no one and you're dead before it's time to go.

We resume our walk and talk about the life surrounding us—the flowers, the birds, the babies in strollers—all safe subjects that remind us that there's still beauty and miracles to appreciate, even on a walk around the block. By the time we return to Max's house, we're back to normal. We're just about to say our goodbyes when Ginny blurts out, "I think I'm dating a mobster," and collapses on the lawn.

38

July 1

While I attend to Ginny, Max rushes inside to get some cool towels. By the time she returns, I have Ginny sitting up and taking tiny sips from her water bottle. Max applies the cool compresses to Ginny's neck and forehead. When we try to move her inside though, Ginny hesitates. "Is your nurse home?" she asks.

"Of course," Max says.

"I don't want to talk about this with her in the house."

Max sends the nurse on an errand and sets us up in her kitchen with some crackers, apple slices, and iced tea. "Got anything stronger?" I say, tapping my glass.

"This blend already has a lot of caffeine," she says.

"Not caffeine," I say. "Alcohol."

Max looks at Ginny, who nods. "I could use some sherry."

"Let me see what I've got," Max says and disappears down the hall. She comes back with a bottle of Smirnoff, holding it like it's someone's used Kleenex. "Harold used to like vodka tonics," she says, putting the bottle on the table. The glass is a bit grimy but I unscrew the cap and pour a little into our iced teas. Max places a hand over her glass before I can pollute it.

Ginny takes a tentative sip and winces. "That's awful," she says, and drinks some more. The concoction brings some color back into her cheeks and loosens her tongue.

"Well, as you know, I've been helping Cristóbal set up his new restaurant in Oakland. It's been such a joy to feel useful again. Ever since Colin passed, I've been so lonely. You spend all your life making friends and building a community and then one by one those people move away, or pass on, or just stop talking to you. I wasn't prepared for how alone I'd feel. If it weren't for you two, I don't know what I would have done."

Ginny pulls out a Kleenex from her fanny pack and dabs her face. Without her sunglasses, I see her eyes are puffy and red. Ginny doesn't suffer from allergies, so I know this is the result of a lot of crying and sleepless nights.

"Cristóbal made me feel a part of something again. It wasn't just being a couple. We were building something together. I kept picturing myself as some larger-than-life hostess, greeting people at the door and showing them to their table. Recommending meals and drinks. I wanted everyone to come to my party, to feel popular for a change. I was so caught up in this fantasy that I overlooked the red flags you two were begging me to see. I actually bragged to the bank tellers about the Cuban themed restaurant I was opening with my boyfriend. They were so happy for me, they didn't question the large sums of money I was withdrawing from my account. For every withdrawal I had a story about what the money was paying for: a top-of-the-line refrigerator unit, a handcrafted bar top, a set of leather-bound chairs for the cigar room in the back."

"So what changed?" I ask.

Ginny finishes her glass and Max refills it with more tea, leaving no room to spike it with more Smirnoff.

"Two days ago, Sharon's daughter came to Xanadu looking for her."

"Who's Sharon?" Max asks.

"She's a neighbor," Ginny says. "One of Barbara's friends."

"A real wackadoo," I say, before realizing the woman is probably dead. "May she rest in peace."

Ginny takes a sip of her tea and continues. "Her daughter hasn't heard from her mother in weeks and has opened a missing persons case. She came to Xanadu with the police to search her apartment. Now everyone, well, Bernard mostly, is saying she's been murdered. And that her murder is somehow connected to Cynthia's suicide."

"Or murder," I say.

"Yes, that's what people are saying," Ginny says. "So, as you can imagine, all this is terribly upsetting, so I tell Cristóbal about it and beg him to come out so we can finally be together. He makes his usual excuses, and, I don't know, I think of all your concerns about my relationship and how people are dying all around me, and I just lose it. I give him an ultimatum: Either he comes out or we're done."

"Good for you," Max says.

"What'd he say?" I ask.

Ginny sucks in her breath and shakes her head back and forth. She looks like someone on a witness stand, struggling to get through her testimony. I unscrew the top of the vodka bottle and push it in her direction. She stares at it, but doesn't add any more to her glass.

"He said, 'You wouldn't like it if we met face-to-face.' He said, 'Because mine might be the last face you see.'"

Ginny bursts into sobs. We move to either side of her and wrap her in our arms. Her body is trembling and we do everything we can to make her feel safe and protected.

"I'm so sorry you've been going through this," I say.

"We're calling the police right now," Max says.

"No, I can't," Ginny says, grabbing hold of Max. "He knows where I live. If I call the police, he says he'll send out someone to show me the view from the balcony." Ginny bursts into tears again. How has this woman not had a heart attack yet? I wonder. Maybe being a kindergarten teacher toughens you up in ways you don't expect. All those kids screaming and crying all day long. It must make you accustomed to chaos.

"He wants me to withdraw $300,000 from the account we share and hand it over to an associate."

Max and I both gasp.

"When are you supposed to withdraw the money?" Max asks.

"He needs a month to make the deposits so they don't arouse suspicion," Ginny says. "I don't see how this kind of transaction goes unnoticed though. If I'm not killed by Cristóbal, I'll be arrested by the FBI."

"No one's getting killed or arrested," I say, trying my best to sound like Liam Neeson. It's not a very good impression.

"I'm such a fool," Ginny says. "I should have told you both earlier, but I've been too embarrassed."

"Nothing to be embarrassed about," Max says. "These guys are professionals. That FaceTime call fooled me too."

My mind goes straight to Cynthia and Sharon. They must have been in the same predicament as Ginny: First, falling in love on Senior Moments, then becoming money mules for criminals, then murdered when they tried to back out. I don't say any of this out loud of course. I'm sure Ginny has made these connections too and doesn't need them voiced, especially now.

We sit around the kitchen table in silence. Harold starts to moan from the other room and Max goes to check on him, leaving Ginny and me alone with the vodka. I'm dying for another shot, but I need my brain firing on all cylinders now. Unfortunately nothing's coming to me. Either Ginny goes through with it and continues as Cristóbal's money mule until the FBI arrests her, or she goes to the police and has to spend her remaining years in witness protection. I can only imagine where the government sends you to start your new life. It's not someplace glamorous like Manhattan or Miami. It's got to be someplace no one would think to visit because of the snowy tundra and abandoned coal mines.

"I'm going to get you out of this, Ginny," I say. "If it's the last thing I do."

39

July 1

That night, I'm so mad I take out a stack of plates from my cupboard and smash them against the back concrete patio. Breaking things has always been my preferred method of anger management, which I discovered after my first husband left me. When Greg moved out, I took the dining set we had scrimped and saved to purchase and broke it into hundreds of tiny shards, which I then used to create a decorative footpath to my birdbath. This time, I have no creative ambitions; I just want to see something destroyed.

Unfortunately, I'm unable to clean up my mess before Meg comes over. She enters through the side gate and finds me sitting on my back steps. I must look like a crazy person (I think I can use this term to describe myself without offending anybody), hyperventilating, surrounded by my moat of ceramic shards.

"What the fuck, Mom," she says, stopping in her tracks. "That better not be Grandma's good china."

All I can do is growl in response. My exertions have left me exhausted, which is kind of the point. I don't have the energy to put up with Meg's nonsense right now. My daughter must pick up on my mood because she bends down and starts picking up the larger pieces of plateware until her hands are full. Then she goes inside and puts them in the trash can. I hear her shout for Jeremy to come help sweep the rest of the mess up.

"He's visiting his friend," I say.

"What friend?" Meg asks, poking her head out the door.

"Bao," I say.

"Bao?" Meg repeats.

"He's Vietnamese," I say.

Meg comes out a few minutes later with a broom and dustbin. "How'd he meet Bao?"

"Online," I say, not wanting to divulge any more information than I have to.

"Of course," Meg says. "Well, at least he's outside. I hope he remembers how to drive."

Meg sweeps around me doing a half-assed job as usual. She's left all the tiny slivers, the debris that will do the most damage because you don't see it waiting to cut you up.

"What brings you by?" I ask.

"What? Can't I visit my own mother?"

"Of course you can," I say. "It's just . . ."

"And what's with the lock on the front door?" Meg asks. "My key didn't work."

"I changed the lock," I say.

"Why'd you do that?"

I shrug. "Just thought it was time. Now that it's just me and Jeremy, I worry about security. He's going to help me install surveillance cameras too."

I can see Meg doesn't like this at all. "That's nice of him," she says.

"He's been a real help," I say.

"Did you make me a key?" Meg asks.

"For what?"

"For the new locks, dummy."

"No, I didn't," I say.

"Don't you think I should have one?"

I don't, I want to say, but know that if I object, I'll have to tell her why and I'm too exhausted from smashing objects to pick a fight with my daughter. "Sure," I say instead.

We sit there in silence. The late afternoon is the nicest time to be in the backyard, even though the space is a mess. I used to love spending time back here, tending to our narrow strip of lawn and my rosebushes along the back fence. After placing Meg in front of the TV, I'd come back here with a beer and cigarette and take such pride in how the place looked. Everything else in my life was such a mess, but I hadn't managed to screw up this little sanctuary. Now, the lawn is full of dandelions and my rosebushes are wild, thorny monstrosities, something out of a Grimms' fairy tale. I've got one bloom right now, a bloodred rose whose petals have turned black from sun exposure.

Meg clears her throat and breaks the silence. I probably should be asking her how things are going with Craig, but I don't really want to know. If she says things are going great, I won't believe her, and if she says things are miserable, it will break my heart.

"So, Craig and I wanted to talk to you about something," Meg begins. "A business opportunity."

"Oh, Meg," I say. "You know I'm on a fixed income."

"But this could *make* you money, Mom," she says, standing in front of me, making her sales pitch like I'm one of those investors from *Shark Tank*. I could really use more of Harold's vodka right now.

"You know my catering company is doing great," Meg says.

"I don't know that."

"Well, it is. People love my bespoke picnics, especially after the pandemic made outside dining so popular. But I can't do it all on my own. Craig helps as much as he can, but he's got his own business selling for Boost a Move so it's mostly me doing all the setup, cooking, and cleaning. I need to hire an assistant and build a larger inventory of product so I can expand my client base."

I look at Meg for any of her tells that she's been using. She looks good, dressing professionally for her sales pitch in a pink blouse and gray slacks. I look to her cuticles, which are always bleeding when she's back on the booze and pills. I see a few red dots, which could just be a sloppy application of polish. Her energy is a bit manic and speedy, but that could just be nerves. I won't know if she's fallen off the wagon until I do something to upset her.

"Honey, I have no money to invest," I say, ripping off the Band-Aid.

"You have the house," she says.

"You want me to sell the house?"

"Not *sell* it. Just refinance. It's a great time with interest rates so low."

"I've already refinanced twice," I say. "The last time to pay for your rehab, remember?"

This sucks the air out of Meg's presentation. She looks like one of those daytime talk show guests being confronted with the results of a paternity test. She's torn between pleading for forgiveness and fighting the booing studio audience.

"That's not fair, Mom," she says. "I was sick."

"I'm not complaining," I say. "I'm just explaining why refinancing's not an option for me anymore. The bank owns more of my house than I do."

"Have you heard of reverse mortgages?" she quickly pivots. "They allow you to sell your house to the bank and keep living in it for as long as you like."

"You need at least fifty-percent equity in your home to be eligible for a reverse mortgage," I say. "Have you gone to a bank and presented your business plan to them? That's who you should be talking to."

"You know my credit is lousy," she says.

"What about Craig?"

Meg just sighs, which tells me all I need to know.

"Do you have any friends who might be interested?" Meg asks. I can see she's growing desperate. Her arms flap about like those dancing tubes in front of car dealerships. "You know it's a good idea, right?"

"It's a great idea."

"So, do you think you could pitch it to the ladies in your walking club?"

"They're even more desperate than me right now, dear," I say. One's got a dying husband who's sending her into bankruptcy and the other might be assassinated. I don't say this last part out loud, of course.

"You just don't believe in me," Meg says.

"That's not it," I say. "They're just not in a position to lend money right now."

"Craig says they're rich."

"How would Craig know that?"

"You can't live in Xanadu and not be rich."

"Tell your boyfriend to leave my friends alone," I say.

"What's that supposed to mean?" Meg asks.

"Is he on Senior Moments?" I ask.

"The dating site for old people? You're joking, right?"

"Ginny's boyfriend tried to get her to buy Craig's bullshit vitamins."

"That doesn't surprise me," Meg says. "They're amazing at promoting gut health."

"That guy is a loser and potentially dangerous," I say. "You should move home now."

"I'm never moving back here," Meg says.

"Well then I guess this conversation is over."

I stand up and move inside. There's nowhere for this conversation to go but down and I've got bigger problems to worry about now than Meg's catering business. If she wanted to save money, she could have stayed here where it was rent-free. Instead, she chose to move in with the boyfriend she's known for all of two months. My goodness, this woman is in her fifties! She should have her shit together by now.

"You've *never* believed in me," Meg says, following me inside. "That's been my problem my whole life."

"Here we go again," I say. "Blame Mom for all your problems. I thought we were done with this. Didn't your last recovery program encourage you to accept some responsibility for your actions? Isn't that what all those apologies were about?"

"Those apologies were about me making amends for the people I'd hurt through my addiction. You've never apologized to me for anything!"

"I'm sorry I was such a shitty mother to you, Meg. I tried my best but as you know from personal experience, mothering is hard work, especially when your kid hates you."

"I didn't hate you."

"You sure acted like you did."

"That's so typical of you. Blaming the victim."

"And that's so typical of you. Playing the victim. It's pathetic."

"I'm pathetic?"

"Yes, Meg, you are. You blame everyone for your mistakes. That's my biggest fault as a mother. I should have toughened you up so that you'd be able to survive in this world. When I'm gone, who's going to take care of you? Craig? I doubt he'll be around much longer. You have no relationship with your son, which is a shame because Jeremy's actually a sweet, smart kid. He's got all my survival skills. Maybe he can teach a few of them to you if he's feeling generous. I don't know why he'd want to though given how you've abandoned him."

"He's twenty-four years old!" Meg says through tears.

"And you're fifty-three!" I yell back. "But you still need your mommy. You know why I changed the locks? Because I knew you'd be back, just like the times you stole from me before. Only this time, you'd be bringing Craig as your accomplice. That's the next step in this game you're playing, isn't it? Mom doesn't give you any money so you steal her valuables? Well, you can forget that. I'm smarter than you and Craig put together. You come near this house without an invitation and I'll make sure you're arrested for trespassing."

I'm gasping for breath when I finish this tirade. I've fallen into Meg's trap and let her drag me down into her cesspool of anger and recrimination. I look at my daughter's horrified face and wait for the feelings of shame and guilt to flood my body. But they don't come. My fury is keeping them at bay. I'm so tired of Meg pushing me around. I'm tired of *everyone* pushing me around. Cristóbal wants a fight? He's going to get one. We're smarter than he is. He's underestimating us because we're old ladies. And that's what we'll use to our advantage. He'll see soon enough that we're tougher than his hired goons and we've got nothing left to lose.

"Now get out of my house," I say to Meg, who stumbles out the back door into the darkening evening.

40

July 1

After Meg leaves, I shuffle around the house, carrying on the argument with Scampers, who scurries from room to room trying to escape the flames bursting from my eyeballs. I've gone full nuclear. Smashing dishes is no longer enough. I must incinerate everything in my path, including my innocent kitty. "Honestly, what was she thinking?" I say, pulling Scampers out from behind the dryer and holding him close. "I've never been anything but a checkbook for that girl. At a certain point, you figure you've done your bit, you know? How much money have I invested in her education, her medical treatments, her lifestyle choices? And do I ever get more than a perfunctory thank you? Never! She acts as if she's a cat. Like I'll go on taking care of her even though she gives me nothing in return!"

I stroke Scampers's fur gently. It's not fair to take this out on him. Scampers isn't the same kind of dependent as Meg. "You're cute and cuddly and make me laugh with your playful battles with string," I say. "Eventually, you'll turn into a killer who will protect us from rodents. That's more than I can say for Meg. Honestly, most people her age are taking care of their parents, not stealing from them. I tell you, Scampers, if I own anything when I die, I'm giving it all to Jeremy. I'm going to write up a will, just as Max and Ginny suggested, and make sure that girl gets nothing. That'll show her."

Jeremy comes home and a desperate Scampers leaps from my grasp and runs to him for protection. He snatches the kitty up and holds him close to his chest. I can hear Scampers purring from where I'm sitting.

"How was your visit?" I ask.

Jeremy jumps back in surprise. "Jesus, Grandma. Why are you sitting in the dark like that? Trying to give me a heart attack?"

Jeremy flips on the light and comes over to sit with me on the couch. Scampers, terrified that he'll be held hostage again, scrambles out of Jeremy's grasp and runs into the kitchen.

"What's wrong?" he asks.

"Your mom and I had a fight."

"She want money?"

The gratitude I feel toward my grandson just then nearly overwhelms me. He's my ally in this fight and it's all I can do not to wrap my arms around his bony frame and squeeze the breath out of him.

I nod.

"She's nothing if not predictable," he says, picking some cat hair off his skinny jeans.

"Tell me about your day," I say, patting his leg. "How was it meeting Bao?"

"He's amazing," he says. "I think I've been spending too much time with assholes online. I've forgotten that there are genuinely good people in the world. I really think you should date him."

"You killed me off, remember?"

"I killed off Stella LaFayette," he says. "Not Poppy Montgomery."

"Yes, but now you have the problem of being both our grandchild," I say.

"Not a problem," he says. "Stella was my father's mother."

"Why don't you invite him over for dinner? We'll see if any sparks fly."

"I already know I like him."

"I meant between us," I say.

Jeremy laughs. "Oh yeah, sure. Of course."

We go into the kitchen so I can make us dinner. There's not a lot in the fridge, so we settle on pancakes. While I'm mixing the batter, Jeremy recaps his day in the breathless way you summarize a great first date. Bao lives in one of the more industrial neighborhoods in Oakland with homes adorned with bars on the windows and doors. His is one of the nicer bungalows, with a fresh coat of paint and planter boxes full of leafy herbs. They spent most of the day looking through Bao's memorabilia from his childhood—photographs, letters, tokens. To hear Jeremy tell it, it's like he's just met James Bond.

"When he was my age, you know what Bao was doing? He was escaping Vietnam with his wife and daughter on a tiny fishing boat. I'm sure you've seen photos of the boat people, right?"

I shake my head. So much world history has been erased from my memory bank to make room for more immediate needs, like what kind of cat food I need to buy and what my Netflix account password is.

Jeremy pulls up a photo on his phone and thrusts it in my face. In the grainy image, there are people, mostly women and children, crammed into the front of a wooden boat, the kind without sails. I can't imagine how one outdoor motor moved this loaded vessel through any body of water, let alone the South China Sea.

"Bao served in the South Vietnamese army, so of course they wanted to torture his ass," Jeremy says. "He got his family on this boat and they escaped in the middle of the night. The first day they're at sea, they get attacked by pirates. Actual pirates. Can you believe it?"

I shake my head.

"These guys are heartless, they steal everything from these people—their valuables, all the food and water. Bao's wife had to swallow her gold earrings just to keep them out of the hands of these bastards."

I think of Cristóbal and Craig, both modern-day pirates. Wherever there are vulnerable people, there will be people who prey on them. It's not something unique to the US.

"After the pirates left, they sailed for two more days without food or water before a Thai shipping company rescued them and brought them safely to shore. They stayed in a Thai refugee camp for two years before finally making their way to the US as part of the resettlement program. It's fucking amazing they weren't destroyed."

I pour the batter on the grill and listen to it sizzle in butter. When Greg and I ran away from home, we thought we were so brave, but we had nothing on these people, who crossed oceans and continents to build a life for themselves in a new country that only resented them.

I place the stack of pancakes in front of Jeremy and pour more batter onto the pan.

"Bao sounds like an incredible man," I say.

"The dude is a fucking badass," Jeremy says. "What he survived? It would have killed me four times over. Seriously, Grandma, talking to him made me think I need to do something with my life. I think I want to travel."

"Where to?"

"Well, Vietnam, obviously. Bao says he has family there that can show me around. But after that, who knows? Thailand, New Zealand, maybe even Antarctica."

I slide the pancakes onto my plate and join him at the table. "That sounds terrific," I say. "Now's the time to do it too, before you're too attached to anything."

"Would you take care of Scampers?" he asks, tearing off a bit of pancake and holding it down to the cat.

"Of course," I say. "How long would you be gone?"

"I don't know," he says. "I'm thinking about buying a one-way ticket."

I stare at him, trying to maintain my enthusiasm for his new life direction. But I just can't do it. With him gone, who will take care of me? Jeremy doesn't realize how much his company has meant these past few weeks. I've come to depend on him for all sorts of things, not just the online scamming. I'll miss all the sounds of him in the house. The sudden bursts of laughter when he cracks a coding problem. The conversations he has with Scampers, encouraging him to come out of hiding with a bit of catnip or squeaky toy. The way he imitates guitar riffs when he's listening to music on his headphones. This place will be too quiet with him gone. Why did I ever encourage him to move upstairs? If he were still sleeping in the basement, I could lock the door and prevent him from ever leaving.

I push my plate of pancakes aside and drop my head onto the table. "It's too much," I moan.

Jeremy's hand strokes the top of my head. It's a weird gesture that makes me think his experience with PDA has been limited to Scampers. "What wrong, Grandma?" he says. "Did something happen with your friend?"

I get up and dry my face on a paper towel. "I think she's going to be murdered."

41

July 1–2

I don't know if it's fear or desperation that makes me spill my guts to my grandson. I'd like to think it's knowing he has an escape plan if things go south. If Cristóbal comes after us, I feel better knowing Jeremy will be out of his reach, safely hidden in one of Bao's family's homes in Vietnam.

I tell him everything, starting from Cristóbal's demand that Ginny withdraw $300,000 and working my way backward. "He threatened to throw her off the balcony, just as he threw her neighbor off hers," I say. "There's another woman who's gone missing too that we suspect was one of his victims. He probably couldn't defenestrate her without drawing too much attention to himself."

"De-what now?"

"Defenestrate," I repeat. "Technically, it means throwing someone out a window, but I think it can be applied to balconies."

"Holy shit," Jeremy says.

"We need to help her."

"She should just go to the FBI. They can protect her."

I shake my head. "I've seen enough television shows to know that won't end well."

"We're talking $300,000. I know that sounds like a lot to you, but for drug lords, it's chump change."

"You think he's a drug lord?"

Jeremy shrugs. "Let me see what I can dig up on the guy."

He scoots his chair back, excited to get started working. I clear my throat to let him know his work starts with clearing the table, one of the ground rules I established after Meg moved out. Jeremy apologizes and rinses the dishes off in the sink.

"Thank you," I say. "And Jeremy, be careful with this one. He's not an amateur like the others."

Jeremy nods and disappears into his basement workspace.

I don't sleep well at all that night. My mind can't stop spinning with all the emotions generated from the day's events. I end up taking a Benadryl and Tylenol PM to help me nod off. I'm out for only a couple of hours before I jolt upright from a nightmare where my house is being overtaken by pirates. I stumble into the kitchen and make myself a cup of coffee and wait for Jeremy to emerge from his basement lair and tell me what he's found.

"It's not good, Grandma," he says, pulling out a frozen pizza and preheating the oven. What is happening to us that we're having pancakes for dinner and pizza for breakfast? The norms of civil society no longer exist in this house.

"Is Cristóbal a ruthless drug lord?" I ask.

Jeremy shakes his head. "As far as I can tell, he's a legitimate restaurateur. But that means nothing. Whoever is scamming your friend is using this guy as an alias, knowing that an eighty-year-old woman won't run a background check on him."

"I'm sure Ginny Googled him," I say.

"Right, and she probably found all these articles confirming what he told her. That's because Cristóbal is a real person, I just don't think he's the person your friend is dating."

"So who is he?"

"My guess is that he's a more dangerous criminal than the guys we're dealing with. Our swindlers just want your money. This guy wants an accomplice. He's washing his money through your friend's account, which means he's into some scary shit. Usually it's drugs but it could also be human trafficking. Those guys don't mess around."

"Oh dear," I say. "Maybe Ginny should go to the police."

"Here's more bad news I found," Jeremy says. "Three months ago, a woman living in a retirement home in Bellevue was found dead in her apartment. Her kids thought she died of natural causes, until they discovered she'd been helping her 'boyfriend' open a restaurant in Seattle. One of her last texts to him was a threat to report him to the FBI."

I start to hyperventilate. Usually, I like confirmation that my paranoia is prescience, but not when we're dealing with a serial killer. Jeremy stands and gets me a glass of water, which I guzzle down. Now that Meg's out of the house, I should really stock up on my alcohol for times like this.

"What do we do?" I ask.

Jeremy shakes his head. "I don't know."

42

July 2

I call the girls and tell them I can't make our walk today. I hate letting them down like this, but I can't face Ginny after what Jeremy's just told me. All I'd see was that poor woman from Bellevue, probably smothered by a pillow in her sleep. I suppose that's better than being tossed off a balcony like Cynthia or whatever happened to Sharon.

There has to be a way out of this. My feeble brain just hasn't figured it out yet. Part of me is still distracted by my fight with Meg. Now that my anger has abated, I'm left with all these conflicted feelings that are making it hard to focus. What if Meg is like Ginny? Trapped in a relationship with a brutal man who's threatening to kill her? She'd never come to me with her "business plan" unless she was pushed (or threatened) into it. Meg still has some pride, I think. I need to make sure she's safe. Maybe while I'm visiting, I can search Craig's apartment for any clues that he might be Cristóbal.

But first I need to make some banana bread.

The process not only helps me get rid of the rotting fruit but distracts me from my insurmountable problems. When it's done, I've got a nice loaf and a sweet-smelling home. Lemonade from lemons. Before I'm tempted to cut myself a slice, I wrap the bread up in cellophane and attach a note telling Meg I'm sorry.

I punch Meg's address into my phone and see that she lives forty minutes away by bus. Lucky for me, the apartment complex is on El Camino, a large boulevard with lots of routes. I don't have to wait long at the bus stop for my shared chariot to arrive. I find a place in the front and feel like a proper old lady, sitting in my tracksuit transporting baked goods on my lap to my daughter. I doubt this peace offering will make much of a difference with Meg, but I'm hoping it makes me feel better about myself. I don't want my last words to my daughter being *Get out of my house*. I'd rather they be something more generous, like *I made this for you* or even *I'm sorry I'm such a bitch*.

Lots of people hate taking the bus, but I don't mind it so much. It's nice having someone deal with traffic, giving you time to relax and observe people not in your usual orbit. Everyone in my section is plugged into their devices. Two Asian girls share headphones and giggle at something on their screen. A middle-aged Black woman stares out the window, mouthing the lyrics to whatever song she's listening to. An obese white man wearing large headphones smiles every time we make eye contact. Would we interact if these devices didn't exist? Probably not. And maybe that's for the best. The only one talking right now is a mentally ill man telling us all about his tapeworm.

I get off at my stop and walk a few blocks to Meg's apartment, passing gas stations, fast-food chains, and appliance centers. Eventually, I get to her building, a three-story stucco complex painted the color of oatmeal. I walk in the lobby and the place smells like being stuck in a warehouse filled with Christmas trees. The pine scent is overwhelming and I have to take baby steps to the elevator to make sure I don't breathe in too much of the toxic air freshener. It's better inside the elevator. On the wall next to the buttons, there's a sign asking residents to please stop feeding the crows.

The elevator takes me to the third floor, which is lit with a flickering light that hums in the empty hallway. I walk down to 307 and knock, bracing myself to have the door slammed in my face when Meg sees it's me. After a minute, I knock again and place my eye to the peephole, trying to detect movement inside. As far as I can tell, the room is empty, which makes sense as it's the middle of the day and both Meg and Craig are probably working or working out. Did I know this subconsciously? Maybe. I place the loaf of bread with my apology against the door and walk back to the elevator.

Just as the elevator doors are about to close, I hear the sound of a door opening. I poke my head out and see a shaft of light coming from the open door directly across from Meg's. A bent old woman sneaks out, snatches my loaf of bread, and disappears back inside before I can yell for her to stop. I storm back down the hallway and pound on her door. "I saw you!" I say. "Give me back my banana bread, you criminal." I stand there for another five minutes demanding justice, but no one comes to my aid. The television inside the room gets turned up to ear-splitting levels and before long my shouts are competing with a game show contestant guessing the right price of an air fryer.

I ride back home fuming. Now I'm the crazy person on the bus talking to herself. "Is everyone a criminal these days?" I ask my fellow passengers, who are all plugged into their devices and ignoring me. I take out my phone and start a text to Meg. **I dropped off some banana bread at your apartment but your neighbor across the hall stole it. You need to report her to the landlord!**

I hold off pressing send and preview the conversation that might follow:

Why are you bringing me banana bread? Meg will ask, missing the point entirely.

To say sorry for yesterday. I was too harsh.

Have you changed your mind about the money then?

No, I told you, I don't have that kind of money.

So you brought me banana bread instead.

Yes, and your neighbor stole it. You should tell your landlord.

What's he going to do? Evict her? You want her thrown out on the street?

Of course not. But people should know she's not to be trusted. Why don't you send Craig over to get the bread back? That'll scare her.

You want my boyfriend to threaten an old lady?

She's a thief!

There's no way Craig's going to win that fight.

You fight with me all the time.

That's different. You're family.

I erase the text and pocket my phone. There's nothing I can do. Meg will never see my banana bread and she'll never see my apology. I'll have to find some other way to reach out to her. Maybe send her a card with some of Ginny's mobster money.

But then something clicks in my brain. An idea. More of a question: What if we could get someone else to take Cristóbal's money instead of Ginny? What if we could have our banana bread and eat it too?

When I get back home, I go immediately to Jeremy's door. I call down and ask him to come up as soon as he's finished. I don't know what he's doing down there and I don't want to know. I pour myself a glass of water and wait for him at the kitchen table.

He emerges a few minutes later, a bit sweaty and out of breath. His plain white T-shirt with the armpit stains clings to his bony frame.

"You exercising?"

"Push-ups," he says. "Trying to get in shape."

"For what?"

"For life," he says. "What's up?"

"How do you feel about helping me bring down a mobster?"

43

July 2

The plan is simple but hinges on what Meg implied in my imaginary text exchange: People believe old ladies are feebleminded and weak. We need to use that stereotype to our advantage. It's worked for me so far with my Internet dating scams. It can work for Ginny too.

All she has to do is to allow herself to get scammed.

Again.

But this time, Jeremy and I will be pulling the strings. We create a fake profile on Senior Moments to woo Ginny out of her (i.e., Cristóbal's) money. Ginny can then report the scam to the FBI without implicating Cristóbal and his cronies. If we do it right, Cristóbal will just think Ginny's an idiot who lost his money, which he's primed to do anyway since she was stupid enough to let him turn her into a money mule. Once the bank and police are alerted to the theft, he won't be able to use her anymore without coming under their scrutiny. He'll disappear from her life for good, hopefully accepting his loss as the cost of doing shady business with the elderly. Like Jeremy said, $300,000 is probably nothing for their money laundering operation. Surely not enough to risk prison.

"But won't this put you in danger?" I ask. "What if Cristóbal figures out you're behind the fake dating profile?"

"He won't." Jeremy smiles and not for the first time do I wonder if he's got a Guy Fawkes mask hidden somewhere in his closet. I've heard that's the preferred disguise of social disrupters.

"You think your friend is up for this?" he asks me. "She's the one who'll have to convince Cristóbal she wasn't behind the scam."

"Let's ask her," I say. "How would you like to get some more exercise?"

44

July 3

When Ginny picks me up for our walk, I leave the house with Jeremy, who's suited up in shorts and a fresh T-shirt featuring a scary clown. Ginny's eyes widen when she sees us, probably because we're such opposites. Jeremy's tall, bony, and pale, and I'm none of those things. With my gray hair and lavender sweatsuit, I probably look like I've brought the grim reaper along for a morning stroll.

I introduce Jeremy to Ginny and she pretends to be thrilled that he's joining us. All the way over to Max's she keeps saying how exciting it is to spend time with someone so young. "You can explain TikTok to us," she says. "And crypto!"

Max's reaction is less enthusiastic. "Why would you want to walk with us?" she asks point-blank. "We'll just slow you down."

"Don't worry about me," Jeremy says. "I'm in terrible shape."

This only makes Max scowl, his implication being that he's a good match for someone like her. After doing some deep knee bends, she marches off at a brisk pace to prove him wrong. Ginny and I struggle to keep up, whereas Jeremy, whose stride is twice ours, has to take baby steps to not get too far ahead.

The ladies pummel Jeremy with questions, to which he responds mostly with terse, one-word answers.

"What do you do for a living?"

"Coding, mostly."

"Did you go to college for that?"

"Didn't need to."

"What about high school?"

"I went to Mountain View."

"Do you have a girlfriend?"

"Or boyfriend?"

"No."

"Would you like one?"

"Sure."

"Dating must be hard."

"I wouldn't know."

"Do you like living with your grandmother?"

"She's great."

"And we hear you have a cat."

"Yes."

"What's its name?"

"Scampers."

"That's a nice name."

"Yes. It is."

It's clear Jeremy doesn't like being the center of attention. Or he's not used to making conversation with his mouth. At one point I look down and see his fingers twitching, like they're in withdrawal, having never been separated this long from a keyboard. I decide to jump in and save him from any more interrogating.

"Jeremy's here because he's going to help us save Ginny."

This stops Max in her tracks. She spins around and faces us, her expression reminding me a little of Margaret Hamilton in *The Wizard of Oz*. The actress was only thirty-six when she played the Wicked Witch of the West. Thirty-six! I spent my whole life thinking she was an old crone in that film only to discover she was in her sexual prime.

"Save her how?" Max asks, suddenly looking at Jeremy not as a guest but as an intruder.

"Can we sit down?" I ask, pointing to the picnic tables in the park we're passing. We walk over to one with some shade from an oak tree and I spill my guts about the Internet scam Jeremy and I have been running out of my basement.

"The money in Max's GoFundMe account?" Ginny says. "That's where it came from?"

I nod.

Ginny turns to Max. "I'm so sorry," she says. "I had no idea."

Max stares at me and I do my best to maintain eye contact with her. I don't want her to think I feel ashamed or guilty for stealing from these assholes, because I don't. The only thing I feel slightly bad about is not telling her I was using her charitable account to wash my dirty money. That's something I probably should have gotten permission to do first. But you know what? I don't even feel that bad about that. Isn't the governing ethos of Silicon Valley "move fast and break things"? Well, I was just keeping up with the times. Ask forgiveness rather than permission. It's the mantra that's made everyone filthy rich in this town.

"I've got no problem with it," Max says finally.

"You don't?" Ginny says.

Max turns to Ginny. "And you shouldn't either," she says. "For God's sake, Ginny, you have a man threatening to throw you off a balcony if you don't become his criminal accomplice. Why should you care what happens to him?"

"Because two wrongs don't make a right," Ginny says.

"That may be something you teach your kindergartners but the real world's more complicated," Max says.

"I disagree," Ginny says. "There is right and wrong. Stealing is wrong."

"It's stealing *back*," I say. "You can't let the bastards win."

"Then report them," Ginny says. "Let the police punish them."

"How would that work for you, huh?" I say. "Either Cristóbal kills you like he killed Cynthia and Sharon, or you spend the rest of your life in witness protection. They could send you to Wisconsin. Wisconsin, Ginny!"

Ginny starts to hyperventilate. Max grabs her hands and gets her breathing under control. When she's calm, I explain my plan in the clearest way possible. "I call it Operation Banana Bread," I say. "We get a thief to steal Cristóbal's money, only the thief in this case is us. After we've drained the account, you tell Cristóbal that you've been scammed by your new boyfriend."

"What happens to his money?" Ginny asks.

"We give it to Max."

"How do we give it to Max without alerting the authorities?" Ginny asks. "Or Cristóbal?"

I turn to Jeremy. "I know people who can help with that," he says.

"All we need Ginny to do is break up with Cristóbal and start dating Jeremy," I say.

"Not me," Jeremy clarifies, "but a fake dating profile I create and control."

"Here's the most important part," I say, grabbing Ginny's hand. "You have to act like a ninny."

"That's not difficult," Ginny says. "But what's to stop Cristóbal from killing me like Cynthia and Sharon? Doesn't this make it *more* likely he'll come after me?"

"Because we'll report the fake scam to the police," I say. "Cristóbal won't risk a third murder if he thinks the police are involved."

"What if the police start asking questions about the money in my account?" Ginny says. "Couldn't I still get in trouble?"

"That's a risk," I say.

"The story we tell Cristóbal won't be the same story we tell the police," Jeremy says.

"I'm sorry, dear. I don't follow," Ginny says.

"You'll tell Cristóbal you lost $300,000. You can tell the police you lost $300. They won't investigate the loss of that kind of pocket change. The point is to be seen talking to the police in case Cristóbal has eyes on you."

"What about the bank?" Max asks. "How do we keep them out of this?"

"The bank has been letting Ginny withdraw money without asking questions. We'll have to come up with a story that satisfies them for the $300,000. After we've taken Cristóbal's money out, you put a freeze on the account, so Cristóbal thinks it's been shut down as part of the investigation. He'll probably keep an eye on you for a while, but as long as the money doesn't turn up in any of your accounts, I think he'll buy your story."

Ginny turns to Max. "You okay with us turning you into a money mule?"

Max nods. "I can't think of a better way to spend a criminal's money," she says, grabbing hold of Ginny's hand and squeezing. "How do you feel about it?"

Ginny looks at the three of us and sighs. "Okay," she says finally. "I guess it beats getting thrown out the window."

"Or moving to Wisconsin," I say.

"My whole family's from Wisconsin." Ginny laughs. "It's really lovely there."

45

July 5

The first thing we have to do is get Ginny a new boyfriend. That means letting the old one down, gently.

"I told Cristóbal that I changed my profile back to single," Ginny says when I get to her apartment. I thought she might need some emotional support for the breakup, but here she's initiated it on her own. Relationships really are easier over fiber-optic cables.

"What was his reaction?" I asked.

"*LOL*," Ginny says. "That's all he wrote."

"Bastard," I say.

"It was pretty hurtful."

I try to keep from smiling, but it's hard. Cristóbal's reaction is exactly what I was hoping for—a sign that he assumes Ginny's an idiot because she's old. Only in this case, I'm not sure Ginny's age has anything to do with creating that impression. What gal goes back to online dating after being scammed into a money-laundering scheme?

"I told him that despite how our relationship ended, I'm not ready to give up on love," Ginny says. "He said he didn't care who I 'effed' as long as I went through with the drop-off. Only he didn't say 'effed.'"

I shake my head.

"You know, it would serve him right if I met my next husband on Senior Moments. I'd send Cristóbal a wedding invitation and tell him he's NOT invited."

"You know what would be even better?" I say. "Stealing his money. Let's focus on that."

We make some edits to Ginny's profile beyond her relationship status. We change her interests to philanthropy, ballroom dancing, and dressage. We highlight her status as a widow with no dependents. When we suggest retaking her profile picture to show off her ample bosom, Ginny finally objects. "People at Xanadu might see this," she says.

"Who cares?" I say. "You don't like them anyway."

"I still have to live with them. I don't want them thinking I'm a floozy."

We compromise and take the photo with Ginny wearing her most expensive jewelry—a gold chain necklace with matching earrings. Thirty minutes after posting, the number of hearts by her name tick upward to three hundred.

"I should have consulted you when I first got on this dating site," Ginny says, watching her ranking shoot up. "I never got more than fifty hearts before."

❖

We all agree to stay away from each other during the week we steal Cristóbal's money. He's been slowly making deposits into Ginny's account, careful to keep the amounts low to avoid any red flags. By next Friday, he'll have reached the $300,000 he wants Ginny to transport to his business associate, who will be parked across the street from the bank in a gray Tesla Model 3. My guess is Cristóbal wants his partner to blend in because those cars are everywhere these days.

I miss our daily walks, mostly for the contact with Ginny and Max but also, I'm embarrassed to say, for the exercise. I know I could go out and walk on my own but the activity seems so pointless without companionship, like dining alone or rock climbing. So, I go back to the YMCA, where my membership is still active. Part of me goes hoping to bump into Meg fresh from an endorphin rush that tricks her into thinking she's happy to see me.

I return to water aerobics and am greeted with an enthusiastic welcome from Lina, my old instructor. She's doing the same routine, with the same soundtrack. The only thing different now is me. I'm not nearly as winded as I was when I first started the class. Now I feel more like Max, wanting Lina to work us out a little harder. It doesn't seem like that long ago I was meeting Ginny and releasing cake frosting into the pool. I've really grown since then, advancing not only in stamina and strength, but also in my ability to pull off nefarious schemes.

After showering and getting changed, I go to the lobby, looking for other classes I might try now that I'm in better shape. I'm browsing the offerings at the check-in counter, hoping to see Meg somewhere in the weight room. I still haven't found a way to apologize since my botched banana bread attempt. I'd like for us to find a way back to some kind of relationship, given that I'm putting her son in danger of getting arrested or killed.

Peering through the glass that separates the weight room from the lobby, I only see unemployed men lifting dumbbells. I shouldn't make that assumption anymore now that everyone is working remotely, but none of these guys strike me as tech workers. Maybe I've come to associate that body type with Jeremy though. Most of the men here look like they could grab my grandson by the neck and ankles and deadlift him without breaking a sweat.

"Fancy seeing you here," a deep voice says from behind. I spin around and come face-to-face with Craig. He's still got his stupid greasy ponytail and mustache, although both look a little darker than I remember, like he's dyed them with a cheap shoe polish.

"Hello, Craig," I say. "Is Meg with you?"

Craig laughs and then follows it up by saying "ha" in case I didn't get the mockery.

"That's a no then," I say, turning to leave. He steps quickly, blocking my exit.

"You've got a lot of nerve showing up here," he says.

"To the gym?"

"After what you did to Meg," he says shaking his head.

"And what exactly did I do?" I say, taking a step back so that his peanut butter oat breath doesn't reach me.

"You abandoned her when she needed you most," he says. "She's working two jobs now thanks to you."

"And what's *your* job, if you don't mind me asking? How are you able to be at the gym in the middle of the day?"

Craig pokes a stubby finger in my face. His fingernails look like the kind you'd see on a water buffalo. "Don't you worry about me," he says. "I provide."

"Then why come to me, begging for money I don't have?"

"You have money. I've seen your friends, their homes, the kinds of cars they drive. Don't tell me you don't all have money because I know you do."

I push past him and storm out the door, wishing I could plunge into the pool and wash the stench of that interaction off my body. What has Meg gotten herself into? I ask, hustling away from that man as fast as I can. When I reach the bus stop, I'm too agitated to sit on the covered bench so I pace back and forth on the sidewalk. What is Craig doing? Stalking us? Thank God I changed the locks on the front and back doors. Even with those precautions, I don't feel safe. It's one thing to deal with thugs and gangsters online, quite another to be confronted with one in person. The bus arrives and I instinctively grab a seat in the front. Even being this close to the driver, my body trembles all the way home.

46

July 13

I spend the rest of the week flirting with Ginny online as Jackson Livingstone III, a Texas oil tycoon who supports public libraries and Planned Parenthood. Once Jeremy sets up his profile on Senior Moments, I take over to spare Ginny the embarrassment of fake-dating my grandson. Over the course of the first week, I woo her with compliments on her purl stitching and puzzle completion. We bond over episodes of *The Great British Bake Off*, cheering on the contestants who display the proper balance of skill and humility. We swap stories of physical ailments and talk about sleeping patterns. We wonder aloud if we'll die before we see a female president.

By Friday, I think it's time we take our relationship to the next level.

"I think we need to spice things up a bit," I tell Ginny over the phone.

"I like our chats," Ginny says.

"I'm going to send you a picture of me on a motorcycle."

"Can you make it a horse?" Ginny asks. "Like that photo of Putin only with your shirt on. Maybe unbuttoned just a bit."

This little insight into my friend's sexual fantasies is unsettling, but I comply. After that, I lift most my communication out of romance novels.

I was out riding today. The wind carried the scent of wildflowers, which mingled with the salty tang of sweat as it streamed down my brow. The relentless rays of the sun were nothing compared to the fiery determination that burns within me to see you.

Unfortunately, Ginny has a hard time responding in kind. *Thank you,* she writes after each of my passionate declarations. *I feel the same.*

By week two, we start referring to each other as soul mates. Week three, I suggest we take our relationship offline and meet in person. I tell her I'll be staying at the Fairmont in San Francisco in a few days and would love to meet for lunch. Ginny accepts my proposal and we sign off with heart emojis.

The day of our "date," Ginny goes to the bank and withdraws Cristóbal's money. It's the most dangerous part of the scheme because it requires her to act in front of a real human. The morning of her scheduled appointment, she's a nervous wreck, so we take an extra-long walk to help her rehearse her story.

"Mrs. Anderson, this is quite a big withdrawal," I say, playing the part of concerned bank manager.

"Yes, Frank, it is." Ginny knows the bank manager because she makes friends wherever she goes. She knows all the checkout clerks at Safeway, the pharmacists at CVS, even the men in the taco truck parked around the corner from the YMCA.

"Won't you please let us write you a cashier's check instead?" I say.

"That's so sweet of you but the artist insisted on cash."

"This just seems like a lot of money for a painting."

"It most certainly is. But it's an original ZamZam. Have you heard of him?"

I shake my head because no one's heard of him because we made him up.

"Oh, you'd love his work. He's a very avant-garde mixed media artist. He's like the Turkish Banksy."

I smile at Ginny's delivery. It's taken her all morning to say ZamZam and Banksy without giggling.

"We're getting his latest piece, *Mindscape Garden*, for half the price if it were to go to auction. It's going to be the focal piece at the new restaurant."

I nod. It's important she mention the new restaurant as that's been the reason for her previous withdrawals. "But why make the transaction in cash?" I ask.

"Oh, you know artists," Ginny says. "They're so antiestablishment. ZamZam doesn't trust banks. At first he wanted to be paid in Bitcoin but we thought that would raise too many red flags with you all."

I hand over the imaginary bag of cash and we all applaud her performance.

"Won't I need help carrying that much money to my car?" Ginny asks.

"Three hundred thousand dollars in one-hundred-dollar bills is only six to seven pounds," I say. "Your purse is heavier. Max will be waiting in the handicap spot just outside the door."

Max nods, happy to be driving the getaway car. She's already picked out a cute scarf and sunglasses as her disguise.

"Okay," Ginny says exhaling. "I think I'm ready."

Everything goes according to plan.

"You were tougher on me than Frank was," Ginny says when we rendezvous at Max's house afterward. She places the bag of cash on the kitchen table and we all marvel at how inconsequential it looks, like someone's doggie bag. We toast ourselves with iced tea and lemon. "It helped that I interrupted his lunch. He seemed more concerned that his burrito was getting cold."

Jeremy takes the money off our hands and reminds Ginny to call the bank tomorrow and have them freeze the account.

"If they ask, just say you think a man saw you enter your PIN at an ATM," Jeremy says. "But they probably won't ask."

Ginny nods, stifling a tiny smile. I think she's enjoying the starring role we've given her in this play. I just hope she stays in character a little while longer. Her big scene with Cristóbal is about to begin.

47

August 4

I make plans to come over to Ginny's when she calls Cristóbal to tell him about the theft. I don't want her to be alone if / when he starts threatening her. Someone needs to watch for that tiny red dot that appears on a victim's forehead just before they're assassinated by a sharpshooter. We decide to call him when everyone on her floor is at dinner just in case we need the privacy. Max surprises me by asking if she can come along as well.

"What about Harold?" I ask.

"He'll be fine with the nurse," Max says. "I'll bring a veggie platter."

I spring for an Uber to Max's house and arrive at 4:20 P.M. She bursts out the front door like a woman who's just quit a job she hates. It's strange seeing her dressed in something other than sweats. She looks almost elegant in black slacks and a cerulean blue top covered with a matching long knit jacket. I look at my own getup—jeans and a sweatshirt—and feel the chasm between our social classes. Even our food plates seem indicative of our different backgrounds. Hers is a beautifully rendered kaleidoscope of cut vegetables arranged on a ceramic platter from Pottery Barn, whereas my frosted scones look like they've been sneezed on in their Tupperware container.

"You know this isn't a dinner party, right?" I say, pulling myself into her sport utility VW. She's wearing perfume, something that smells of nectarines and honey.

"Of course," Max says. "I thought I'd feel more at ease if I pretended I was going to my book club."

We arrive at Xanadu and scan the lobby before entering. Most of the residents are in the dining hall, which gives us the all clear. We enter the building, get our visitor passes, and make haste to an open elevator. Max can't help looking around, taking in the surroundings. "Smells like Bolognese sauce," she says, wrinkling her nose.

The elevator arrives on the ninth floor without stopping and before we know it, we're safely ensconced in Ginny's apartment.

"This is much nicer than I expected," Max says, which I think she means as a compliment. She walks over to the wall of windows and stares out at the distant foothills. The sun lights the whole room, which seems wrong given the sense of impending doom I feel. I half expect to see a mushroom cloud arise from behind the hills, followed by a radioactive shock wave and shattering of glass.

Ginny must be nervous too because she goes immediately for one of my scones, which I score as a small victory. It isn't until she's halfway through that she remembers to offer us drinks. She bounces off the couch and comes back holding two bottles, one wine, one mineral water. After taking our orders (Max opts for mineral water, leaving the chardonnay for Ginny and me), she pours our drinks and we get down to business.

"The goal here is to have him walk away," I remind Ginny. "You need to convince him he's working with the dumbest accomplice ever."

"Got it," Ginny says.

"Ready?" I ask.

Ginny nods and starts texting from the couch. Max and I hover from behind to coach like Cyrano if she needs it.

Can we talk? she begins.

Three dots appear at the bottom of the screen. We don't have to wait long for Cristóbal's response.

Busy

It's important

What is it?

Ginny holds her breath. **The money's gone.**

Three dots. This time, they linger a bit longer before the words appear.

What do you mean?

I've been scammed.

The texts stop. Ginny turns around and looks up at us with panicked eyes. Max bites down on a finger carrot with a hard snap.

A minute later, the phone in Ginny's hand rings. It's like the device has electrocuted her. She drops the phone and scrambles to pick it up off the carpet. When she finally retrieves it, she holds up the screen for us to see: **Unknown Caller** it says. Ginny accepts and puts the caller on speaker.

"Where's my fucking money!" a voice bellows. Max and I scramble around the couch and stand on either side of Ginny, protecting her like *Charlie's Angels*. I hope I'm the Kate Jackson in this reboot, the smart one with the sensible haircut.

"I'm so sorry," Ginny cries. "This is all my fault."

"I know it's your fucking fault," Cristóbal, or the man playing Cristóbal, screams. "What happened?"

I put my hand on Ginny's back to calm her. She's breathing in short bursts, like after one of our more strenuous workouts. I look over at

Max, who's clenching and unclenching her fist, the way you do when you give blood.

"Well, I was upset, as you know. You wouldn't come out and help me with this money transfer. So, after we broke up, I met someone new," she stammers. "On Senior Moments. A really nice gentleman. Or so I thought."

Ginny starts crying. I give her a thumbs-up for authenticity and then realize she might actually be upset, either because of the breakup or the fact that she's talking to a potential murderer.

Cristóbal says nothing, so Ginny keeps talking.

"He came to San Francisco last weekend and took me to a lovely lunch at the Fairmont. Just as we're finishing our meal, he tells me he's a federal agent, tracking cybercriminals, and that he suspects that my identity has been stolen. He had a badge and everything."

Silence.

I give Ginny a thumbs-up and encourage her to keep going.

"He had all my information—my bank account, my social security number, even my address. He said the FBI was going to freeze all the bank accounts associated with my name that afternoon. I nearly died of a heart attack, I'll tell you."

"Did you say anything about me?" Cristóbal says.

"I didn't. I was about to confess to everything but then he tells me he knows I'm not involved. The whole reason he came to San Francisco was to confirm I wasn't some drug lord. Can you imagine?"

"So what happened?"

"He said if I wanted access to my money, I would have to withdraw it and place it in a government account where they could monitor it. So I did. We drove to the bank together and he waited outside. Before

I handed over the cash, he showed me a photo of a Treasury check for $300,000 and said it would be delivered tomorrow. But I never received the check."

"You fucking idiot," Cristóbal says.

I think Ginny is about to lose it but instead a smile creeps across her face. She's enjoying this, I realize, the way a child might delight in torturing an overly strict teacher. It's a tipping of scales that throws everyone off balance and for just a moment, Ginny is relishing the feeling of weightlessness.

"Don't worry," she says, suppressing her glee. "I reported it to the bank, who froze the account immediately. Then I made a full report to the police."

"You did what?" Cristóbal says, explosive again.

"Well, I felt so bad. This is all my fault. So I spent all day at the police station answering their questions. They were so nice and helpful. I have complete confidence they are going to figure this whole kerfuffle out."

"Did you give them my name?"

"Of course not," Ginny says. "I mean, they already have your name because it's on the bank account so they might try to contact you, but don't worry, I took all the blame because, really, this is all my fault. I can't apologize enough."

The line goes dead.

"Cristóbal?" Ginny says. "Cristóbal?"

Ginny hangs up and throws the phone onto the couch, like it's something dead and rotting in her hands. Max and I wrap our arms around her and hold her tight. I suddenly realize we're standing in front of her window. We're nine stories up but that won't protect us from a sniper or drone or helicopter. After Ginny calms down, I walk over and close her blinds, blocking out all the light in the room. Max turns on a table lamp and we huddle in silence. It's like we're all waiting for Cristóbal's response—a phone call, a knock on the door, a rocket launch. But nothing happens. All we hear is the sounds of our breathing.

"I'm impressed with your performance," Max says, filling her empty glass with a splash of wine. "You really sounded like an idiot."

"I've had practice," Ginny says laughing.

Max holds out the bottle to us and we encourage her to pour generously.

"We did it," I say, holding up my glass for a toast. "We scammed the scammer."

"You think so?" Ginny asks, touching her glass lightly against mine and Max's.

I nod. "Why don't you stay with me tonight?" I say. "I worry about you being alone."

"I'd like that," Ginny says.

Ginny hustles into her bedroom. We hear the closet door slide open and a bag unzip. I turn to Max and see her scowling.

"What?" I whisper, so Ginny won't overhear.

"It's not over," Max says. "You know that, right?"

"What do you mean?"

"That was too easy," she says.

"It wasn't easy," I say. "A lot of work went into pulling this off."

"I'm not arguing with that," Max says. "I'm just saying, criminals don't lose this much money without some kind of response. We need to be ready when it comes."

"Ready how?"

Max thinks about this. "I don't know," she says. "But Ginny's safer here than at your house. There's a security guard at the entrance and other personnel to come to her aid if she needs it."

"That didn't stop Cynthia and Sharon from getting killed," I say.

"They weren't expecting a killer," Max says. "We need to be ready." She yanks open Ginny's cutlery drawer and removes a bread knife. "Sleep with this."

I almost laugh at the feebleness of the weapon. "Ginny, stop your packing," I say loud enough so she can hear me in the other room. "I'm spending the night here."

"All overnight guests have to be cleared with administrative staff," Ginny says, emerging from her bedroom.

"Let's go clear me then," I say.

We walk to the elevators, hoping to catch one before the other residents start their ascent from the dining hall. We descend in silence, unsure of what awaits us down in the lobby. What if the doors open and Cristóbal is standing there, with a sinister smile and gun in hand? He could shoot all three of us without a silencer and none of the residents would probably hear it.

The door opens to an empty lobby. Ginny pokes her head out and gives us the all clear. As soon as we're out the doors, we hear a commotion, just outside the entrance to the dining hall. Bernard and Alfonse have each other by the shoulders and are doing the kind of slow dance you might see in a middle school gymnasium. Each is trying to shake the other into submission but neither has the strength to throw the other off balance. "Stop it, you two," Barbara says, slapping each of them on the forearm. The two of them break contact and face off, huffing and puffing.

"You malignant swine," Alfonse says.

"Jackal!" Bernard counters.

It's like watching *Masterpiece Theatre* perform WWF.

Ginny instinctively moves toward the commotion (she still has the instincts of a kindergarten teacher), but I hold her back when I see Bernard dust himself off and storm into the cafeteria, leaving Barbara and her cronies attending to Alfonse.

I feel all eyes on us as we move toward the exit. Suddenly, I'm less confident in Max's theory that we're safer in Xanadu than my home. *Keep walking*, I want to say as we approach the receptionist. Keep walking until we're far, far away from this place.

"You two going to be okay?" Max asks before she leaves.

"We'll be fine," Ginny says and checks me in as her overnight guest.

By the time we're making our way back to the elevators, the lobby has returned to normal, but my state of mind is still in a tailspin. I can protect Ginny from these Xanadu bullies, but how am I going to stop an assassin if he wants to break into her apartment and throw her off the balcony?

48

August 11

The next week we live like frightened deer, alert to every sign of danger. Ginny's nerves are wrecked, the buzz of the scam having turned into the hangover of getting caught. Every day she waits for an email, phone call, or knock on the door that will signal the beginning of the end. Besides a few follow-up calls from the bank and police, she's left pretty much alone. Cristóbal's profile has disappeared from the Senior Moments dating site and he no longer responds to any of her texts or emails.

Still, there's some lingering paranoia.

Ginny is sure she's being watched. There's a strange car parked across the street that she's never seen before. She can't use her computer without thinking that someone is monitoring her every tap on the keyboard. The other night, she woke up in the middle of the night (i.e., 10:00 P.M.) and sensed someone standing outside her door. When she went to check the peephole, the hallway was empty. She now sleeps with a can of hair spray.

We insist she keep walking with us.

The exercise calms her nerves. Seeing normal life continue reminds us that we aren't living in a Raymond Chandler novel. There are still people walking their dogs, pushing their children in strollers, and sometimes pushing their dogs in strollers. Max alters our route so we explore new neighborhoods, ones with gardens we can admire and lives we can imagine. Why does that place have so many cars parked in the driveway? Imagine living next to that construction project. Why is this person giving away a perfectly good end table?

Focusing on other people's lives helps us avoid thinking about our own. Max doesn't have to worry about the deteriorating health of her husband. I don't have to worry if Meg will ever forgive me. And Ginny doesn't have to worry about being bound and gagged and thrown into the trunk of a car.

Like Max always says: Exercise is restorative.

We try not to think about the money trickling into Max's GoFundMe account. Jeremy is managing that side of things, making small, untraceable deposits every other day to avoid suspicion. The balance is nearly at $200,000, something Max can really use to defray Harold's medical costs. Unlike Ginny, she's only grown lighter since stealing all of Cristóbal's money. That's not to say she's turned into a beacon of hope and optimism; she just doesn't point out our failings with the same frequency as before.

"Did I tell you I went back to the YMCA?" I say as we take off from Max's house.

"When?" Ginny asks.

"Before. When we were . . . you know." I don't want to say, *Back when we were keeping a low profile to avoid arrest or assassination*. That will just send Ginny into a tizzy. I'd rather have that elephant stand quietly in the room than trample us in a stampede. "I went back to water aerobics."

"With Lina?" Ginny asks.

I nod. "It was so easy."

"That's because you're in better shape," Max says. "Thanks to me."

I look at Ginny and roll my eyes.

I don't tell them about running into Craig. Part of me doesn't want to bring him into this nice walk we're having. Another part doesn't want to admit how badly I've failed my daughter. I've complained to the girls about Meg before, but this time feels especially painful because I cut that frayed rope that might allow her to crawl out of the crevice she's fallen into.

"It's strange to think how far we've come from that class," Ginny says.

"Are you talking about your blood pressure?" Max says.

"I'm talking about our friendship," Ginny says. "When I think back to that first class, I'd never have guessed we'd be where we are today."

You mean running from the law and mob? I want to say but don't. I just smile instead.

"I knew you had it in you," Max says.

"To do what?" Ginny asks.

"To be better," she says.

"And what about you, Max?" I ask. "Do you feel like you're better too?"

Max thinks about it. "I do," she says finally.

We wait for her to elaborate, but she doesn't. "How so?" I ask.

"I'm more tolerant of people's flaws," she says finally.

49

August 12

"Barbara invited me to dinner," Ginny says over the phone.

"Did you make an excuse?" I ask.

"I did. I said we already had plans."

"That's good."

"So now *we're* having dinner with Barbara."

Apparently, Barbara was not going to be put off by Ginny's previous engagement so now I'm rifling through my closet looking for something to match Barbara's effortless glamour. It's impossible to find anything that doesn't make me look like some charity case, so I go with the loudest print I can find. When I show up at Ginny's she stares at me like I just stepped out of a Roy Lichtenstein painting.

"You're making a bold statement with that dress," Barbara says when she sees my outfit. I take pleasure in the idea that my attire might cause her some embarrassment. She's dressed in a sleek navy blue dress with pearls. In her dainty hand she carries a small pink Prada purse.

Alfonse and Patty meet us at the elevators, each carrying plastic totes of chilled wine.

Everyone lapses into silence while we wait for the elevator to arrive. Unfortunately, it's stopping on every floor, probably to pick up passengers for the dinner rush.

"Patty told us the funniest story today," Barbara says to break the ice. "She was at the spa getting a massage and her masseuse, an Asian, smelled of garlic, like she'd just come from working a shift at the Chinese restaurant next door. None of the essential oils they use could hide the odor. Patty says, at the end of her hour session, she felt like a steak that's been seasoned and tenderized."

"I can still smell it on me," Patty says, extending her arm as proof. All I smell is her obnoxious perfume. A bit of garlic would be a welcome substitute.

Neither Ginny nor I laugh, which throws some doubt that Patty's story is "the funniest." Luckily, the elevator arrives to break the tension and we all pile in, Ginny and I in the back and the Barbara trio up front. When we stop on floors going down, Barbara acts as bouncer and refuses entrance to a lady in a wheelchair, even though we could have squeezed together to accommodate her. Two floors down, she allows a dapper gentleman with a neatly trimmed beard on with a flirtatious coo, "Good evening, Dean," which makes Dean decidedly uncomfortable. When the elevator doors open in the lobby, Barbara steps off first and leads us into the cafeteria.

She weaves between the tables until she finds one that's in the center of the room and takes her seat. Once we're all sitting down, she raises her hand and snaps her fingers to call over a waitress. "Five wineglasses, please," she says and then shoos the girl away.

"I was so sorry to hear about Sharon," I say. "Do the police have any leads?"

Barbara laughs off my concern. "Oh, I wouldn't worry about Sharon," she says. "I'm sure she's just paying her daughter back."

"For what?" Ginny asks.

"The ingrate filed for conservatorship based on the few times Sharon got a little drunk and made some poor financial decisions. I think this whole disappearance is her way of showing her daughter who's boss. She's probably on a cruise somewhere in the Bahamas as we speak."

"Didn't you say she left you a note saying she was going to visit her daughter?" I ask.

"A misdirection," Barbara says with a wave of her hand. "Designed to throw us off her trail."

Alfonse uncorks the bottle of wine and pours everyone a glass. "To Sharon," Barbara says, raising her glass. "Wherever she may be." She tosses back the wine with a hearty gulp. "Oooh, that's good. Has a hint of peach, don't you think?"

Alfonse and Patty take a sip and nod their heads in agreement.

The server comes back and takes our order. I follow the ladies' requests for the spring salad even though what I really want is the chicken ricotta. Ten minutes later when our dinner arrives, I've already reclassified it as grazing. I'll fix myself a peanut butter and banana sandwich when I get home.

"So, Poppy," Barbara says, emptying the bottle into her glass. She nods at Patty, who bends down and retrieves her bottle from its chilled carrying case. This one's got a twist-off cap so no need to snap her manicured fingers for assistance. "You're becoming a regular around here. You interested in moving to Xanadu?"

"No," I say and reposition my napkin in my lap. "I just come to see Ginny."

"We all love Ginny," Barbara says, patting Ginny's hand. "I couldn't ask for a better neighbor."

Just then, Bernard appears, grinning from ear to ear. "Hello, ladies," he says, doing a small bow. He doesn't look at or acknowledge Alfonse and I wonder if he's still angry about their fight a week ago.

Ginny and I greet Bernard with considerably more enthusiasm than the rest of the table. Patty begins stabbing her salad in earnest, while Barbara tears into a dinner roll.

"Barbara, I just got off the phone with Sharon's daughter. She told me the most interesting bit of news. Want to hear it?"

Patty stands up dramatically and excuses herself to use the restroom.

"Can't you see we're eating," Alfonse says testily.

"This will just take a second. I'm sure you'll want to hear it. Turns out, Sharon's credit card was charged at 2:13 A.M. for an Uber ride to the airport the night of her disappearance."

"See, I told you Sharon's just taking a short vacation," Barbara says to the table. "There's the proof."

"Thing is, she wasn't there when the Uber arrived," Bernard says. "So she was charged the no-show fee, not the quoted fee to the airport. Don't you think that's strange?"

There's a loud crash from the other side of the room. Alfredo, our befuddled waiter from last time, has dropped a trio of dishes onto the floor and is apologizing profusely to the surrounding tables that've been splashed with spaghetti sauce and salad dressing. Some woman with her hair in a tight bun and crisp button-down hurries out and tries to help manage the situation.

When it looks like they have everything under control, we turn our attention back to Barbara for her response to Bernard's news. Barbara gets ready to speak, but she's got something caught in her throat. Her eyes bulge out in panic as her breathing becomes more labored. She shakes her head and starts digging through her purse, dumping its contents onto the table in a mad fury. When she doesn't find what she's looking for, she grabs Alfonse's arm and wheezes something I can't make out. Alfonse jumps into action and starts looking frantically around the table and floor. Finally, he shouts, "EpiPen! Does anyone have an EpiPen?"

Barbara drops to the floor and starts writhing, gasping for breath. I can see her skin turning a grayish blue as she struggles for breath. Is this the moment I've been dreading my entire life? The moment I have to jab a straw into someone's throat to save their life? I look around to see if there's a straw on any of the adjacent tables, but those things have probably been banned from Xanadu just like everywhere else.

Barbara's beautiful long legs kick furiously like she's a drowning swimmer. Ginny drops to her knees and tries to calm her down, but Barbara's clawing her throat in a desperate attempt to get air. I look over at Bernard, who's watching the scene with a sort of bizarre fascination. He's the only one in the room who isn't moving and for a terrible moment we lock eyes. I wish I could say I saw concern or compassion in his gaze, but all I get is a dull stare, like someone waiting for a pot of water to boil.

Next thing I know, the manager who had been helping Alfredo clean up his mess is by Barbara's side with a tiny red bag, which she unzips. She removes a large syringe and jabs it into Barbara's naked thigh. Within seconds, Barbara is gulping for air. The color returns to her face, while Alfonse holds her head in his lap. "You did this!"

he screams at Bernard, who's still standing there speechless. "You monster!"

A few minutes later, two men in nursing uniforms come in and take a shaken Barbara away on a rolling stretcher. Alfonse doesn't leave her side as they disappear out the doors.

50

August 13

The next day, we're on our usual walk when Ginny gives us an update.

"Barbara nearly died," Ginny says.

"Poison?" Max asks.

"Peanut oil."

"Was it some mistake made in the kitchen?" I ask. If the chef is as incompetent as Alfredo, I'm surprised the whole place hasn't been hospitalized.

"The manager says they follow a strict protocol to keep peanuts and shellfish out of the meal prep because so many people have allergies."

"Then someone added it at our table," I say.

"And removed Barbara's EpiPen from her purse," Max says.

"But Barbara isn't on Senior Moments," I say.

"She was," Ginny says. "That's how she met Alfonse, remember?"

"Do people suspect him?" Max asks.

"People think it was Bernard," Ginny says.

"He does hate Barbara," I say.

"Not enough to wish her dead," Ginny says.

❖

When I get home, the place is empty. Jeremy must still be visiting Bao. The two of them have been spending more time together these past few weeks, which is sweet. Jeremy has helped Bao wire his home in exchange for language classes. Jeremy is serious about his trip to Vietnam and wants to learn how to communicate before he leaves. I listen to him practice his pronunciation downstairs with some online language program. It sounds like I have a very dull Vietnamese couple living in my basement.

With Jeremy gone, Scampers greets me at the door, wanting to play. I pick up the feather on a string toy Jeremy bought and dangle it in front of the cat's face, which sends him into a paroxysm of springs and swipes. We do this for about five minutes before it wears me out. I toss a mouse-shaped chew toy across the room for him to retrieve and that's when I notice something's off. I can't pinpoint it exactly. It's like the whole front room has shifted from a minor earthquake.

I'm being paranoid, I tell myself. But can you blame me? There are too many nagging questions swirling in my head: Cynthia could have killed herself or she could have been pushed. Sharon could be vacationing in Aruba or she could be at the bottom of the ocean. Barbara could have eaten something tainted with peanut oil or she could have been intentionally poisoned. Everything feels too connected to be coincidental. What these women had in common is Xanadu and Senior Moments. If those places are the circles in my Venn diagram, then Ginny is in the overlapping oval. She's in danger, especially now that she's "lost" Cristóbal's money. My only hope is that her police report has given her some protection. But how long will that protection last? It's not enough to steal Cristóbal's money. We need to find out who he is and put him away before he comes after Ginny. Maybe there's a way we can trace Cristóbal's communication, although Jeremy's already told me it's nearly impossible to do through the dating or messaging apps Ginny's been using.

I do a quick tour of the house and don't notice anything missing from the shelves or cabinets. Everything looks okay with the exception of the window in the bathroom—it's open just a crack. Jeremy might have left it ajar before he went to visit Bao, I rationalize. I walk over, shut it, and make a mental note to replace the faulty lock. I'll talk to Jeremy when he gets home about installing those surveillance cameras too. Maybe we need a few inside as well as outside the house.

It's terrible not feeling safe in your own home. Normally, I'd go to my bedroom and take a nap after my walk, but when I stand in front of my door, I realize it's only got one escape route. If someone blocked it, I'd have no way to get around my attacker and nothing besides my clock radio with which to defend myself.

I go back to the living room and curl up on the couch in front of the window. The room is bright and warm and impossible to imagine as the setting for a kidnapping or murder. I call to Scampers to come rest with me but he's in the throes of a deep catnip trance and doesn't budge from his place on the opposite armchair. I fall asleep listening to the construction crew working on the remodel two houses down.

❖

Jeremy wakes me up when he comes through the front door. He looks at me quizzically, the way he does when he thinks I'm having a senior moment, which he defines as anytime I've forgotten to buy his favorite soda.

"Why are you on the couch?" he asks, walking over to Scampers and scooping him off his resting place.

I sit up and try to find a reasonable answer to his question. "I was sleepy" is all I can come up with. "Did you leave the bathroom window open?" I ask.

"I don't think so," Jeremy says.

"It was ajar," I say.

"Ajar?"

"Yes, ajar."

Jeremy puts Scampers on the floor and leaves the room. I go to follow him, but I'm still a little foggy from my nap. I was having a strange dream in which I was talking with Harrison Ford about filling a pothole in front of the house.

So, I'm sitting on the couch when I hear Jeremy make his discovery. First, the creak of the door leading to the basement, then the slow walk down the stairs, then his terrified scream.

"What is it?" I yell.

When he doesn't answer, I hoist myself up and hurry over to the basement door. I'm halfway down the stairs when I see what has caused Jeremy's panic: Every single piece of technology he owns, even the cables and power strips, is gone.

51

August 13

Jeremy springs immediately into action using the only device he now has access to: his phone. He's so furious, I leave him alone and walk upstairs to make dinner. But I'm too distracted to even crack an egg. I walk out the front door and stand in front of the house. I don't know what I'm hoping to discover, exactly, but I don't want to be inside any-more knowing that someone has robbed us. What if they were hiding in the basement when I went to take my nap? The whole thing feels like a violation. Whoever broke in must have been watching us awhile to know our schedules. Jeremy has less of a routine than I do so they must have taken a chance he wouldn't come home before they grabbed his stuff. Either that or they had someone following him.

I walk down to the construction crew down the street, a trio of Spanish speakers who break from their work with two-by-fours to answer my questions. No, they didn't see anyone enter or leave my house while I was away. They point to the Neighborhood Watch signs posted on a lamppost. I'm embarrassed to say I don't know how this particular security detail works, exactly. I thank them for their help and start knocking on my neighbors' doors, hoping to find someone bored and nosy enough to watch the street while the rest of us are out. I find her in a racist woman my daughter's age but all she does is complain about the Mexican construction workers I just spoke to.

The first person I call is Meg. She doesn't pick up, as usual, so I leave a message that I mean to be conciliatory but quickly becomes accusatory. "I don't know if you and Craig are behind this," I say at the end. "But if you are, return Jeremy's computers now. I'll pay whatever you want. His whole life is on those machines. Please don't wipe them clean and sell them."

I sit on the front steps and start to weep. I feel so hopeless. And scared. And sad. Not for me as much as for Jeremy. How are we going to get his beloved computers back? My home insurance should cover the cost of the stolen items, but only if I report the theft to the police. I don't know if we can do that, given what Jeremy and I used the computers for. What if the police start asking questions: *Why'd the thieves only take the computers? Why would they target you of all people? Not to be rude, but look at the other homes on this street. They're WAY nicer than yours, probably with two working parents who send their children to summer camps for weeks at a time. What have you got that anyone would find of value?*

The police in my imagination are a little rude, but their questions are the same ones I have and they lead me to two scenarios: Either this is a simple home robbery or Cristóbal knows where I live.

Scenario 1: A burglar broke in and stole the only items worth anything: Jeremy's computer equipment. This feels about as convincing as the stories that Cynthia jumped, Sharon is on vacation, and Barbara's meal was contaminated by a clumsy chef.

Scenario 2: If the computers were stolen by Cristóbal, it means he's connected me to Ginny and knows we scammed him. Stealing my grandson's computers will help him learn *how* we scammed him and maybe get his money back.

I add my house as another circle to my Venn diagram of murder. Now the only person that appears in the cross section is Craig. He's done workshops at Xanadu. He's selling his vitamins on Senior Moments. And he's been in my house. But is he smart enough to run a money laundering operation? And is he capable of murder?

Jeremy's still in crisis mode when I return home, typing into his phone like he's dismantling a bomb. I think I can see the adrenaline surging through his body.

"Jeremy?" I say.

"Not now, Grandma."

"Are we in danger?" I ask.

The fear in my voice cuts through his panic. He looks up at me standing at the foot of the stairs, clutching the handrail, trembling in the chill of the basement, and purses his lips. "I don't know," he says.

He explains to me the various threat levels, depending on who stole the computer and for what purpose. Most of what he does is safely hidden in the cloud, he assures me, but there's always the chance that he left some evidence on his computer. "When I pee, it goes in the bowl, but there's always a chance something splashes on the seat" is how he explains it to me, a metaphor I understand but wished I didn't have to hear.

"I'll get dinner ready," I say, and trudge up the stairs.

What have I done? This is all my fault. I thought I was so smart. It was pure hubris to think I could outwit these people. Now I've put Jeremy, Ginny, and probably Max's lives in danger and for what? So I could rip off a scam artist?

I open the refrigerator door and stare at the empty shelves inside. I've got some very basic food groups, but nothing beyond that. I take out everything I need for a Caesar salad, minus the anchovies, and start making the dressing. This with some garlic bread is about all I can handle right now.

Halfway through my whisking, a teardrop splashes into the bowl and I realize I'm crying again. It's like I'm pouring all my failures into this recipe, infecting Jeremy even further than I already have. Is it not enough that I've given him all my loser DNA, now I have to poison him with my cooking?

I sit down at the kitchen table and stare at the head of lettuce in front of me, its outer leaves already shriveled and browning. Whoever said wisdom comes with age was an idiot suffering from dementia. I am making worse mistakes now than I ever made in the past. I've always thought I could outsmart people, only to be proven wrong every time. Only this time, I not only ruined my life, I may have brought down the people closest to me as well.

I peel off the lettuce leaves, recounting each failure as I go.

When I was in seventh grade, I stole a girly magazine from the house where I babysat and charged the boys in my brother's fifth-grade class ten cents a peek. One of the boys told on me and in addition to losing the babysitting gig, I nearly got thrown out of school.

One time, I took Meg to a fancy swim and tennis club and used a member's ID I had found in the bathroom to order us an enormous lunch of BLT sandwiches, French fries, and chocolate malts. Just as we finished, the member arrived and asked us how we enjoyed our meal. I sent Meg to the pool and worked off the lunch by cleaning the man's Lamborghini.

My second husband's friend, a photographer with a trust fund, offered to pay me to pose naked from the waist down. I thought, sure, why not? Two months later, my vagina *and* my face were on full display in a gallery my husband passed every day on his way to work. We divorced shortly thereafter.

Most recently, I resold the office computers I was supposed to leave in the company's e-waste bin. I was so confident I'd outsmarted those tech geniuses with their degrees from Stanford and MIT. All it took was some janitor to rat me out and force me into early retirement.

I finish this walk down this memory lane and realize I've torn this head of lettuce into shreds. Staring at the loose leaves, I come to the conclusion that I've always been a hustler, no better than the guys scamming old people on the Internet. Only those guys are smart. They only punch down; they know better than to punch up. It would be better for everyone if I just died right now. Can you die by giving up? Maybe all I have to do is lay my head on this pile of wilting lettuce and let go. I can see the headline now: *Woman Dies in Salad of Her Own Making.*

"No," I say to the empty room. I'm not going out that way. I reach over to the wooden block holding my knives and pull out the largest one I have and start vigorously chopping the lettuce. The only thing worse than dying with your head in a salad is leaving behind a mess for the people you love to clean up. I'm not doing that to Ginny, Max, and Jeremy. I got them into this mess and I'm going to get them out.

52

August 14

I start the next day by contacting the girls and telling them what happened and what my plan of attack is. "The most likely suspect is Craig," I say. "Which means Meg may be in real danger. I have to get her out of that apartment."

"Do you think she'll listen to you after what you said?" Ginny asks.

"No, which is why we're going to confront her where she least expects it." Max agrees to help, as does Ginny. It's a simple plan really, that only requires them to agree to a picnic.

We meet as usual at Max's house and start our walk through the neighborhood toward the public park. The ladies are full of questions regarding the break-in and I try to walk that fine balance of alerting them to the danger while minimizing their stress. This works better for Max than it does for Ginny.

"Craig's been in Xanadu," Ginny reminds us. "He knows the place."

"Then why not steal your computer?" Max asks. "If he's looking for evidence of our scam, that would be logical to start."

"That's true," I say. "Craig only took Jeremy's stuff because it's expensive. And to get back at me for not dying and leaving Meg the house."

"He wanted me to start taking Boost a Move," Ginny says. "You warned me, remember? When Cristóbal suggested I take it? Do you think I was dating Craig the whole time?" Ginny goes suddenly pale and I can see her mentally inventorying all the embarrassing things she said over the span of their relationship.

"Craig's an idiot," I assure her. "No way he could pull that kind of scam off. Best case scenario, this is just Meg fencing stolen goods to pay for her drug habit."

Ginny and Max look at me with alarm.

"I mean, not 'best case scenario' but 'most likely scenario.' Trust me. I've lived through this before. Addiction makes you do terrible things. When Meg's using, all she cares about is getting high. She doesn't care who she has to hurt."

The ladies shake their heads and offer their condolences.

"You can't blame yourself," Ginny says.

"Addiction is hereditary," Max says. "Your father was an alcoholic."

I accept these well-meaning pardons while at the same time dismissing them. I've heard them before, mostly from myself, and they don't help. "I was terrible to her last time we fought," I say. "Now she's not accepting any of my calls and I'm forced to ambush her through her place of business."

Max submitted the order to Meg's website for one of her bespoke picnics. I figured it was safer to have her be the client since Meg had met Ginny at the gym. If Meg suspected a trap, she'd probably refuse the job, even if it meant a loss of income I'm sure she needs.

Max ordered one of the Tuscan picnics complete with a bottle of prosecco, bread, cheese, and assorted vegetables. "Everything looked delicious," Max said after she placed the order, an uncharacteristic compliment from our militant nutritionist. I told her not to get her hopes up. If Meg was on a bender, we'd be lucky if we got box wine and snack packs.

We reach the park and scan the area for our picnic table. Families have already claimed most of the wooden benches. There's one birthday party complete with balloons, piñata, and screaming children. We wander through the crowds looking for Meg but don't see her or our food anywhere. *It's worse than I imagined*, I think after we've checked every picnic table and found them occupied. Now Meg's taking people's money and not even bothering to show up.

"Is that it?" Max asks, pointing to a table set up on the other side of the wide, expansive lawn, as far away from the playground as possible. A woman dressed in a white linen shirt and apron waves us over. As we approach, we realize she's picked the best place in the park for us to dine. The spot is in a shady grove of trees, sheltered from the noonday sun and away from the crowds that cluster near the rec center building. It's secluded and empty, mostly because there's no picnic table or barbecue pits nearby. The woman—I can't believe it's Meg—has brought her own table and chairs and created a different world than the one crowded with kids and confectioners' sugar. It's charming.

As soon as Meg recognizes me, the smile disappears from her face. Her warm greeting turns into her usual look of disapproval. Even with her scowl, she still looks lovely, dressed as a hostess in a fancy restaurant. Her hair's pulled back in a ponytail she's tamed with some gel. She looks healthy with a light tan and lipstick that highlights the full lips she inherited from her father. The apron accentuates her curves while hiding her belly. It's the best I've seen her look in ages and it's all I can do not to wrap her in my arms and squeeze the life out of her.

Meg's expression tells me it's better to stay away.

"Don't be mad," I say, approaching. Ginny and Max hang back for their own safety.

"I can't believe you tricked me like this," Meg says in a barely controlled whisper.

"You weren't answering my calls," I say.

"I didn't want to talk to you."

"That's not acceptable."

Meg laughs and shakes her head. I notice she's wearing the gold hoop earrings I bought her for her fortieth birthday, which gives me some confidence that I haven't been completely worthless as a mother.

"We've always fought and we've always made up because we talk to each other," I say.

"Well, not this time," Meg says.

"Meg, I'm sorry," I say. "I shouldn't have said those things."

"It was very hurtful," Meg says, brushing away a tear. I can't tell if it's real or imaginary.

"I brought some potential investors," I whisper. "Why don't you show them what you can do?"

Meg takes a few deep breaths, shakes her head, and clicks her heels together to prepare for her performance. Then she pushes past me and welcomes the ladies to their dining experience. Max and Ginny take their seats at the table, which is set with a cream-colored linen cloth, white bone china, and champagne flutes. Once everyone is seated, Meg removes the chilled bottle of prosecco from an ice bucket, pops the cork, and slowly fills our glasses as she tells us about the assortment of meats, cheeses, and olives on the table, overdoing it a bit with all their origin stories. I'm simultaneously proud of her and ashamed of myself.

When she's finished, Meg goes to her car, telling us to call if we need anything. As soon as she's gone, Ginny and Max heap praises on the spread, the décor, and Meg's professionalism.

"Am I being biased or is this pretty great?" I say, raising my flute for a toast.

"Lovely," Ginny says, clinking her glass against mine.

"I agree," Max says.

We sip the cold, sweet, bubbly liquid, which tickles the throat as it goes down. I'm just about to forget all my troubles when Max generates a rain cloud over all our heads.

"Clearly, your daughter's healthy," she says. "Which means Craig stole Jeremy's computer equipment for Cristóbal or because he is Cristóbal."

"My daughter may be doing great," I say. "But she's still living with a dirtbag. We need to find out what she knows."

"How are we going to do that?" Ginny asks.

"I need to ask her," I say, standing up from the table. I finish the rest of my liquid courage and head off to where Meg's car is parked.

53

August 14

I walk the football field of park lawn, impressed that Meg hauled all the picnic gear on her own. Meg sees me approach and opens the passenger side door. Before I can sit down, she sweeps the fast-food containers and wrapping paper off the seat and onto the floor.

"Well done, Meg," I say, plopping onto the worn upholstery.

"Surprised?" she says.

"A little. I've never seen you at work before. You're different."

"Well, I hope your friends like it."

"They are impressed," I say. "Send me your business plan and I'll share it with them."

"Really?" Meg says, brightening for the first time in my presence.

I nod. "Let's start with Ginny."

"She's the one at Xanadu?" Meg says. It bothers me that she's so quick with this information, but I let it slide.

"Yes. She has some disposable income and can introduce you to other wealthy seniors."

"Oh, Mom, that would be so great."

I can't help it. My heart warms hearing the word *Mom*. It always has and always will.

"Now I have to ask you about Jeremy's computer," I say.

"I didn't take it," Meg says, turning away from me. "How could you even think that?"

"What about Craig?" I ask.

Meg hesitates, staring out the window. I follow her gaze and see she's tracking a couple of women pushing baby carriages along the gravel path that snakes around the park. I wonder if she ever had that experience. Like me, she had her child in her early twenties, not the easiest time to forge alliances with other mothers. Nowadays, there are all kinds of support groups and ways to connect. When I had Meg, I had to chase a stranger pushing a stroller down the street to get someone to talk to me.

"He wouldn't do that," Meg says finally.

"You sure?" I say.

She runs her hands along the steering wheel before answering. "Craig's got his issues," she says. "But he wouldn't sink that low."

I sense she's holding something back. She can't tell me about Craig's "issues" and of course my mind goes straight to some kind of sexual deviancy, like he enjoys watching Meg eating hot dogs in her underwear. "I want you to move back home," I say, placing a hand on her knee.

Meg flinches me off. "Jeez, Mom, is that what all this is about? You'll get your friends to invest in my company if I leave Craig?"

"What? No. Well, maybe? That guy is dangerous, Meg. You're not safe there."

"I'm an adult, Mom. I can handle Craig on my own."

Meg's heating up so I back away before I get burned. I open the door and exit the vehicle. "We'll call if we need anything," I say and head back to the picnic.

I recount the conversation for the girls, turning Meg into a partner rather than an adversary. "She's going to help us," I say. "Be our inside woman."

The lie works and Max, Ginny, and I go back to eating, drinking, and chatting in that shady grove of the park. It's a nice escape from our worries and Meg attends to our every need, bringing out an almond tart with grapes for dessert and serving us hot coffee she's made from a French press. The whole experience is delightful and it's all I can do not to curl up on the grass and take a nap. Max reminds me that women our age can't nap in public without people thinking we've collapsed from heatstroke, so we gather our things instead.

Before we leave, we offer to help Meg pack up but she refuses, saying you don't help the waiter clear the table at a restaurant, which I guess is true. Out of politeness or concern, she offers us a ride back to Max's house, which we decline. "The walk will help digestion and reduce our blood sugar levels," Max explains. Ginny and I could stage a coup, but we follow her lead, believing she's got no motive to want to kill us.

We drag our feet all the way back to Max's. It's nice to see her more relaxed about leaving the nurse alone in the house with Harold. That either means she has more faith in Harold's caretaker or less faith in Harold's recovery. The money is still being deposited into her GoFundMe account. I guess Jeremy's contact on the dark web isn't afraid of exposure. Those guys who live in basements must have a whole underground network that protects them from any prying eyes from above.

"That really was a nice afternoon," Max says as we're leaving. "I forgot its whole purpose was to discover who broke into your house."

Ginny drives me home so I can take a proper nap. As I'm getting out of the car, Ginny grabs my arm and asks, "Do you really think Craig broke into your house just to steal computers?"

The worry on her face reminds me of when we got caught sabotaging Max's ankle weights and I take full responsibility for it. "I do," I say. "If it were Cristóbal, he wouldn't start with me."

"He'd start with me," Ginny says, nodding.

Fifteen minutes later, I get a call from Ginny just as I'm dropping off to sleep. Someone's broken into her apartment. Her laptop's been stolen.

54

August 14

Jeremy drives me to Xanadu but doesn't come in, although at this point I don't know if keeping a low profile matters anymore. Whoever is stealing our things has obviously made a connection between us. The only one left to hit is Max, although her house is never unoccupied. "Neither is Xanadu," Jeremy reminds me. "And they still managed to break in there." I call Max and tell her the bad news, which she takes with the stoicism of a New England fisherman.

"I've got nothing worth stealing," she says.

I remind her that she's currently holding all the stolen cash in her GoFundMe account. "If they trace the money, you could be in real danger."

"I'll sharpen my kitchen knives."

People at Xanadu are on high alert when we arrive. In the lobby, there's a cluster of women berating the portly Filipino man at the check-in desk. Carlos tries to assure these busybodies that everyone who checked in today was a guest of a resident, but the women aren't having it. They accuse him of leaving his post and allowing a stranger to enter the building to murder them.

"I didn't see you when I left the dining hall this morning," one of his accusers says.

"I was here, ma'am," he says, turning his attention to me, trying to appear as competent as possible. He asks my name, who I'm visiting, and hands me my guest pass. On my way to the elevators, I hear one of the ladies continue her interrogation.

"Who's watching the door when you're signing people in?" she says.

I get in the elevator with two men, who are discussing the need for more surveillance.

"On *Sleuthing in Somerset* they've got cameras everywhere," one man says.

"That show's terrible," his friend replies. "All the inspectors do is watch videos."

"That's how they solve cases nowadays," he says.

We stop at the fourth floor and Bernard walks in, looking as dapper as usual in his cardigan and corduroys. (*Now that's a great name for a* Masterpiece Theatre *mystery*, I think. *Cardigans and Corduroys*, featuring a kindly, old Irish gent who plays fiddle in a pub and solves crimes between pints.)

Bernard sees me, smiles, and steps past the men trying to figure out the best corner for the elevator camera. "I was just on my way to check in on Ginny," he says. "Mind if I accompany you?"

"Not at all," I say.

By the time the elevator reaches the ninth floor, I half expect the crime scene to be roped off by a slew of detectives dusting the area for prints. But the hallway is empty and quiet, as it always is. Ginny ushers us inside her apartment, which is disappointingly not ransacked.

"My dear," Bernard says. "How are you doing?"

"I'm fine," Ginny says, but I can tell she's not. She looks exhausted as anyone would be after a day of drinking and robbery. She returns to her easy chair and wraps herself in a blanket. To think, a few hours ago we were toasting to our health with prosecco in a public park. How quickly life can force you to change lanes. One minute you're on cruise control, the next a high-speed chase.

Of course, we weren't coasting when we picnicked in the park. We were just enjoying a brief respite from terror. The only reason we were dining alfresco was to find out if Craig was behind my house burglary. Now I have to wonder: Did Meg call Craig to tell him Ginny would be out of her apartment for a few hours? It's certainly plausible. Craig's a familiar face around Xanadu thanks to his fitness workshops. Maybe he told Carlos he was here as someone's personal trainer. Or maybe he knows some secret entrance and slipped in unnoticed?

A loud knock startles us all. Bernard springs from the couch (*That man is very spry for someone who walks with a cane*, I think again) and goes to answer the door.

Barbara stands in the hallway holding a bottle of wine. "I thought you could use a restorative," she says, pushing past Bernard, who tries to block her entrance. She walks over to the kitchenette and starts opening drawers, looking for a bottle opener. After digging around, she finally finds one, pops out the cork, and starts pouring. Ginny doesn't have four wineglasses, so I get mine in a coffee cup.

"What a fright," Barbara says, plopping down on the couch next to me.

"How are you doing, Barbara?" I ask. *The last time I saw you, you were flopping like a fish on dry land*. I don't say this last bit out loud of course.

"Much better since Alfonse and I decided to move out," Barbara says.

Bernard can't hide his pleasure at hearing this news. I think I see him do a little jig where he's standing.

"Because of the . . . murders?" Ginny asks.

"Of course because of the murders," Barbara says. "This place isn't safe anymore."

"So, you believe me now?" Bernard says, marching over to where Barbara's sitting and standing in front of her like some prosecuting attorney.

Barbara leans back and takes a slow sip of her wine. "I know you hold a lot of anger against me, Bernard," she says. "But I find the pleasure you take in my misfortune very unsettling."

"Oh, that's rich coming from the woman who blackballed Rosalyn Blather from choir."

"We didn't need another soprano."

"And you took down all my Pride decorations."

"I don't see why we must be subjected to rainbows for a full month just so you can feel good about yourself."

"What about St. Patrick's Day?" Bernard says.

"It's not a real holiday and you know it," Barbara says. "Besides, leprechauns are creepy."

"Leprechauns are adorable!"

"Let's not forget, we're here for Ginny," I remind them.

"Of course," Barbara says, redirecting her focus back to Ginny on the easy chair. "How are you, dear?"

"I'm fine," Ginny says. "I feel silly complaining after everything you've been through."

Barbara nods. "Doctors said I was seconds away from heart failure."

Bernard mumbles something I don't pick up, but Barbara does. "That's it," she says, standing. "Ginny, I'm here if you need anything."

Before she reaches the door, I ask her, "Did you see or hear anyone enter Ginny's apartment this afternoon?"

"I was gone all day at a matinee of *Midnight Requiem*," Barbara says. "Very avant-garde. I do not recommend it."

Barbara leaves, closing the door behind her. As soon as she's out of the room, Bernard starts to sing, "Ding dong, the witch is dead." He plops down next to me and raises his glass in a toast. "To Barbara leaving," he says. Neither of us join his celebration.

"Oh, come on," he says. "You hate her as much as I do. Admit it."

"She nearly died, Bernard," Ginny says.

"You know her own son didn't come to check on her?" he says.

"I didn't know Barbara had kids," I say.

"It's the one thing she doesn't brag about," Bernard says. "You think he's in prison?"

"I think he lives overseas," Ginny says. "There's a photo in her apartment of them standing in front of a temple."

"But nothing online," Bernard says. "All those Facebook posts and not one photo of him."

"That is odd," I say.

"No, it's not," Ginny snaps. "Max's kids live overseas and she doesn't post about them. They haven't come to see Harold."

That's odd too, I want to point out, but I can see Ginny getting angry. It's not an emotion I'm used to seeing on her and both Bernard and I back away like we've just encountered a hissing bunny.

"Join me for dinner?" Bernard says, finishing his glass and standing.

"I'm not hungry," Ginny says.

I walk Bernard to the door. Before he leaves, I ask, "What was that fight you and Alfonse got into the other night?"

Bernard chuckles. "I was defending Alfredo's honor," he says. "Alfonse lit into the boy for no reason. I mean, the man just lost it. So, I suggested he step outside to cool down. I may have poked him in the ribs to get him moving. The jury's still out on that one. Anyway, things pretty much went downhill from there."

"Good for you," I say, leaning in to hug him. I notice he's got a tiny pinprick of a hole in his lobe. "Do you wear an earring, Bernard?"

"Not since Alfonse started wearing one."

I close the door. The FaceTime call with Cristóbal. He had an earring. And facial hair. Just like Alfonse. Just like Bernard.

55

August 14

The call is coming from inside the house. I don't know where that phrase comes from, but it rings in my head and makes me grip the doorknob tightly in my fist. I feel an intense need to fling open the door and run to the elevators. I need to get Ginny out of this place where the women are poisoned, thrown off balconies, or just disappear.

"Come on," I say, rushing back to Ginny. "Let me take you to Subway."

"Honestly, I'm not hungry."

"Let's do drive-through then," I say. "It will be good to get some fresh air."

Ginny doesn't move from her chair. In fact, she seems to sink into it, like a cute hamster sliding down a snake's gullet. "I want to confess," she says.

"Confess? To whom?"

"To Cristóbal. Tell him we took the money."

I sit back down and attend to Ginny like an overzealous therapist. "Are you crazy?"

"It worked with Max, remember? We apologized and she forgave us and now we're good friends."

"You think Cristóbal's going to want to start a walking club after you tell him you stole his money?"

Ginny leans back and covers her eyes with her hands. "I'm just hoping he won't murder me."

"No one's getting murdered," I say, but not very convincingly. How can I share my suspicions of Alfonse and Bernard now? If Ginny thinks Cristóbal lives in Xanadu, she'll be even more inclined to confess and I can't have that. We need to act as normal as possible so no one suspects us of doing anything shady.

"They have our computers," Ginny says, staring up at the ceiling. "They know our secrets."

"We don't know that," I say.

"I'm going to text him," Ginny says pulling out her phone.

I lean over and snatch the phone out of her hands. "Ginny, you can't."

"Give that back."

Ginny lunges toward me but I dodge her outstretched hand. I stand before she can and retreat behind the couch. "Promise me you won't text Cristóbal," I say.

"We need to return his money."

"No we don't."

Ginny lets out an exasperated sigh. "Why did I ever listen to you? Fool me once, shame on me, fool me twice . . ."

"I wasn't trying to fool you."

She turns on me with a look of disappointment I've never seen on her face before. Suddenly, I feel like one of her kindergarten students who's just been caught using the F-word on the playground. "You made me believe we could get away with this," she says.

"Ginny, I'm sorry. I'm going to make this right."

Ginny gets up and walks over to the kitchenette by the door. She empties her wine out in the sink and fills the glass with water. "You like to think you're smarter than everyone else, Poppy, but you're not. You're just not. You remind me of the kids I had in my class who always thought they could get away with lying and cheating. Their confidence didn't lie in their abilities but in their belief that everyone except them was stupid."

"I don't think everyone except me is stupid," I say. "I don't think you're stupid."

"Yes, you do," Ginny says. "You think kindness is stupid. You think I let people take advantage of me."

"Like Cristóbal?"

Ginny snaps her fingers and points at me. "See? There it is. You can be so . . . arrogant. But you know what? I bet I've made fewer mistakes in my life by trusting people than you've made by not trusting them."

"Ginny, you can't trust Cristóbal to do the right thing."

"What matters is that I'm doing the right thing."

"Giving Cristóbal's money back is not the right thing. It's the *easy* thing. That money came from drugs or worse. If you help him launder it, you're complicit in all his crimes."

Ginny turns her back on me and starts washing the glasses and silverware in her sink. I remember using housework to avoid a fight when I was married. Most of the time it resulted in a lot of broken dishes and scorched dress shirts.

I gather my things and walk out the door, pausing to place Ginny's phone on the counter before I leave.

56

August 15

The next day Ginny texts me saying she isn't feeling well and to go to Max's without her, as if that's an easy thing for a person with bad knees and a suspended license to do. I wake up Jeremy to have him give me a lift. While he gets ready, I go down to the basement thinking I might discover a clue as to who robbed us. Jeremy's work cave looks so empty without all the screens and cables connecting him to the world. I picture him as the last employee to leave a bankrupt company. And yes, I'm the bankrupt company in this scenario.

Jeremy enters the kitchen, dressed but unshaven, his beard growing in little tufts like face fungus. I feed him some toast and coffee, which seems like a paltry lunch. I suppose it's technically breakfast, given it's his first meal of the day. I give him one of my yogurts in case he needs something with a little protein.

"Would it be possible to trace a FaceTime call?" I ask.

"That depends," Jeremy says. "Do you have the device the call was made on?"

"It's Ginny's phone," I say. "I want to see if the call she made to Cristóbal was coming from Xanadu."

"Shit," Jeremy says, sitting down. "You think Cristóbal lives in Xanadu?"

"I don't know," I say. "Maybe." I don't share that my suspicion is based on a brief glimpse of a man's earring because I don't want to sound overly paranoid. Lots of men my age probably wear earrings, right? I hear my father laugh in some dark recess of my brain in response to this question.

"If I had her phone, I could probably capture the IP address involved in the call. It wouldn't give us an exact location, but it would tell us if it's close."

"There's only one problem," I say. "Ginny's mad at me. It may take me awhile before she trusts me again."

Jeremy must see the wretchedness on my face because he jumps up from the table and wraps me in a hug. The embrace keeps me upright but doesn't absorb any of the guilt I feel. I need some form of physical punishment for that to happen, which is why I'm looking forward to Max's workout.

On the way over, I tell Jeremy about seeing his mother, only slightly exaggerating the pride I felt in her professionalism. He nods but doesn't ask me for any details. This is typical of him when we're talking about anything personal. Jeremy's conversational skills are most fluent when he's in a position to lecture me about technology. When he's not behind a metaphoric podium, he tends to clam up. I don't know if this is the result of him being male or being Jeremy, but when it comes to feelings, my grandson is about as conversationally fluent as he is when speaking Vietnamese. After dealing with the emotional volatility of my daughter, it's kind of a relief to not have to worry about someone screaming or crying at me for no reason. The only downside is that Jeremy tends to be a bit clueless when it comes to thinking of others. Case in point:

After dropping me off in front of Max's house, he takes off before we can discuss how I'm going to get home.

Max and I keep a brisker pace without Ginny. The physical pain of the workout takes my mind off the emotional pain I'm experiencing. When we get back to Max's house, I suggest we keep going, despite my aching joints.

"What's wrong?" Max asks.

"I just don't feel tired, is all."

Max eyes me skeptically but then suggests we circle her block a few more times. As soon as we're off again, she pinpoints the reason I've suddenly become a fitness enthusiast. "You and Ginny have a fight?"

I nod, actually starting to feel a little winded.

"Did she want to confess to Cristóbal?"

"How did you know?"

"Because she's a good person."

"And what am I?"

"You're more concerned with doing what's right than doing what's good."

"I don't see the difference."

"Of course you don't."

We walk in silence as I try to figure out if I've been insulted or not. I find this happens a lot when talking to Max. Her bluntness is open to a surprising number of interpretations.

"I know I'm an asshole, if that's what you're implying," I say.

"That's not what I'm implying at all," Max says. "I don't think you're an asshole. You just put principles over people. Ginny's not like that."

This seems like a generous interpretation of my character.

"How do I put principles over people?" I ask, genuinely curious.

"You didn't like it when I took over the water aerobics class, so you put a stop to it."

"I've apologized for that," I say.

"You asked for examples."

"Are you saying I shouldn't have done anything to stop Cristóbal from taking advantage of Ginny?"

"Not at all," Max says. "I think what you did was smart and appropriate. Maybe even a little brave. But it's not something I would do because the principle I live by is that people need to clean up their own messes. I take care of myself and don't go out of my way for others. If you're looking for assholes, she's right here."

Max points to herself in case there's any confusion.

"You're not an asshole," I say.

Max shrugs. "I'm not wired to care about people the way you are."

"I don't believe that," I say. "If that were true, then why make us walk with you?"

"That was selfish," Max says. "I needed an escape from Harold."

"It wasn't just that," I say.

"You and Ginny interested me," Max says. "You seemed like such an improbable pair: angel and devil."

"Thanks a lot."

"I mean devil in the mischievous sense, not the Christian sense."

"You don't have a relationship with your kids, do you?" I ask. The best part of being friends with a blunt person is it allows you to be blunt yourself.

Max shakes her head.

"That's sad."

"Is it? I don't see your relationship with your daughter as a healthy alternative."

I sigh. She's got me there. "There's got to be a happy medium."

"We get the children we deserve," Max says. "You think everything's unfair, so you got a daughter with a persecution complex. I like to stand alone, so I got children who are rugged individualists, to the point of rejecting their parents entirely."

"It's so depressing."

"What is?"

"Being old and realizing you haven't evolved."

"Biology is destiny."

"If that's true, then there may be some hope for our kids. They're only half of us."

"In my case, it's the better half."

"Mine too," I say laughing, although I don't know if it's true. Greg had some wonderful qualities, none of which I can remember at the moment.

"Can I stay for dinner?" I ask as we finish our first lap around the block. "My grandson kind of abandoned me here."

"Of course," Max says. "I'm grilling salmon."

"We need to talk about what we're going to do if Ginny confesses to Cristóbal."

Max sighs. "I suppose we'll have to kill her."

"You really are a cold-hearted bitch, aren't you?"

"You better believe it."

57

August 15

Max and I work well in the kitchen together. She's in charge, obviously, and does most of the heavy lifting, but she delegates sous chef tasks to me that I can manage, all of which put me in more contact with vegetables than I'm comfortable with. She needs to instruct me how to chop broccoli when I present her with florets the size of carnations.

Working in her clean and spacious kitchen with her Williams Sonoma utensils and a glass of chilled wine, I'm reminded that meal preparation can be almost as enjoyable as the meal itself. I wonder if Max would let me move in after Harold dies, but then banish the thought as soon as it enters my head. Leaping from a nice dinner date to cohabitation is what got me in trouble with my second husband. Turns out, one romantic, candlelit meal is not an accurate preview of married life, especially to a person who can only demonstrate his flexibility by biting his toenails. Not that I think Max has any bad habits, unless you count being good at everything, which, admittedly, is pretty annoying.

"Where are we eating?" I finally ask.

"On the back patio," Max says, pointing down the hallway. "Outside Harold's room."

I walk out the back door and onto a stone patio that stretches like a strip of beach in front of an ocean of green. How Max manages to keep her garden looking this verdant and lush in the middle of a drought is beyond me. The grass in the yard looks too manicured to be real, but with Max, you never know. I can see her trimming these stalks with nail clippers to get them to stand up so uniform and straight.

I look right and see that Max has set up a table and chairs outside Harold's bedroom. His sliding glass door is open, but his room is dark, save for the flickering light of the television. A retractable awning keeps the patio in shade so none of us will roast in the late afternoon sun.

I set the plates and silverware down and peer into Harold's room. It seems rude not to say hello, even to someone who can't speak, so I poke my head inside and am immediately struck with the odor of urine and some medicinal ointment I can't identify. Max has placed a fan to circulate the air, but it doesn't hide the smell of dying and decay.

"Evening, Harold," I say. "I'm Poppy. Max's friend."

Harold lies motionless on the bed. Oh lord, he's dead, I think, until his body spasms as if in the midst of a bad dream. I'm struck by how much he's shrunk since I saw him being pushed in a wheelchair at the YMCA. Max has kept him well groomed, like her garden, which makes him look a bit like a wax dummy whose face is melting.

He emits a low moan and opens his eyes. He looks at me with great pity, like I'm the one suffering and there's nothing he can do to offer me comfort. The connection I feel is jarring. It's almost as if Harold's boarding a plane and looking back at me waiting at the gate, hoping to get off the standby list.

I sit down at the edge of the bed, being careful not to touch his legs or feet, and study him. What's it like in there? I want to ask. Do you see the light? Hear voices? If he really is between worlds, maybe he can provide some travel tips for someone like me who will be making this journey soon.

But then Harold's beatific expression changes to something that resembles a zombie transformation. His body jerks and he lets out a low moan. I stand up and make low shushing sounds to soothe him. "It's okay," I repeat, without much conviction. Harold starts to thrash and I call out to Max to help. She comes rushing in and holds him down while I retreat to a corner of the room. She speaks to him in German. At least, I think it's German. It could be Afrikaans or Hungarian for all I know. The language calms Harold's grunts down to whimpers, which are almost harder to listen to, so I step outside, back into the light and warmth of the backyard. I finish my glass of wine waiting for Max to emerge from the crypt.

When she doesn't appear, I decide to go back to the kitchen and finish assembling our dinner. Max has already plated our meal so I put everything on a serving tray and bring it outside. After transferring the plates to the table, I go back to the kitchen and grab the bottle of wine. I really shouldn't have another glass, but Harold's fit has shaken something in me that needs calming. After refilling my glass, I take a large sip and feel a quiet numbness flow through my veins. I look out at Max's garden and feel grateful for every flower, leaf, and blade of grass staring back at me.

I'm halfway through my glass when Max emerges from Harold room. Harold's moans have been replaced by the sound of British voices coming from the television. Max sits down without a word and starts cutting into her salmon.

"I overcooked it," she says.

I go to refill her glass of wine, but she stops me.

"I have to go to the pharmacy," Max says. "Can you babysit while I'm gone?"

I don't do a good job of hiding my reluctance to accept this job offer. I take another sip of wine to give myself time to think of a reason I can't help out my friend. Unfortunately, the alcohol doesn't inspire any great ideas. *I have to feed the cat*, is all my feeble brain comes up with and even I know that's a weak excuse.

"But I don't know German," I say, hoping it will disqualify me.

"Don't be silly," Max says.

"What . . . what . . . what would I have to do, exactly?"

Max stabs a broccoli floret and holds it in front of her mouth. That's me at the end of her fork, I think. Pinned down and unable to escape.

"Nothing. Just be here in case he stops breathing."

"Oh, is that all," I say finishing off my wine.

"Fine, you can clean up," Max says, gesturing to the dinner in front of us. "By the time you're done, I should be back."

"But what if he stops breathing?" I say.

"His monitor will alert you," Max says. "All you have to do is press a button."

Max removes a medical alert pendant from around her neck and hands it over to me. The device is the size of a locket with a large, green button at the center. I put it on, feeling only slightly more confident in my ability to manage the care of a dying man. I really wish I hadn't had that second glass of wine. It's made me sluggish and lightheaded. Why did that judge have to suspend my license? Then I could drive to the pharmacy and leave Max at home to attend to her husband. Alcohol is not my friend, I decide for the hundredth, possibly the thousandth, time, pouring myself a tiny glass. A soupçon, if you will. Something to take the edge off. After this, no more.

We finish our meal and strategize about Ginny.

"If she confesses to Cristóbal, we'll have to give back the money," I say.

If Max is distraught by this, she doesn't let it show. "Fine" is all she says.

"What will you do?"

"I'll manage," Max says. "The money doesn't worry me as much as Harold's quality of life. He never wanted to live like this. But we're stuck. He's neither animal nor vegetable right now."

"I'm sorry," I say, both for the situation and my unwillingness to help Max when she needed me. I really am an asshole.

Max stares out at her garden. A squirrel runs along the edge of her back fence, pausing for a moment above a camellia bush. It eyes a flower bud for a moment and then quickly scurries away. Max smiles to herself. Nature's not going to get the best of her out here. It may think it's in control, but she's the one who's going to bend all creatures great and small to her will.

Third Victim

After Max leaves for the pharmacy, I start clearing the dishes. It doesn't take me long to clean up, as Max is one of those people who can cook and clean simultaneously. The kitchen is already spotless by the time I enter so all I have to do is load the dishwasher and I'm done.

I peek into Harold's room to make sure he's still breathing and see him resting, bathed in the glow of the television. I can't tell from where I'm standing if his eyes are open or not. How many people die like this? I wonder. Their last human voice coming from some second-rate actor doing a guest stint on a crime show? I guess there are worse ways to go.

I walk around Max's house in the fading light of the day. The sun has set, but the sky still glows pink and blue. I can feel myself getting sleepy, the result of too much exercise and too much wine. Laying down on Max's bed feels like a bad idea, both because it's an invasion of privacy and because it will only make it harder to stay vigilant in case Harold's monitor starts beeping. I decide to sit in the front room and play solitaire or do a crossword but there's not a deck of cards or newspaper to be found anywhere. Max doesn't even have a puzzle to keep her entertained. What does she do in those hours when she's not nursing, gardening, cooking, cleaning, or exercising?

I scan the bookshelves, hoping to find a light beach read, but all that lines the shelves are indecipherable epidemiology texts and Marcel

Proust. I grab *Swann's Way*, and before I even crack its spine, I'm curled up on the couch in a deep, deep sleep.

I wake up and find Max wrapping me in a warm, heavy blanket. The room is dark, except for the glow of the streetlights that stream through the front window. They illuminate Max's face and my sleepy brain recasts her as my mother, the only adult who ever took care of me.

"Mama?" I mutter.

Max shushes me and tells me to go back to sleep. "Get some rest," she whispers and disappears down the hall. I come to and realize where I am. I wonder momentarily if Jeremy is worried about me, but the thought of digging out my cellphone and texting him feels like one of the trials of Hercules, so I lay my head back down on the soft cushion and fall back asleep.

I don't know what wakes me up a few hours later. I've often thought that the years of parenting a rebellious teenager trained my unconscious to alert me to the slightest change in my environment. A doorknob turning, a floorboard creaking, a refrigerator door opening—all of it sounded like those tests from the Emergency Alert System. Meg accused me of booby-trapping the house, but my stranger danger is probably the result of an overactive imagination and too many horror movies.

When I wake up it takes me a moment to orient myself. I'm in Max's house, on her couch, under a weighted blanket. The moonlight streaming through the window behind me illuminates the far wall of the room, making the framed print of an English landscape a blur of dark greens, browns, and gray. I listen for the sound that woke me but the house is quiet. I grab a large, glass paperweight off the coffee table in case I need a weapon.

The next sound I hear comes from the kitchen. *It's just Max*, I tell myself. She probably wakes up in the middle of the night remembering some leftover she didn't wrap properly. Or maybe she's a sleepwalker—one of those women who devour whole cartons of ice cream in their sleep. I resist the urge to grab my phone and videotape her as I'm a guest here and want to be polite.

But then a man steps into the doorway.

The moonlight illuminates his body, which is covered in black clothing. It's definitely not Harold. The man's frame is a dark triangle with broad shoulders and skinny legs. His face is covered with some sort of ski mask that makes it impossible to see any features except his eyes. I wait for him to react to my presence in the room, but I must be cast in shadow on the couch. Quietly, I curl up and pretend to be a bulky throw pillow. As I'm doing so, I feel Harold's medical alert pendant on my chest. Slowly, I move my hand over and hit the oval call button as gently as I can.

The man takes a step in the room. The fear surging through my body must make me hyperalert to his presence. I swear I can hear his breathing and smell his deodorant—some sour mixture of lime and rotted wood. He moves toward the bookshelves that surround the fireplace and scans for valuables. He picks up a gold watch that's housed under a domed glass display and pockets it.

Then he turns to me and sees I'm not a throw pillow.

I hear his breathing quicken as he assesses the situation. I figure my best chance of surviving this encounter is to lay still and pretend to be asleep. I start to snore, very softly, hoping it will convince him that I'm unconscious or pretending to be unconscious. Either way, he's got no worries about my screams waking up the neighbors.

He stands there frozen for what feels like hours. Finally, he takes a few steps, until his body is inches from my face. I suddenly realize that this guy may not be here to rob Max's house at all. If Ginny confessed to Cristóbal, he may have dispatched one of his assassins to kill us in retaliation. If this is the case, I may as well prepare to be smothered by a pillow.

This is it, I tell myself. The end. I'm about to die.

This isn't the way I thought it would happen. I always envisioned dying in some cataclysmic car crash. Never this. This man's going to take my life. I'll die alone, in a strange environment, just like I always feared. For a second I think death will come as a relief. I'm ready, I think, to let all this go. All these worries and the guilt and sorrow and pain. This man will be doing me a favor, taking something from me I could never give up willingly.

I wait for my life to flash before my eyes. Nothing. All I hear is the man's heavy breathing. I will some images to appear: The time Greg and I ran away from home, making love in the back seat of his car after we crossed into California. Meg's birth. Our family's first camping trip to Big Sur. Seeing my sleazy boss get put in handcuffs by the police. The time I won ten grand at the roulette table in Reno. My walks with Ginny and Max. It's a great reel actually and I'm suddenly filled with something that feels almost like gratitude that I was given these moments. Life feels suddenly precious to me. Something I'm not going to just give up just because some asshole is pissed that I outsmarted him. My eyes snap open.

Before the man can get his hands on me, I reach out and grab him in the only place I can do any damage. Luckily, my vantage point makes this easy. He's standing right over me, his crotch just above where I'm lying. In a flash, I thrust my hand out from under the blanket, latch onto his balls, and squeeze as hard as I can.

I've got to say, it's been awhile since I've touched this part of a man. I've never been much good at knowing what to do down there, but it's pretty easy to imagine that sack as a lemon that needs juicing. I do my best to imitate Max and squeeze with all the strength I can muster.

The man groans loudly and collapses on top of me.

Now is the time for screaming.

I get one good shriek out before the man's weight pushes all the air out of my lungs. Now I can sense every aspect of this guy, from his potato chip breath to his calloused hands to his pomegranate-sized biceps. He's old. Not old like me but definitely over fifty. Don't ask me how I know this given his mask stays on as we grapple on the couch. Maybe it's his breathing. My sock in the balls has knocked the wind out of him, but now I think he's struggling like an older man who suffers from chronic back pain.

I can feel him recovering from the blow I delivered. He's got enough breath back to grunt "fucking bitch" in my ear. There's no way I'm going to slide out from under him now. He's regained control of his arms and uses them to pin mine to my sides so that my blows won't land on his head and shoulders. In a few moments, he'll be able to position himself to trap my arms under his legs so he can free his hands to strangle me.

That's when I see Max rise up from behind him with a fireplace poker and swing.

She must be a great golfer because she knocks the man off me with a single blow. The man lands on the carpet between the couch and the coffee table. It doesn't take him long to get up on his hands and knees but as soon as he does, Max whacks him again across the temple and he falls backward onto her carpet. This time he stays down.

I scramble off the couch and rush over to the door.

"Call 911," Max says, raising the golf club in anticipation of another swing.

"I already did," I say, pulling out the medical alert pendant.

Max and I stare at the motionless body in front of us and all I can think about is how those bloodstains are going to ruin the carpet.

"Maybe we should put a towel under his head?" I offer.

"We shouldn't tamper with the crime scene," Max says, her voice flat and monotone.

"After the EMTs arrive, we'll clean the carpet."

Max walks over and places the fire poker back in its stand by the fireplace. I think she's in shock, but this could just be her natural inclination to tidy up. Ginny and I have long speculated that her obsessive cleaning is a form of aggression.

"Do you have any Dawn liquid soap?" I say. "I used that on a blouse after a nosebleed and it worked wonders."

"Hydrogen peroxide is a better cleaning agent," she says, turning her attention to the bloodstain that's spreading at her feet.

"Is this a synthetic or natural fiber?" I ask, running my foot against the carpet.

"Natural."

"You want to be careful the hydrogen peroxide doesn't bleach the color."

"I'll do a test strip under the couch."

"Good idea."

We stand there in silence waiting for something to happen. We just killed a man. Shouldn't the earth split and swallow us up in a fury of hellfire or something? What's taking the EMTs so long to arrive? I press the Life Alert button resting against my chest and wonder, not for the first time, if this thing is just another scam aimed at defrauding the elderly.

"I'm going to check on Harold," Max says.

Before she can walk out of the room, I grab her by the arm and squeeze. "It's not your fault," I say. "He was going to kill us."

Max looks out the front window. The moonlight bathes the street in a silvery glow. Anyone driving by would think this is a quiet, peaceful neighborhood, which it is. I'm the one responsible for turning it into a war zone.

Max walks out of the room. I debate going with her but figure she may want some alone time with her spouse. How much of the fight did Harold overhear? I wonder. Poor man. I can't imagine a worse fate than listening to your wife getting attacked and being powerless to stop it.

I feel my wrists, still sore from where the man gripped them. Is this enough evidence to convince the police that we killed him in self-defense? My papery skin's prone to bruising but no one ever died from a wrist squeezing. It would be better if these marks were on my neck.

"Don't be ridiculous," I mutter, my words breaking the silence like a frozen lake cracking. I didn't realize how much the quiet had consumed the room. Off in the distance, I think I hear the wail of a siren but it could just be my imagination playing tricks on me.

We need to be sure the police see this as a case of self-defense. If they start digging into why the man was in Max's house, we're sunk. We could be charged with fraud, theft, and possibly manslaughter. This is California, after all, not Florida. There are no stand your ground laws here that allow you to shoot someone for making you uncomfortable.

Everything will depend on whether the jury sees this man as a threat. It helps that Max and I are two old ladies, but not if the only injury I sustained is a bruised wrist. There needs to be more incriminating evidence against him or we could all go to jail.

I stare at his prone body on the floor. He's dressed head to toe in black, giving the impression of a shadow abandoned by its owner. In the darkness of the room, it's hard to see if his chest is moving so I kick him lightly with my foot. Nothing. All I need to do is bend down and position his hand around my neck to make some purple bruises.

Now I definitely hear the sounds of sirens off in the distance. So, this little button works after all, I think, finally removing the fob from around my neck. Of course, now I wish the ambulance would slow down a bit to give me more time.

Without thinking, I kneel next to the man on the carpet, grab his wrist, and lift his hand to my neck. I feel a little like a circus performer putting my head in the jaws of a lion. Please, please, please, be dead, I think as I wrap his fingers around my throat. The leather glove he's wearing feels cold and slick against my skin. I'm just about to squeeze when a thought pops in my head: Is this man right- or left-handed? That could be important. A good detective might wonder why a right-handed man tried to strangle a woman with his left hand. Or vice versa. What hand am I even holding anyway?

The sirens are getting louder and any minute now Max is going to walk into the room and wonder why I'm tampering with evidence. Fuck it, I decide. This isn't worth it. I'm doing what I vowed to never do again: making a situation worse by trying to make it better.

I'm just about to stand up when the hand I've been holding suddenly jerks and comes to life. I try to move out of its grip but it's faster than me. Before I know it, its grip is so tight around my throat I can no longer scream out for help.

I try to pull his hands off with my own but he's too strong for me. His arms haven't locked into position, which gives me some mobility. I flail about, reaching for anything I can use as a weapon to bash him unconscious again. My hand lands on the paperweight I stashed between the couch cushions earlier. Grabbing it by its smooth, rounded top, I lift and bring it down as hard as I can on the wound Max inflicted earlier. The man groans and releases me to protect his skull from further damage. As soon as I'm free, I call out to Max, who rushes in, grabs the fire poker, and whacks the guy a few more times until he's motionless again.

"I guess he wasn't dead," I say.

As soon as she catches her breath, she yanks an extension cord from its socket and ties the man's ankles and wrists like a rodeo cowboy roping a calf.

The ambulance pulls up in front of the house and I stumble to the door to let the paramedics in. The EMT duo look around, trying to make sense of the scene. I'm sure they've seen some pretty grisly situations but I bet they've never responded to a call where two old ladies are hog-tying a man dressed in black and bleeding on a beige carpet. The young man and woman stand before us holding their medical tool kits and probably wonder if their training has equipped them to respond to this particular emergency.

"This man tried to kill me. I hit him with this," I say holding up the paperweight.

"And I hit him with this." Max holds up the fire poker, which thankfully doesn't have bits of skull and brain on it.

The pair call for police backup and approach the unconscious man to attend to his wounds. The female paramedic bends down and gently removes the man's ski mask. There are multiple lacerations on the back and side of his head, which she starts to clean and dress. As she's working, I hear the police sirens down the block. Pretty soon this place is going to be chaos with all the neighbors out speculating about the disaster that brought all these flashing lights to their block.

Before the police barge in and push us outside the crime scene, I peer over the paramedic's shoulder to catch a glimpse of the man who almost killed me. The first thing I recognize is the mustache. Then the scar from the removed neck tattoo. It's Craig, my daughter's boyfriend.

58

August 15

The paramedics wheel Craig, still unconscious but alive, out on a stretcher. My injuries are not significant enough to warrant a trip to the hospital, which makes me feel grateful and disappointed. I'm exhausted but want there to be no doubt that we acted in self-defense. Before the police officers start their interrogation, I make them take photos of my neck and wrists, even though they're not the shade of purple I was hoping for.

My report to the police officers does not go well. I want to present them with a tight-knit sweater of a story, but the whole thing unravels under their questioning until all I'm left with is a hand full of cat fur and dust bunnies.

"He hit my house first and stole all my grandson's computer equipment," I say.

"Did you report it?" Officer Dunbar asks. He's a tall, handsome Black man who looks about ten pounds too heavy to be chasing down criminals. He's got the laid-back, doughy charm I associate with people who spend a lot of time in front of a barbecue.

I stare at him, debating between telling the truth or playing the forgetful old lady, a role I've performed before to get me out of traffic tickets. I decide this isn't one of those situations where you want law enforcement to question your mental stability, so I go with the truth.

"I didn't," I say. "I suspected Craig and wanted to talk to my daughter first to make sure she had nothing to do with it."

"And did she?" Officer Bell asks. He's the younger of the two. Not much older than Jeremy, but with blond hair and the jawline of a cartoon character.

"She did not," I say.

I wish I said this with more confidence. I want to sound like a witness for the defense, someone with 100 percent clarity about the innocence of the accused. But I say my line like a bad actor, with a shaky voice and darting eyes. The officer writes something down on his notepad and waits for me to continue.

"He then broke into my friend's condo at Xanadu and stole her laptop," I say.

"Did you report that?" Dunbar asks.

"Gah," I say. The two officers and Max look at me like I'm having a stroke.

"You'll have to ask her," Max says, coming to my rescue. She provides the officer with Ginny's information.

The two officers look at each other and share some secret communication, probably concerning the reliability of our witness testimony. My mind tries to predict all the scenarios they're imagining right now. The only physical evidence they have is the unconscious body of an ex-felon and a fire poker with Max's fingerprints. How many stories could they concoct to explain that crime? I've seen enough crime shows to know that things are never as simple as they seem. I could have been so desperate to break up Meg and Craig that I lured him here under some pretext only to frame him for burglary and assault.

"He stole a gold watch," I say, pointing to the empty glass dome sitting on the mantel. "Check his pocket."

Dunbar notes that down. Of course, as soon as I've said it, I can see how easy it would have been to plant that watch on an unconscious body. I really should have been a detective or a crime novelist, I think. Another missed calling to add to the list.

"It's easy to connect the dots after the fact," Max jumps in, sensing our declining credibility. "We had no way of knowing this man knew we were friends."

"But your daughter knew you were friends," Officer Bell, the young Dick Tracy, says. That's the connection I was hoping they wouldn't make, even though it's a painfully obvious one.

"Yes, but she has nothing to do with this," I say, feeling more confident. "She wouldn't steal from her own mother and son."

Unless she's using again, I think, but don't say aloud.

"Why were you sleeping on Ms. Schelling's couch?" Dunbar asks.

Oh shit.

"I was watching Max's husband while she was at the pharmacy and fell asleep," I say, tugging at my cotton sweater, which is starting to feel a bit like a straitjacket.

"How long were you gone for?" Dunbar asks Max.

"Forty-five minutes," Max says.

"So, you returned at . . ."

"At 9:15 P.M.," Max says.

"And you were asleep?" Dunbar asks me.

"It had been a long day," I say.

"Had you been drinking?" Bell asks.

"I may have had a glass of wine at dinner."

"Just one glass?"

"I don't understand how these questions are relevant," Max says, losing patience. She steps toward the officers and I see them shrink in response. There's no mistaking the authority she exudes in every situation, whether it's water aerobics or CSI. "A man with a ski mask broke into my house to rob me. When my friend screamed, he attacked her and I subdued him with the only weapon available to me at the time. We've made our statement, now collect all the physical evidence you need and let us get to sleep. It's nearly three A.M."

Max and I walk back to the kitchen, where she pours us each a glass of cheap vodka. It's just the restorative I need. The officers leave us alone as they continue to take photographs and scour for clues.

"We'll be in touch," Dunbar says, putting his card on the table. "In the meantime, if you think of anything else, please call."

We thank him and sit in silence until their patrol car disappears down the street.

"Well, that went south fast," I say, putting my head on my arms. I want to fall asleep right here and wake up to breakfast, but I know I have to call Meg and let her know why her boyfriend isn't coming home tonight.

"We need to tell Ginny," Max says.

"Tomorrow," I say. "I've got to talk to my daughter first."

"You really think she knew nothing about this?" Max asks.

"I do," I say.

"Then you better get her out of that apartment fast before her boyfriend makes bail," Max says.

The conversation with Meg does not go well. Not that I expected it to. It's not easy hearing your boyfriend has attacked your mother in her friend's house at three o'clock in the morning. I give her the basic summary of what happened and promise to go into more detail tomorrow. Or today. Later. Oh my God, I'm so exhausted.

Max lets me sleep with her in her bed to avoid the scene of the crime. By the time I enter her bedroom, she's already passed out. I don't know why it surprises me to see her on her stomach. I guess I imagined Max sleeping like a vampire in a coffin, arms crossed over her chest, ready to bolt upright at the slightest disturbance. I lie down next to her and try to fold myself into a tiny ball so I don't take up much space. Within seconds, I'm asleep.

59

August 16

Max gives me a ride home after breakfast. Unlike me, she looks alert and energized to take on the day. She's done her hair, applied her makeup, and dressed in slacks and a satiny blouse. I feel like a homeless lady sitting next to her. I wonder if she dressed up for her visit to Ginny at Xanadu. She's going to go there after she drops me off to explain what happened. It's nice to know that I'm not the only one intimidated by that place.

When we pull up, I see Meg's car (my car) parked in the driveway. I feel my stomach sink a little anticipating the conversation we're about to have. Wouldn't it be nice if she greeted me with a tearful embrace saying how relieved she is to see me safe? *I picked up your favorite muffin at that bakery you love*, she'd say and sit me down at the table for a nice cup of coffee.

"You okay?" Max asks. "You look like something's stuck in your throat."

"I'm fine," I say.

"Don't be surprised if you experience some PTSD," she says, removing her sunglasses and staring at me intently. "I've got some sleeping pills if you need them."

"You take sleeping pills?" I say, surprised.

"They're Harold's," she says. "But I take them now and again."

I thank her. Before I leave, I ask, "Do you think it's over?"

Max stares out at the road in front of her. "Are you asking if I think Craig murdered those women?"

I nod.

"It's easier to see him as a murderer than a money launderer," she says.

"That's what I think too," I say and close the door.

I enter the house and make a lot of noise to alert Meg and Jeremy that I'm home. Any hope of Meg rushing to my side and pampering me with baked goods quickly vanishes when I hear angry whispers in the kitchen. I make my way down the hall and find Meg and Jeremy sitting quietly at the table. There's no scones or coffee. All that sits in front of them is the morning paper, which neither has bothered to remove from its plastic wrap.

Jeremy stands and Scampers drops from his lap to the floor. Before I know it, he's wrapped his arms around me, asking me if I'm okay. I'm uncomfortable with such close bodily contact, given that I slept in my clothes and haven't showered or brushed my teeth. But then I smell Jeremy's bed sweat and stale breath and figure he's okay with my imperfect hygiene. I hug him back and tell him that I'm fine. He stands back to give Meg a chance to show her concern, but she just glowers at me from the kitchen table.

"Hello, Meg," I say, taking the high road, which will allow me to look down on her. "Nice to see you."

Meg barks out a laugh.

"Jesus, Mom," Jeremy says, shaking his head. He retreats to the doorway leading to the basement and scoops up Scampers, who looks uncomfortable in his new role as shield.

"What?"

Jeremy's bewilderment matches my own and I'm grateful he's here to defend me. After last night, I just don't have the energy.

"Your boyfriend breaks into Grandma's friend's home and attacks her," Jeremy says, stroking Scampers's fur. "You can't take some responsibility for that?"

Meg doesn't respond well when she's cornered, which has made every intervention we've attempted a disaster. She's like a trapped animal in that way, more prone to bare her teeth and growl than flip on her back in submission. To defuse the situation, I walk to the counter and busy myself with making a pot of coffee. I fill the carafe, pour the water into the machine, and dump four heaping spoonfuls of grounds into the filter, all the while thinking, *I told you so, I told you so, I told you so.*

"I'm making coffee," I say, feeling it's better to describe what I'm doing instead of what I'm feeling at this point. Meg waits for my undivided attention before speaking. When I press the brew button, she starts speaking.

"I'm sorry for what happened, but has anyone stopped to think how this is affecting me?"

"Seriously?" Jeremy says. He's so agitated he starts spinning in circles. Scampers squirms out of his grasp and disappears into the front room.

"I'm a victim too, you know," Meg says, rising from the table. "My boyfriend's in some kind of coma, the police suspect me as being his partner in crime, and I'm about to be homeless. That sound serious enough for you?"

"Craig's in a coma?" I say.

Meg nods. "There was some brain swelling from his, uh, injuries."

My legs collapse and I grab hold of a kitchen chair. After falling into it, I drop my head onto my arms and start to weep. If Craig dies, what then? Could we be tried for manslaughter?

"All of this is your fault," Jeremy says, sitting down next to me and gripping me by my shoulders. "You chose to move in with this asshole, after dating him less than a month. How do you not see that?"

I feel sorry and not sorry for letting Jeremy fight my battle for me. As most parents know, children will not listen to their parents even when they are 100 percent correct in their judgment. I could give a speech worthy of Clarence Darrow itemizing all the mistakes Meg has made in her relationship with this psychopath and it wouldn't move her in the slightest toward a confession of guilt. Hearing her behavior criticized by her child, however, is a different matter. Even the worst parents don't want their kids to be ashamed of them. Jeremy's making more of an impact here than I ever could, so I let him continue while the coffee slowly drips into the waiting carafe.

"I didn't know he was a criminal!" Meg says.

"Really, Mom? The neck tattoo wasn't a clue? Or the lack of meaningful employment? Or the fact that every time he visited, he looked like he was casing the joint? None of that triggered any warning signals for you?"

Meg turns and walks toward the door leading to the backyard. I can see she's about to run away and if she does that, we'll have lost her. Maybe for good this time. If she isn't using now, she'll definitely be using later unless we hand her a way to climb out of this hole she's dug. That's the pattern I've seen play out over the years: Meg fucks up, we make her feel terrible, and she turns to drugs and alcohol to cope with those feelings.

"Meg, stop," I say, lifting my head. "Have some coffee."

Meg turns around and stares at me, sensing a trap. I stand, pour her a cup, add just the right amount of cream and sugar, and place it on the table. Then I pour Jeremy his cup—cream, no sugar—before finally serving myself.

This peace offering reels Meg back to us. She sits down and takes a sip and starts sobbing. I walk up behind her and gently rub her back. Jeremy and I exchange glances (just like the police did last night) that communicate more than words ever could. We acknowledge Meg's bullshit, express our fatigue with her failures, and recognize that it's our responsibility to help her because she's incapable of helping herself. We wait for her to quiet down before taking our seats on either side of her, and sip our coffee.

"I'm so sorry, Mom," Meg says finally. She raises her head and it looks like she got struck with a water balloon. "I'm such a fuckup."

"Shhh, now," I say. "You didn't know."

"I swear I didn't," Meg says, swiveling her attention between Jeremy and me. "If Craig is robbing people, he's hiding the goods from me."

"You need to get out of that apartment," I say.

Meg wipes the tears from her cheeks and shakes her head. "No way," she says.

"Honey, it's not safe."

"Why is it me who has to leave?" she says, getting some of the fury back in her voice. This time, her selfishness doesn't bother me. "I like that apartment. Most of the stuff in it is mine. I pay most of the rent. He's the one who has to go."

I look at Jeremy, who seems as surprised as I am.

"Are you sure?" I ask.

"I'm inviting the police over today to search the place," Meg says. "I'll get their advice for how to keep him away if and when he's released from the hospital. I don't care if I have to take out a fucking restraining order, he's not getting back in that apartment."

"He won't want to stir up any trouble before his court date," Jeremy says. "Let's hope he slinks back into the hole he crawled out of and stays there."

"I'll have to find a new gym," Meg says.

"You can join my walking club if you want," I say. "But you'll have to keep up."

60

August 16

We spend the rest of the morning getting an earful about Meg and Craig's relationship, not that Jeremy and I asked for these details. But Meg's in a chatty mood so she tells us all about Craig's weird obsession with some anime character named Sailor Moon. "He goes to, like, conventions and stuff," Meg whispers as if she's outing him as a member of Opus Dei. She tells us how he only eats meat and vegetables and won't stop pestering her to change her picnic menu to keto approved foods. "Deli trays are not my brand," she exclaims. She tells us he talks with his mom at least once a day, sometimes after they've been intimate, which is "super weird." It's interesting that Meg feels these personality quirks are the things worth discussing and not his enthusiasm for grand larceny, money laundering, and murder. She doesn't have any stories of him associating with criminal gangs or disappearing for days at a time on mysterious errands. If he is Cristóbal, she has no idea where he's stashing his loot. Before she leaves, I ask her if Craig has an earring.

"Ugh, yes," she says. "And a tongue piercing."

I cringe, but not for the reasons Meg probably assumes.

❖

Jeremy and I stay in the kitchen, luxuriating in the silence like a couple of vacationers in a resort swimming pool. When I offer to make Jeremy something to eat, he declines saying he's meeting Bao for lunch.

"She didn't ask me," he says.

"Ask you what?"

"Anything. She didn't ask me anything. Not even how I was doing."

"She was upset," I say.

Jeremy shoots me a look, which I understand completely: Meg's always upset. There's no room in her head for anyone but herself. I clasp the boy's hands in mine and squeeze them tight so that he's looking me in the eye. Then I share with him the only words of wisdom I have on the subject. "Your mom," I say as tenderly as I can, "she's nuts."

Jeremy smiles and shakes his head. "Should I even tell her I'm going to Vietnam?"

"That's up to you," I say. "Speaking as someone who ran away from home, I don't recommend leaving without a proper goodbye. You'll always wonder if your parents miss you or not. It's a terrible question to live with."

"Maybe you're right," Jeremy says. He stands up to go.

"When are you leaving again?" I have to ask. I've been a little self-involved myself lately.

"Next month," he says.

"Did you tell me that?" I ask.

"Nope, just found a cheap ticket. One-way."

"Oh, Jeremy," I say, rushing up to hug him. "You can't leave just when I've discovered how great you are. It's not fair."

"Sorry, Grandma," he says. "It's time I see a bit of the world."

The thought of being alone in this house fills me with such dread I'm speechless. The only words my brain can produce are *It's finally happening.* It's what I imagine death feeling like the moment before you disappear forever. This home, the place I've loved for four decades, will become my tomb. When they find me, I'll be slumped over my kitchen table, my starving cat nibbling on my earlobe.

As if sensing my distress, Scampers rubs his body against my ankles. I scoop him up in my arms and squeeze him tight. I hold him out to Jeremy like a ventriloquist's dummy and make him say, "How can you leave me?"

"You'll be okay," he says, to the cat and me. "You've been adopted by a nice family."

The words are a comfort. He's right. I've got friends now. Or friend. I need to work on repairing my relationship with Ginny. I've been a bit of a Meg when it comes to her, only thinking of myself, letting my pride get in the way of admitting my mistakes. Now that we've caught the criminal responsible for stealing our laptops, we can all breathe easier, until Max starts us on a new, more rigorous workout routine, that is.

"You have to let me throw you a going-away party," I say.

"You don't have to do that, Grandma," Jeremy says.

"I want to. I'd like to meet Bao before you go. Who else would you like to come?"

Jeremy hesitates. "Most of my friends are online," he says.

"Want to invite your mom?" I ask. "We can have her cater so she has to serve you all night."

"I'd be okay with that," Jeremy says with a lopsided smile.

"How does Friday sound?"

Jeremy gives me a thumbs-up and disappears downstairs.

61

August 16

As soon as Jeremy leaves, I realize the huge mistake I've made. I've never hosted anything, including my daughter's birthday parties. (It was a different time when Meg was little. There was none of this pressure to throw themed parties with elaborate gift bags *for the guests!* Kids were happy if you took them to Sizzler and let them build their own sundae.) I suddenly feel all this pressure in my chest (Is this the PTSD Max warned me about?) when I think about the guest list, the menu, the clean house, etc. Even if I do manage to check off each of those to-dos, I'll still have to sweat through the actual party, making sure everyone's glass is filled and that no one gets stuck with the drunk/bore/pervert (although in this case, that person will most likely be me). All this responsibility negates any fun I might have. And what am I rewarded with at the end of the night for all my efforts? A messy house I have to clean. Honestly, I don't know why people bother.

But a promise is a promise and it's time I start using my manipulative powers for good instead of evil. If I can figure out a way to steal $300,000 from a criminal, I can open my door to my closest friends and relatives and pour them a few drinks.

After lunch, I start by preparing the guest list, which is easy because I can count the invites on one hand.

- ✓ Jeremy
- ✓ Bao
- ❑ Max
- ❑ Ginny
- ❑ Bernard
- ❑ Meg (as caterer)

Sheesh, I think. No wonder Jeremy is eager to leave the country if these are the people at his going-away party. When I was his age, the only old folks I knew were my grandparents, and I certainly didn't party with them after birthday number 12. Maybe I could hire some young people to come over, throw a little something extra to the one who flirts with Jeremy a little. *That's a prostitute*, I tell myself. *The young person you're thinking of right now is a prostitute.*

I decide to go down my list and confirm everyone's RSVPs in person, starting with Max. It's nearly 3:00 P.M. and she must be back from her visit with Ginny by now. It suddenly dawns on me that I missed my afternoon nap. Strange, I would think after the drama of last night I would pass out after lunch, but the thought of lying down in an empty house is not as appealing as it normally is. I'm like a shark right now, moving through the house as I attack people over the phone.

"But I don't even know your grandson," Max says when I invite her.

"That doesn't matter."

"I don't know if Harold's nurse can stay late."

"I'll wait while you check."

This is something Max would say and I'm happy to see it works. I listen as Max walks into Harold's room and asks the nurse. I don't hear her answer but a few seconds later Max says she can make it. "But only for an hour."

"Great. How'd things go with Ginny?"

"Fine. She didn't call Cristóbal."

"She didn't? Why not?"

"She didn't say," Max says. "I don't think she's left her apartment since we last saw her."

"Did you tell her what happened with Craig?"

"Of course. That was the purpose of my visit."

"He's in a coma," I say.

"Brain swelling?" Max says.

"How'd you know?"

"Educated guess," she says.

"Meg has the police searching the apartment for evidence."

"They won't find anything," Max says definitively. "I don't think Craig is Cristóbal."

"Why not?"

"Because Cristóbal wouldn't risk arrest breaking into an old lady's house," Max says. "He'd send a hired goon to do that. That's all Craig is. Muscle."

"Unfortunately, we won't know until he's out of the coma."

"And even then, he may not talk if he's more afraid of his boss than the police."

I decide to call Ginny next. This is going to be the hardest call to make because I know she's still mad at me. I know this because if she wasn't, she would have called me by now to see how I'm doing. I was attacked last night, after all. At one point, I thought I was going to die. Holy shit, Ginny, does that not merit a phone call? I am now storming up and down the hallway, bouncing between the kitchen and front room. Scampers tracks my movements trying to figure out this new game we're playing. Eventually, I throw my phone onto the couch in frustration.

And this is when the PTSD makes its first appearance. I suddenly realize that everything I've done today—managing Meg, planning Jeremy's party—has been an elaborate exercise in denial. I collapse over the arm of the couch and sob uncontrollably. Some internal dam has been opened and I can't stop the tears from falling onto the carpet below me. I try to choke out some words, but all that emerges from my mouth are gasps for air.

I sit up and stumble into the kitchen to pour myself a glass of water. After drinking it down, I wipe my face with a dish towel and take some deep breaths to calm my nerves. When my heart stops racing, I walk back to the living room and pick up the phone off the couch.

Fuck it, I think. *I'm going to Xanadu.*

It's a three-mile hike to the murder palace, as Bernard affectionately calls his retirement community. The walk helps calm my nerves and give me time to rehearse my apology to Ginny.

I'm sorry I tried sticking up for you. No, too passive-aggressive.

I'm sorry you're such a ninny, I had to save you from a mobster. No, too aggressive-aggressive.

It takes me several blocks before I find the right words. *I'm sorry I let my need for revenge put you in a vulnerable position*, I'll say. *After nearly being strangled to death, I now understand why you might prefer to involve the police.*

Maybe it's time I tell her about my negative associations with law enforcement, starting with my father, who I always saw as a bigger threat than any of the "criminals" in my small town. You grow up watching a police officer continuously break the law for his own benefit and it only makes you fear the badge. Even last night, after I'd been assaulted, the police didn't leave me feeling confident that they were on my side.

Halfway into my walk, I realize I should have timed it better. The heat of the afternoon sun saps my energy and I forgot to bring my water bottle. This part of my suburb doesn't have any supermarkets or corner stores, so I'm left with drinking out of water fountains in playgrounds and public parks. The detours slow me down but eventually, I make it to Xanadu. I'm glad I stopped to hydrate along the way, because when I see the police car parked outside the entrance, I break into my fastest speed walk. *Please don't let it be Ginny*, I think as I pump my arms. *I'll never forgive myself if it's Ginny.*

62

August 16

I reach the parking lot and scan the area for tape outlining the dead body. If someone had died, there'd be an ambulance or fire truck parked outside, but all I see is the parked squad car. Everything seems normal otherwise. The valet even looks a little bored, standing behind his station and flipping through his phone. He barely looks up when I pass him and enter through the automatic doors.

The lobby is full of people, gathered in tight circles, sharing information. Something has set this place abuzz and it's not tonight's dinner specials. I turn to the receptionist, the same gentle Filipino man who was here last time I visited. "What's going on?" I ask him, showing my ID. The man looks at my license, types my information into the computer, but doesn't say anything as he hands me my badge. I'm just about to leave when I notice the crowd watching the floor countdown above the elevator. When the monitor reads *1*, there's an audible ping and the doors slowly slide open.

The crowd parts in anticipation of the perp walk, I assume. The first person out is Ginny, who's a mess of tangled hair and puffy skin. She looks like she hasn't slept in days. In fact, she's wearing the same outfit I saw her in on the night of our big fight, and that was two days ago. She looks around the room with a wounded expression, wordlessly begging those standing on either side of her to show some mercy.

Then Bernard steps out of the elevator, followed closely behind by two police officers, neither of whom I recognize. Bernard stops when he sees the crowd in front of him, like a student stepping into the wrong classroom on the first day of school. He smiles and mutters something about this being a big misunderstanding. "I'll be back by dinner," he says, raising his cane a little. The announcement draws nothing but a low murmur from the people surrounding him. I notice that he's not handcuffed, which is kind of the officers.

When Ginny sees me standing by the receptionist, she loses what composure she had and stumbles into my arms. I hold her tightly and pat her back as she sobs. Over her shoulder, I make eye contact with Bernard, who nods in my direction. "Take care of her," he says, as he's led out the doors and placed into the back of the squad car.

Suddenly we're surrounded by busybodies, all of whom want Ginny to tell them what she knows. I wrap my arms around her and do my best to shield her as we make our way to the elevator. As soon as we're in, I punch her floor button and hold her tight as we ascend with the others who squeezed in before the doors closed.

"I never trusted him," a short woman says, gripping her walker like it's a safety bar on an amusement park ride.

"That cane is a weapon," a bald man mutters. "Probably uses it to whack his victims."

"You know he's hacked into all our emails," a woman shaped like a question mark says. "He can do that, you know."

Eventually, Bernard's accusers vacate the elevator, leaving Ginny and me alone when we reach her floor. We hurry down the hallway to avoid Barbara, in case she's lurking behind her door waiting to pounce as we pass. As soon as we're inside Ginny's apartment, I sit her down on the sofa and make her comfortable with some pillows and blankets and hot tea.

"Let's split a Xanax, shall we?" Ginny says.

First Max with her sleeping pills and now Ginny with Xanax. What's next? Fishnet stockings and thong underwear?

I get her pills from the medicine cabinet and Ginny cuts one in half with a butter knife.

"It's not him," Ginny says, swallowing. "I don't believe it."

"What happened?"

"They found my laptop in Bernard's apartment."

"Who's 'they'?"

"Well, me, I guess," Ginny says. "I used the Find My app on my phone to see if my computer appeared. It was a long shot, but sure enough, it showed my computer in the building."

"Did they search everyone's rooms?"

"They didn't need to," Ginny says. "The cleaning people found it."

"That seems convenient," I say.

"They also found peanut oil," Ginny says. "A tiny vial of it on his countertop."

"What did Bernard say?"

"He said he's been set up. He's blaming Barbara, of course. But nobody believes him."

"Do you?"

Ginny takes a sip of her tea. "I do," she says. "Not that it was Barbara, necessarily, but that someone is setting him up. Bernard's not a murderer."

I tell her about Craig's attack. After going into graphic detail about him strangling me, I make my apology, hoping my near-death experience will soften Ginny toward me. It does.

"It's not your fault," she says, grabbing my hand. "It was an impossible situation."

"But I made things worse."

"I thought so too at first," Ginny says. "But all you did was try to solve a problem I created. I didn't have the strength to end it myself. I was too scared. But you weren't. You stood up to those bullies. You're kind of my hero."

"That's the Xanax talking."

"I mean it. The only reason I haven't called you sooner is because I was so ashamed of my cowardice. I was so close to calling Cristóbal and confessing to everything."

"What stopped you?"

"I didn't want to disappoint you and Max. If you two weren't afraid, then I wasn't going to be either."

"I'm proud of you," I say. "And nothing from Cristóbal?"

"Nothing," Ginny says. "Of course, that doesn't mean he's not out there waiting for me to leave the building."

"Speaking of leaving the building," I say. "I'm throwing a party on Friday for Jeremy. He's leaving for Vietnam and I'd love for you to come."

Ginny hesitates.

"I'll have Max pick you up and drive you home," I say. "She'll bring her fire poker."

Ginny sighs. For a second I think she's going to decline but then she says, "Okay. What can I bring?"

"Nothing," I say. "My daughter's catering. Just bring your brave self."

63

August 16

I don't want to trouble Ginny for a ride home, so I call Meg, hoping she still feels bad that her boyfriend tried to murder me. She shows up ten minutes later with a big smile on her face and a water bottle for me in case I get thirsty. Her Uber driver demeanor lasts until I inform her that Jeremy is leaving for Vietnam in three weeks. Then we're back to playing the blame game.

"I'm his *mother*," she says. "Why am I the last to hear about this?" Her sour mood lifts a bit when I ask if she's free to cater the going-away party and that I'll pay extra for Vietnamese food and drink. "Oh my God, I love banh mi sandwiches," she squeals. "Can we invite Officer Dunbar?"

"Who?"

"The officer assigned to Craig's case," she says. "I think we hit it off today."

"You're flirting with the cop investigating your boyfriend?" I ask just to make sure I'm understanding her correctly.

"*Ex*-boyfriend," Meg says. "Officer Dunbar spent, like, four hours in our apartment questioning me and looking for evidence."

"You make that sound dirty."

"There's something there," Meg says, biting her lip. "Here, let's call him now."

She passes me his card and I look at her like she's lost her mind. Then I think, maybe it won't be such a bad thing to have a cop on my side for a change. I liked Dunbar's attitude when he questioned me the night of the attack. He was much kinder than his Terminator partner, who looked like he was sculpted out of liquid metal. I dial the number.

Dunbar doesn't pick up his phone so I leave him a message. "Hello, Officer Dunbar. This is Poppy Montgomery, the woman who was assaulted by her daughter's boyfriend last night? I was so grateful for your help and attention. I'm just calling to see if you've had any luck finding the stolen goods. I know it's early, but my grandson is leaving for Vietnam next week and we'd love to get his computers back before he goes. By the way, we're throwing him a little going-away party this Friday and would love it if you could come. I know that's probably not the kind of thing police officers do but I figure you can come over and call it official business. Collect some overtime, perhaps. Hope to hear from you soon."

I hang up.

"Nice job, Mom," Meg says. "That all sounded very natural."

I don't want to tell her I've had a lot of practice lying to men recently. "This will be your chance to show him you can cook and clean."

"Fuck, Mom. This isn't the fifties."

"I don't care what you do," I say. "Just win him over. We need him on our side."

64

August 23

The day of the party, Meg comes over early looking professional in a crisp, white button-down and with her hair pulled back in a neat ponytail. As she unloads the food and decorations from her car, I escape to the bathroom and try to make myself look presentable.

One look in the mirror and I wish I had outsourced this task to Meg as well. My face looks tired and old, which is why I try to avoid reflective surfaces as a general principle. These days I feel like every mirror comes with the caption, *How did this happen?* When I was young, I could never imagine myself as this old; now that I'm this old, I can't remember myself as ever being young. I can't tell if that's a blessing or a curse.

I destroy a small layer of the ozone in my attempts to give my limp gray hair some body. Then I draw all over my face so people can see my lips, cheekbones, and eyebrows. After the makeup is complete, I go into my bedroom and try to find something that's a little more festive than my usual elastic attire. I opt for a pair of slacks I bought for my DUI court date and pair it with a creamy silk top. I'm going to have to crank the heat to be comfortable in such thin attire, which I feel okay doing since this is a Vietnamese themed party and I'm sure summers there are unbearable.

Meg once again impresses me with her catering work. I don't know how much of her décor is authentically Vietnamese, but she's transformed my drab interior into something warmer with paper lanterns, red tablecloths, and a silk cherry blossom floral centerpiece. She's brought over a portable speaker and plays the kind of Vietnamese music you might hear in a spa. In the corner of my living room, she's lit a stick of incense, which adds an aromatic, spicy scent to the air.

Meg's wisely prepared foods that she could make in advance and serve at room temperature—there's a bowl of papaya salad, a plate of mini banh mi sandwiches, and a tray of chilled vegetable rolls. The only thing she needs my oven for is to warm up some fried shrimp rolls. It amazes me that this woman can be so good at planning and executing a meal but can't balance a checkbook to save her life.

"I figured your guests aren't adventurous drinkers," Meg says, pushing bottles and cans into a white metal party tub filled with ice. "So I'm just putting out two bottles of sauvignon blanc and some Vietnamese beer I got at Whole Foods." I cringe at the mention of the supermarket, knowing it's going to cost me. Maybe Ginny can set up a GoFundMe account for me when Meg presents me with the bill for this soiree.

Max is the first guest to arrive, which is no surprise. She rings the bell at five o'clock, the exact time I told people the party was starting. She's dressed in a steel blue, tea-length dress that shows off her figure nicely. She's wearing lipstick, something I've never seen her put on before.

"I brought this for Jeremy," Max says, thrusting a wrapped box into my hands.

"What is it?" I ask.

"Tide travel sink packets," she says. "For washing his clothes."

"How practical," I say.

"I also went to the bank and got him some dong."

"What's that?"

"It's the currency," she says. "Always good to have some cash on hand. Plus you get a better exchange rate here than in Vietnam."

"That's really thoughtful," I say. "Thank you."

"It's not for you," Max says.

"Can I get you some wine?"

I lead Max to the dining room and pour her a glass of sauvignon blanc. Max can't help but peek into the kitchen to see what Meg is up to. Meg, sensing a future investor or client, puts on her happy face and greets Max with two light kisses on the cheek. "So nice to see you again," she says. "How's Harold doing?"

I'm gobsmacked, as the Brits say. Meg not only remembered Max's husband's name but that he's sick. Who is this woman and what has she done with my daughter?

The doorbell rings again and I go answer while Meg and Max chat. Ginny greets me with a long and strong hug, her floral perfume smothering the aroma of burning incense. She looks so much better than when I saw her last. Her face is round and pink and full of joy. She dressed up in a glittery silver top and matching knee-length skirt. She's also wearing heels, which makes me think she's lost her mind a little.

Ginny hands me a package for Jeremy. "I bought him a book," she says.

"I can see that," I say, turning the paperback-shaped object in my hands.

"It's *The Mountains Sing*," Ginny whispers, as if Jeremy is standing right behind me. "Have you read it?"

Of course I haven't read it, I want to say. I'm still on the letter *G* of the Sue Grafton mysteries and I started those ten years ago.

"It's a multigenerational story about a Vietnamese family, written by a Vietnamese poet. It's fantastic and really gives you a sense of the country, not just the war."

"That's so thoughtful," I say and lead her back to the food and beverages.

Ginny oohs and aahs at the décor and the spread. "Meg, you've done it again," she says.

"Ginny!" Meg says, spreading her arms wide for a hug. "So nice to see you again. You look fantastic. Clearly, you're getting a better workout with Max than at the Y."

Again, all I can do is shake my head in disbelief. I pop a spring roll in my mouth and it's delicious. Could it be this confident, capable person has been in Meg all along? Has she just chosen not to show her to me? I feel cheated all of a sudden, resentful of the fact that I never got to spend time with this Meg, only the obnoxious one. But I don't let myself get sucked into this emotional black hole. Instead, I turn away and fire all my thrusters toward the light, which is this party and my friends.

Jeremy and Bao are next to arrive. When they walk in the door, we're all there to cheer, which I hope makes Jeremy's guest feel welcome. I must say, I'm surprised by Bao. I haven't had much interaction with Vietnamese people other than the movies, which is why I probably pictured a short man wearing a silk robe and conical straw hat. Bao is very sporty in a powder blue polo and khaki pants. His clothes don't balloon out, making him appear shrunken under too much fabric. Whatever he does for exercise must keep him in good shape. I catch a glance of Ginny checking him out, a shy smile brightening her face.

Jeremy introduces Bao and I feel a self-consciousness settle over the crowd. What if Bao thinks all this food and decorations are for him?

Like we think this is what it takes to make him feel at home? And what if we got all these details wrong? What if, like some of those Japanese symbol tattoos I hear about, we've put something ridiculous on full display?

If Bao is offended, he doesn't let it show. He steps up to each of us and shakes our hands with a strong grip that feels rough and calloused.

"What can I get you to drink?" I ask.

"I'll take a beer," he says, his voice deep and only slightly accented.

I pull a Vietnamese beer out of the ice and show it to him. "This okay?" I ask.

Bao nods and I pour him a glass.

"All this is for Jeremy," I explain. "I hope it doesn't offend you."

"Grandma!" Jeremy says.

"I like it," Bao says, taking in the room. "Very festive. Although we usually light incense at the shrines of the dead."

Meg walks out of the kitchen, holding a plate of spring rolls. She sets the food down on the table and extends her hands to Bao. "So nice to finally meet you," she says. "Thank you so much for encouraging Jeremy to go to Vietnam." She looks at her son with genuine warmth and a little bit of sadness. "You're a better influence than me."

"He is a good boy," Bao says.

Jeremy squirms under the spotlight, unused to this much attention. Meg gathers everyone around and tops off their glasses before filling her own with sparkling water.

"I'd like to take a moment to toast my wonderful son," she says. Everyone raises their glasses. I want her to end her speech here, but Meg, unlike her son, enjoys being the center of attention so she continues.

"It's hard raising a child when you're a child yourself. As a young mom, I never really fit in anywhere . . ."

Meg was 29 when she had Jeremy. I start to interrupt, but then hold my tongue, realizing she probably lied about her age while flirting with Officer Dunbar. If he comes to the party, she'll need others to confirm her invented backstory.

". . . I was always the youngest mom at any play date or birthday party. People judged me. I didn't have the stability they had. Jeremy's dad was always touring and all my friends had moved away. It was just me and mother. Is it any wonder I started drinking?"

This last line gets a laugh but I'm hurt and mortified and just want her to shut up.

"Seriously, Mom," she continues. "I know I've been a pain in the ass, but you'll never know how grateful I am that you stuck by me and Jeremy all these years. We're all here because of you and I'll never be able to repay you for all you've given us. So while this party is for Jeremy, I also want to toast my mother, who's seen me at my worst and never given up on me. I love you."

Meg steps over to where I'm standing and wraps me in a one-armed hug while everyone raises their glasses. Damn this girl, I think. There she goes again. Making me feel bad for thinking the worst of her. Why does it take a special occasion for her to be nice to me? Maybe some people need an audience to speak from the heart. Without some kind of buffer, that kind of intimacy can get awkward real fast.

I encourage everyone to fill their plates with Meg's delicious food, which they do with enthusiasm. Jeremy opens his presents and thanks Max and Ginny with stiff, slightly awkward hugs. He shows off the gift Bao gave him, a vintage coin Bao held on to throughout his journey from Vietnam to the refugee camp in Thailand to the United States. "Now it makes its return journey," he says. "Don't spend it on bubble gum."

Bao is shy and reserved in our presence. Ginny attempts to draw him out by asking him about his gardening.

"It's a relationship," Bao says, nodding. "Some plants require a lot of effort."

"What do you grow?" Ginny asks.

"Tomatoes, lettuce, squash, a little marijuana," Bao says smiling at our shock and surprise. "I discovered its therapeutic powers after my cancer treatment. It's an interesting plant. Lots of varieties to experiment with."

"Is that why you love going over to Bao's house?" I ask Jeremy, who flushes red with embarrassment.

"We're not given much space to grow things in Xanadu," Ginny says. "It's a shame really, because I think it might give people something to do. At the very least, a community garden reminds you of the cycle of life."

"Do people want to be reminded of that at a retirement home?" I ask.

"Someone gave me an orchid after Colin died and it's still alive," Ginny says. "People told me to throw it out after it lost its flowers, but I kept caring for it and it bloomed again."

"Ginny's our hopeless romantic," I say, which makes her blush.

"What is Xanadu like?" Bao asks.

We all pause, wondering how we should answer that question.

"Show him the website," Max says. She probably wants to buy us some time so we can find another way to describe Ginny's retirement home than a place where old ladies go to get scammed and then murdered.

I pull up the Xanadu site on my phone and hand it to Bao.

"Very nice," he says, scrolling through the images.

Meg picks up the tray of spring rolls on the table and brings them over in case people want seconds. "Hey, I know that lady," she says, catching a glimpse of my phone when Bao hands it back to me.

I look down at the screen and see Barbara staring back at me. She's holding a ceramic cup and smiling like an actress in a coffee commercial. *Barbara never had a second cup before Xanadu*, the voiceover says in my head. Of course Xanadu would use her as their model of someone leading an active, fun, meaningful life.

"How do you know Barbara?" Ginny asks.

"She and Craig were partners," Meg says.

Ginny's plate tips, nearly sending her food cascading to the floor.

"Partners, how?" I ask.

"In his vitamin business," Meg says. "I saw the two of them in her car when I moved in but she drove off before I could introduce myself. Craig said she was an angel investor."

Back in the day before Spotify, this would be a good moment for the record to scratch. We all stand there, holding our spring rolls limply in our hands as our brains process this information. Meg stares at us thinking it's her appetizer that's caused our sick expressions, not the news she's just delivered. "Oh, I forgot the dipping sauce," she says and scurries back to the table. When she returns, we're all still standing there, shell-shocked.

"She sent Craig after us," I say. "She saw us together the night we stole her money."

"What now?" Meg says.

"She must have thought there'd be some evidence on one of the computers," Jeremy says.

"Or she was setting Craig up to take the fall," Max says.

"Just like she set up Bernard," Ginny says.

"What are you all talking about?" Meg asks.

"What's Barbara's last name?" Jeremy asks, phone at the ready.

"Vosovic," Ginny says.

"Did she poison herself?" I ask. "Make herself look like a victim instead of a criminal?"

"Or did someone else poison her?" Ginny asks. "Maybe to get rid of her."

"Alfonse?" I say. "He has an earring, just like the one I saw on our FaceTime call."

"He's got the most to gain," Max says. "If he's Cristóbal, then he must know it's time to make a quick getaway. Maybe he was tying up loose ends."

"Xanadu sounds like an exciting place," Bao says, dipping his spring roll into the sauce Meg's holding and taking a bite.

Just then the doorbell rings. I'm still reeling from our discovery so Meg beats me to the door and opens it. Officer Dunbar is standing there, dressed in khakis and a striped button-down shirt, holding a bouquet from Trader Joe's. He hands them to Meg, even though I'm pretty sure they're meant for me. "Oh Glen, they're lovely," Meg says bringing the roses to her face and inhaling. *Glen?*

She ushers him inside and introduces him to everyone as her friend. She pours him a beer and then leaves to put the flowers in water.

"Officer Dunbar," I say. "I think we may know who's murdering those old ladies at Xanadu."

65

August 23

It takes the rest of the party to convince Ginny she's living next to a crime syndicate.

"It's not possible," she says. "They play bridge every Thursday."

"Think about it," I say, trying to channel that detective in those Sue Grafton novels. "Barbara's in a prime location to find easy marks. She targets widows living at Xanadu because they're lonely and vulnerable. She gets them on Senior Moments where they meet a handsome entrepreneur who needs help opening a new restaurant or café or sports arena—something that requires a lot of cash up front. He convinces his new lady friend to help him open a joint bank account so he can deposit money that she can use to pay these 'contractors' in cash."

"It's a good scam," Max adds. "Because the victims are shamed into silence. Once the woman realizes she's being used, she's too embarrassed to tell anyone."

"But they'd get caught eventually, wouldn't they?" Ginny looks to Dunbar for an answer.

"It depends," Dunbar says. "They may know just how long to use these women before they're caught."

"Or not," I say. "Maybe that's why Cynthia and Sharon were killed."

"Or maybe they're running different scams on different people," Jeremy adds.

Dunbar nods. "These cyber criminals are tough to track down and prosecute because most of them live outside the country."

"I think I'd know if Barbara was a money launderer," Ginny says.

"Not her," Jeremy says, excitedly assembling the pieces of this puzzle. "Her son."

He holds up his phone and shows an image of a middle-aged man being escorted into court by a uniformed officer. The man looks off camera, as if trying to intimidate a surprise witness or aggressive prosecutor. He's dressed in black, which only highlights his pale skin. He's bald with dark eyebrows and the wide, thick lips of a fish. The only place I see any resemblance to Barbara is in the eyes, which are catlike and icy blue.

"That looks like the man in the photo Barbara has in her apartment," Ginny says.

"It's Nikola Vosovic," Jeremy says. "He's wanted for drug trafficking. Authorities suspect he's somewhere in Taiwan."

"How can we prove that she's behind the Senior Moments scam?" I ask Dunbar.

Meg hands him a plate of food, which he looks at with surprise and some hesitation. He bites into a banh mi roll and acknowledges its deliciousness with a grunt of pleasure. After devouring the rest, he takes a sip of beer, and addresses the crowd gathered around him like the authority figure he is.

"Besides you, how many other people have been targeted by this woman?" he asks.

"And man," Max says. "Let's not forget about Alfonse. Barbara can't pull off this scam without his help. He's probably an equal partner in crime."

Everyone waits for Ginny to respond. "I have no idea," she says.

"That's what you'd have to figure out first," Dunbar says.

"Why isn't it enough that Ginny was a victim?" Max asks.

"It could be," Dunbar says. "But elder scams happen so often, police don't put a lot of resources into investigating them, which means you'd have to connect these scams with the murders you say happened at Xanadu."

"If Cynthia and Sharon were going to the police, it would provide motive to kill them," I say.

"That's a headline that would interest my captain," Dunbar says, chomping down on another banh mi sandwich.

Jeremy signals me to change the conversation by swiping his fingers across his neck. Either that or he's choking. His eyes are bulging out a bit, so I go over to check.

"You should be careful with this," he bends down and whispers in my ear.

I pull him into the adjacent room and point at an imaginary crack in the ceiling. Actually, it's not imaginary. That crack has been a source of concern for quite some time.

"You may not want the police to investigate this crime since you're holding three hundred thousand dollars of Cristóbal's money."

"Barbara's money," I correct him.

"Whatever," Jeremy says. "You don't want to initiate an investigation that will lead the police to you. We got away with our scam because we underreported the amount of money lost to the police. If the police or the Feds think there's a crime syndicate operating out of a retirement home, they may dig a little deeper."

"I don't want to put you in any danger."

"I covered my tracks pretty well," he says. "Plus, I'm leaving for Vietnam in two weeks, which will make it harder to arrest me if it comes to that."

"This is the first time I'm glad you're leaving," I say, wrapping my arms around him and squeezing him tight. "But I want you to be able to come back."

"It would help if you got Barbara's laptop," Jeremy says. "A good forensics person could trace those Senior Moments posts back to her."

"That bitch," I say.

"Grandma," Jeremy says, putting a hand on my shoulder. "She did the same scam we did, just on a larger scale."

"No," I say, shaking my head. "She terrorized vulnerable women to make money. We just robbed a few assholes."

"The crimes are the same, even though the victims are different."

Damn it, he's right. And Barbara was able to get away with it for the same reason we did: because she's old and no one saw her as a threat. The invisible cloak I was hiding under to scam assholes out of money was the same one Barbara used to pull off her crimes. But I can't admire her for that, just as I can't take pride in the scheme we pulled off. Maybe Ginny's simple morality is right after all. There is right and wrong. I was wrong, just like Barbara. Maybe it's time to make a full confession. I have a police officer in my house right now. I could walk up to him, hand him my papaya salad, and tell him everything. It would probably throw a damper on the party, but at least I'd die with a clear conscience.

Ginny joins us from the other room, looking as perky as when she got her new label maker. "We can't let Barbara swindle someone else."

"I'm ready to make a full confession," I say.

"Are you crazy?" Ginny says, lightly punching me on the shoulder.

"You were right, Ginny," I say. "What I did was wrong."

"Tell that to your priest," she says. "I think I know how we can stop her without implicating ourselves," Ginny says.

"How's that?" I ask.

"We tell everyone Barbara pooped in the pool."

66

August 23

I've got to hand it to Ginny: She's a quick learner. Four months ago, she would have never been able to come up with a scheme so devious. I guess I really have been a good influence on her. Her plan is perfect and only requires one embarrassing public confession. After troubleshooting for a few minutes, we return to the party and tell our assembled guests what we plan to do. They're all on board, even the cop, who sees the scheme as a means of career advancement.

"You are a brave woman," Bao tells Ginny at the end of the evening, which for us is seven o'clock. Max extended her stay for thirty minutes but when she left, the remaining guests started filing out the door.

"I'm really not," Ginny says. "I just don't like to see bad deeds go unpunished."

"Jeremy will be gone soon," Bao says. "Can I call you to hear if your plan was a success?"

"Of course," Ginny says, and gives him her number.

I nudge Jeremy as we watch the two "swap digits" as the young people say.

"We don't say that," Jeremy tells me.

After everyone leaves, I go inside and find Meg and Dunbar cleaning up. With Meg still wearing her catering apron, they look like a nice interracial couple from the fifties. I back out before I spoil the intimacy of the moment. Forget about candlelit dinners, finding a man who helps clean up is where the real romance lies.

I walk through the house and gather all of Meg's decorations, snuffing out each of the candles in the paper lanterns. I don't know why I got so worked up about hosting this party. It's nice to welcome people into your home and show them how grateful you are for their company. I should have done this years ago, instead of hiding from everyone, like Jeremy in his basement. Do I have water aerobics to thank for what feels like a happy ending? We'll see. I make a wish on the last candle before blowing it out. "Please let Ginny's plan work," I say to the glowing lantern in front of me and then extinguish the flame.

67

August 28

Ginny's right about the lecture. It's very easy to set up and advertise. She speaks with the events coordinator at Xanadu the following day and by late afternoon the lobby and elevators are plastered with flyers announcing Officer Glen Dunbar's talk on *Cyber Scams! How to Avoid Losing Your Dignity, Your Money, and Possibly Your Life!* This is exactly the kind of community outreach Dunbar's captain has been pushing for and he commends Glen for his initiative. He and Jeremy spend the day at Meg's apartment creating the presentation. When they show me the script, it's much too reasonable.

"You need to scare the shit out of us," I say. I punch up a few lines and have Glen watch twenty minutes of Fox News to capture the right tone. After doing a few run-throughs, Glen is ready to go. "Make sure you're wearing your uniform," I remind him. "Maybe have one of those bullet sashes draped across your front."

"You mean an ammo belt?" Glen asks. "Those are for machine guns."

"Perfect," I say. "Bring one of those too."

On the day of the lecture, Ginny does her best to fill the seats. She talks it up at breakfast, at lunch, and at dinner, reminding people that their life's savings are at stake. She's fighting against Barbara and her crew, who are protesting the visit.

"They're saying it's fearmongering," Ginny says. "I don't know if they're going to come."

"They have to come," I remind her. "If we can't separate Barbara and Alfonse, the whole thing falls apart."

By the time Dunbar's talk starts, the lecture hall is full to capacity, with the staff bringing in extra foldout seats to accommodate the late arrivals. I guess our scare tactics worked. After everyone is seated, Max and I sneak in the back to watch the drama unfold. I spot Ginny and Bernard, who's making his first public appearance since being questioned by the police, sitting strategically in the middle. Dunbar might be the one lighting the match, but it's Ginny who needs to make sure the fire spreads.

It's a great crowd, but the guest of honor still hasn't arrived. I stand in the doorway, waiting for the elevators to burp out Barbara. She has to come. She will come. I'm sure of it.

With every scam, there's a psychological element that helps you trick your victim. In the case of the men Jeremy and I swindled, it was their greed that allowed us to steal their money. With the Senior Moments scam, it's the lure of romance. With the scam we're pulling off tonight, it's Barbara's queen bee complex that will be her undoing. If there's an event happening at Xanadu, even if it's an event that might incriminate her, she must be at the center of it. Of course it makes more sense for her to stay away. The talk is warning people away from her criminal enterprise. But if I know Barbara, and I think I do, it's her hubris that will make it impossible for her to miss this. Like me, she thinks she's the smartest person in the room. My hope is that she's looking forward to disparaging our speaker and maintaining her dominance over the crowd.

But she still hasn't shown up and the crowd is getting restless. We're five minutes past curtain and Dunbar's standing on stage, ready to go. My phone pings with a text from Jeremy.

Has it started yet?

He's got his own part to play tonight and must time his entrance perfectly or the whole thing will fall apart.

Still waiting, I write back.

Dunbar can't hold the crowd off any longer. He clears his throat and thanks the audience for coming. The lights dim and he begins his presentation.

He's in the middle of sharing his credentials when the elevator pings open and Barbara and Patty emerge, each holding sloshing martinis. I hold my breath for Alfonse to exit with them, but he doesn't appear. That means the first part of our plan is working. It's time to alert Jeremy.

The seagulls have landed, I write.

Barbara and Patty march into the auditorium, laughing like a bunch of Goldie Hawns, and practically dance down the center aisle to the empty seats up front. Barbara's hubris is on full display. Her delayed entrance is clearly designed to make light of the presentation and to throw off the speaker. But these ladies are no match for Dunbar, who commands the stage like a prison guard at a riot. He's in full police gear (no ammo belt, unfortunately) and stares down the drunk duo until they quiet down.

"How many of you have ever been cheated online?" Dunbar states. He cuts an imposing figure walking up and down the tiny stage, staring into the audience. I told him to scare the shit out of us but maybe that's not the best tone for a Q&A. No one raises a hand.

"Really? Well then I must be sitting in the luckiest room in America," he says to nervous laughter. "Because senior citizens lost more than three billion dollars last year to financial scams. Three billion dollars. Now I don't know about you, but I can't afford to lose three dollars let alone three billion!"

Some light coughing. "What'd he say?" a voice says from the back.

"I'm going to walk you through the most current scams my department has been tracking so that you're aware of how to keep yourself safe from these online criminals. These people taking advantage of your good nature are really the lowest of the low. They prey on the sick and the elderly with no concern about the tragedy they leave in their wake. It's hard for me to call them human because they seem to have no regard for people like you. To them, you're just an easy buck."

I wrote that line and I'm proud of how it lands. There's a general rumble in the crowd as they imagine these nefarious villains tying them to the railroad tracks and cheering gleefully as the train approaches.

Dunbar goes through his slide deck, starting with the snatch-and-grab cybercrimes ("Send me an Apple gift card so I can get your nephew out of prison") to the more dangerous identity thefts ("Just click this link to restore access to your Wells Fargo account"). As he describes these various schemes, you can see the audience getting more and more agitated thanks to Dunbar's Tucker Carlson delivery. I keep my eyes on Barbara and Patty and they remain still and quiet throughout the presentation, at times shaking their heads at Dunbar's hyperbole.

"Now I'd like to tell you about the worst predator waiting for you online," Dunbar says, lowering his voice as someone practiced in the art of telling ghost stories around the campfire. He taps a key on the laptop and the logo for Senior Moments appears on the screen. There's a collective gasp from the audience. If this declaration didn't come from an imposing man in uniform, I wonder if Barbara would have stood up and demanded an apology. Instead she just shakes her head and mouths to those around her *Not true*.

"This site has been the place where cybercriminals go to scam seniors," he says. "It takes your desire for companionship and uses it against you. We've seen seniors scammed out of money by suitors who claim they need help with a medical emergency. We've seen seniors share sensitive information with suitors who then open credit card accounts under the senior's name. But worst of all, we've seen seniors turned into criminals through money mule operations that have them unwittingly launder money for drug traffickers."

"I've had enough of this," Barbara says standing up. "Let's go, Patty."

Patty rises unsteadily on her feet, her martini making this show of solidarity a little wobbly. A smattering of people follow their lead and Dunbar for the first time looks nervous that he's lost the trust of the crowd. I'm prepared to tackle Barbara if she tries to leave before Jeremy is through with Alfonse. Just before the exodus happens though, Ginny stands up and says in her most authoritative teacher voice, "It happened to me."

This quiets the room. People stop gathering their things and turn to look at Ginny, who looks like she's about to faint. Bernard makes a show of standing next to her and grabbing her arm. Barbara and Patty have no choice but to retake their seats.

"I met a man on Senior Moments who convinced me to open a bank account and then had me deliver cash to his 'partners,'" Ginny says making the finger quotes. "I stayed silent about it for months because I was so embarrassed, but what Officer Dunbar is saying is true."

"I don't think the people in this auditorium are as naïve as you, dear," Barbara says.

The room goes silent at the insult. This is the moment we couldn't plan for because we don't know how many victims there are at Xanadu. We know Barbara convinced Ginny, and probably Cynthia and Sharon, to go on Senior Moments. We know her son is a crooked lawyer linked to drug trafficking, money laundering, and other financial frauds. We know he lives in Taiwan, a country with no US extradition treaty. We know, or think we know, that it was Barbara who stole Ginny's laptop in an effort to find the money we stole from her. When that didn't work, she planted the device in Bernard's apartment in an attempt to frame him. What we don't know is how many other people have been scammed and silenced by this geriatric bitch. This is the moment we're going to find out.

The house stays silent. Ginny, bless her heart, remains standing, hoping someone will join her, but people are either too scared or too ashamed to rise up. I guess it's easier to take an "I am Spartacus" stand when it's just your life, not your reputation, at stake. We've lost, I think. Barbara's beaten us at our own game. She pulled off the perfect scam by making everyone think old ladies can't be cold-blooded thieves. Part of me respects her, the other part wants to stuff her into that martini glass and stab her with a toothpick.

"I'm sorry, Ginny," Barbara says, rising to leave again. "But maybe you're the only one who needs this lecture."

Ginny looks about the room, but her gaze is like a spotlight that everyone shields their eyes from. She starts to take her seat when a woman two rows down from her stands up and says, "It happened to me too."

Ginny straightens back up and gazes at the woman, encouraging her to talk.

"I let a man I met on Senior Moments string me along for a year before the Feds knocked on my door and told me I'd be arrested if I didn't stop moving money for him."

"It happened to me too," another woman says from the back. She needs the women on either side of her to help her up, but once she's standing she tells a story about how a wealthy philanthropist tricked her into transferring large sums of cash to someone she thought was a high school principal. "He was a hoodlum!" she says. "A hoodlum!"

And on it goes until there are eight women standing.

"I applaud you women for coming forward," Dunbar says. "These operations only work when their victims stay silent out of embarrassment or shame."

"Officer Dunbar," Bernard says, raising his hand. We scripted this part for him as a gift for all Barbara's put him through, and he's milking his moment for all it's worth. He clears his throat and asks, "Is it normal for this many women in one retirement home to be victims of the same cyber scam?"

Dunbar shakes his head. "Not in my experience, no."

The room goes quiet, but it's the quiet of someone trying to figure out if they've just been shot. When people start to realize the blood on their shirt is coming from them—metaphorically speaking—the room explodes in pain, anger, and confusion. Within minutes the whole auditorium is shouting questions and conspiracy theories.

"Who would do such a thing?"

"I thought this was a meeting about the low flow toilets," another says.

"Why go on Senior Moments with all the eligible bachelors living here?" a man shouts and then collapses into a fit of coughing.

"It was her!" a woman shouts, pointing at Barbara. She says it loud enough to be heard by everyone in the room. Heads swivel in Barbara's direction. Barbara's choice to make herself the center of attention now seems ill advised as the angry residents start pressing in on her.

"She talked me into going on that damn site," the woman continues as she makes her way to the aisle. "She's the one who set me up with that hoodlum."

"Me too!" another woman says.

Barbara holds up her hands and tries to calm the mob that's forming around her.

"Listen here," she says. "Patty and I both use the site and we've never had any trouble."

Barbara looks over at Patty, who's slowly backing away from her. She sees Barbara's ship is sinking and like the rat she is, scurries away to avoid being sucked under.

"She made me help her," Patty tells the people around her. "Her son's a mobster!"

Barbara is panicking now, a trapped squirrel with no tree to climb. What will this crowd of octogenarians do to her? I wonder. It's not like we have the strength or balance to knock her down and kick her. Well, maybe Max could, but she's staying put, watching the crowd swell around our tormentor, blocking her exit.

"Officer Dunbar should really do something," I say.

"Yes, he really should," Max replies.

Neither of us moves.

Finally, it's Ginny who parts the bodies gently with plenty of "excuse mes" and "sorrys" until she's standing in front of the crowd. She holds up her arms and creates a little pocket of space around Barbara, who cowers behind her.

"Everyone, please calm down," she says and waves Dunbar over. He makes his way through the crowd and stands next to Barbara. It's hard to tell by his stance if he's there to protect or arrest her.

"We all know Barbara," Ginny says. "Do we really think she's capable of such a diabolical plot to steal our life savings?"

"Her son is wanted for money laundering," Bernard says, holding up his phone with the image of Nikola that Jeremy showed us earlier.

The student has become the master, I think, watching Ginny place her hand over her mouth in mock horror.

Barbara clings to Dunbar and begs him to protect her.

"I'll take you to the station," he says and leads her away, not in handcuffs, unfortunately.

We all follow them as they scurry out the door. Just as they're making their way through the lobby, the elevator doors open and Alfonse exits, escorted by Officer Bell. By the look on Alfonse's face, I can see that Jeremy was successful. While we were keeping Barbara busy at the cybersecurity seminar, Alfonse was answering some "routine questions" from Officer Bell about Bernard. Alfonse was all too eager to help the police build their case against his lover's would-be assassin, until Jeremy called him, disguising his number as Barbara's. When Alfonse picked up, Jeremy deepfaked Barbara's voice (her many posts on social media made it easy for Jeremy to copy her speech), telling him that the police had arrested her and she was making a full confession.

When Alfonse and Barbara see each other in the lobby, each in the company of a police officer, they have only seconds to decide what to do. They're both caught in the prisoner's dilemma and if they were more generous people, they would have stayed silent. But they're not generous people. They're assholes, so they turn on each other in an instant.

"She's the one behind it all!" Alfonse screams, pointing at Barbara.

"Liar!" Barbara screams. "I have proof that he murdered Cynthia and Sharon. He tried to poison me when I threatened to turn him in!"

Dunbar and Officer Bell allow the screaming fight to continue as they place the two in handcuffs.

"She's been using Senior Moments to wash her son's dirty money!" Alfonse screams.

"He ran Sharon over and dumped her body in the Bay!" Barbara says.

Dunbar and Officer Bell walk the two of them out of Xanadu and into waiting police cars parked outside.

68

August 31

With our help, Dunbar pieces together the money laundering scam Barbara has been running for years out of Xanadu and before that, Golden Pines in Belleview. She wasn't washing *all* her son's dirty money. Given the numerous shady enterprises he's involved in, that would take hundreds of retirement homes, each with its own inside man or woman running the operation. It turns out, Barbara's little enterprise was just for her. She had spent her life in the Vosovic crime family, first as daughter, then as wife, and finally as matriarch. When she finally "retired" she quickly grew restless and convinced her son to let her wash some of his money for a little spending cash. That's what Cynthia and Sharon were murdered for—so Barbara could continue shopping at Neiman Marcus.

Speaking of Cynthia and Sharon, thanks to Alfonse's testimony, we learned they were killed for very different reasons. Cynthia found the racy photo she'd sent her Senior Moments sweetheart on Sharon's phone when Sharon left her device unlocked and unattended in the cafeteria. (Apparently, the mean girls took great pleasure in sharing and commenting on these images, proving that some people never leave middle school.) When Cynthia threatened to go to the police, Barbara had Alfonse throw her off the balcony. Sharon became so alarmed that their little game had turned deadly that she tried to flee the country. Unfortunately, she told Patty, who told Barbara, who told Alfonse, who ran her over and threw her body in the Bay.

It wasn't until Sharon's daughter showed up looking for her that Barbara decided she needed an exit strategy, so she upped the ante with Ginny, making her withdraw a large sum of getaway cash from the bank, while throwing suspicion off her with the peanut oil incident. This also made it convenient to frame Bernard when he started spreading the rumors that the women had been killed because of their association with Senior Moments. Bernard never suspected Barbara and Alfonse of being killers; he just liked ruining Xanadu's pristine reputation that Barbara had worked so hard to maintain.

Shortly after Barbara's arrest, Bernard got an offer to join a jazz quartet at the Rancho Mirage Retirement Home in Palm Springs. After the way people at Xanadu turned against him, he knew he'd never feel at home there, so he jumped at the chance.

"With all the murderers gone, life here will be so boring," he said.

He's letting us throw him a going-away party, which Meg agreed to cater.

"I want the theme to be spite," Bernard told her. "Can you handle that, dear?"

Turns out, that theme is right up Meg's alley. Rather than arrange some elegant cocktail party in Ginny's cozy apartment, she turns the Xanadu cafeteria into "the gayest nightclub in fairyland" (Meg's words, not mine). Xanadu was more than happy to inject a little levity after their string of murders and bent over backward (excuse the pun) to accommodate her plans. There might have been some threats to sue on

Bernard's behalf for wrongful search and seizure, but I wasn't in the room when Meg negotiated with the manager.

Meg moves Bernard's piano into a corner of the cafeteria and sets up a mic nearby for partygoers to sing. Above the piano, she hangs a huge banner that reads WE WERE WRONG TO SUSPECT YOU OF ANYTHING BUT KINDNESS in glittery script and surrounds it with decorative fans and rainbow flags. In the corner she puts a huge multilayered cake with inch-thick frosting and a giant penis candle in the center. The pièce de résistance is the velvet rope she puts surrounding the party area, manned, as it were, by two drag queens with clipboards.

"It's everything I dreamed it would be," Bernard says when he sees the setup.

Bernard can't wait for the guests to arrive. He rushes over to where the champagne is chilling and pops a bottle. Loudly. I think the cork lands in someone's macaroni salad across the room.

"I'm so proud of you, dear," I say, squeezing Meg's arm.

"Really?"

I nod. "You could have drummed up more business with a different kind of party, but you put Bernard's needs ahead of your own."

"Crap," she says. "I didn't think of that." Then she smiles to let me know she's joking.

"You're really good at this."

"There's something about serving people that feels right," she says. "Like penance. Although, most of my catering has been for people I care about. I don't know how I'm going to feel when I have to work for an asshole."

"It will be harder for sure," I say. "But I can give you some tips for how to manage them."

"I'm not spitting in anyone's food if that's what you're thinking," Meg says.

I pretend to be shocked and offended. "I would never do something so crass and . . . obvious."

The party is a hit. Ginny, Max, Jeremy, and Dunbar are all there, along with a select number of Bernard's friends who stuck by him during his ordeal. Many residents try to come in for cake and champagne, but are denied entrance by the towering drag queens who tell them they're not on the list.

It's in the middle of our sing-along to "She's a Rainbow" when the authorities come to take Jeremy away.

Two suits enter the cafeteria, one white, one Hispanic, with coordinated steps and shaved heads. Their dress and attitude are so stereotypically law enforcement that at first I think Meg has arranged for strippers to entertain us. It isn't until I see the man walking slightly behind the two that I realize something's wrong. Because I know the man. He's the same age as most of the men at Xanadu but he's in much better shape and his clothes don't bunch or sag around the middle. And his ears. How could I forget those giant ears? It's Bao. And he's smiling just like he did when I met him a few weeks ago at Jeremy's party.

"That's sweet of you to invite Bao," I say.

"I didn't," Jeremy says, and looks at me with wide, saucer eyes.

When Bao reaches the drag queens at the velvet rope, he does a little bow and asks if he might speak with Jeremy.

"Are you alright?" Jeremy asked, rushing up to him. "Who are these guys?"

"They are my colleagues," Bao said. "Or former colleagues. I've been retired for years now."

"Retired from what?" I ask.

Bao smiles but doesn't answer my question. "I'd like to speak with you, if that's okay,"

Jeremy steps over the barrier and sits with Bao at a nearby table while the two agents remain next to the drag queens, who, even with all their feminine wiles, can't get the men to crack a smile.

We all huddle up and try to figure out what's going on.

"What if they know about the money?" I ask.

"If they're here to arrest him, they would have done it already," Max says.

"Do you think Bao was faking being single?" Ginny asks.

Bernard tries to distract us with a rousing rendition of "Gee, Officer Krupke," but it does little to lighten the mood. Eventually, Bao brings Jeremy back to the party and greets everyone warmly.

"I'm so sorry to interrupt," he says. "But I wanted to talk with Jeremy about something important before he leaves on his trip."

"Is he in trouble?" I say.

"No, not at all," Bao says. "A potential job opportunity."

"What kind of job?" Ginny asks.

Bao smiles. "Can I have a piece of cake?" he asks.

While Ginny walks Bao over to the cake table, I sidle up to Jeremy, who's staring off into space. "You okay?" I ask.

Jeremy snaps out of it and smiles. "Right as rain," he says. I'm surprised he gets the idiom right instead of saying "right as cucumber" or some such.

Bao finishes his cake, kisses Ginny on the hand, and then leaves the party with his two escorts. It isn't until they're gone that Jeremy sinks into a chair and allows us to refill his champagne glass.

"He wants me to come work for them," he says.

"Who?" I ask.

"I'm not at liberty to say," Jeremy says.

I pepper him with all the three-letter agencies trying to see if he'll break, but he doesn't, which makes me think he might be a good hire for one of those organizations.

"Can you still go on your trip?" Ginny asks.

Jeremy nods. "I can basically work from anywhere," he says.

"Well, now we have another reason to celebrate," Max says, grabbing the microphone off its stand. "Bernard, do you know 'Ich bin von Kopf bis Fuß auf Liebe eingestellt'?"

"I do not," he says, cracking his fingers. "How about 'I Will Survive'?"

All it takes are the opening chords to get us up and singing.

69

September 10

Living alone isn't as terrifying as I thought it would be, mostly because I'm rarely alone. I've got my cat, my daughter, and my friends whenever I need them. If I get real lonely, I can always chat with someone on Senior Moments. I've come to rely on that dating site a lot lately. When I first got on, I played my old part of Stella LaFayette, flirting with any suitor who seemed shady. What can I say? It scratched an itch. I enjoyed stringing these assholes along, especially after they asked me for money. I wasn't going to steal money from them again, but I could take their time—old people have a lot of that on their hands and it made me feel good that I was keeping this guy occupied so he couldn't seduce someone else. But it didn't take long for me to grow tired of spending time with assholes. Now I chat with a couple nice gentlemen who don't want anything except a little company. That's something I can give away freely, knowing now how much I get back in return.

"My children are coming to visit next week," Max says on our morning walk. The August heat these past few days has been intense. It's caused everyone to huddle inside with their air conditioners. When Max suggested we move our walk to 8:00 A.M., I almost backed out, which is ridiculous because I wake up every morning at six (sometimes earlier if Scampers decides to sleep on my face). Now I kind of like being out when the world is waking up. It's nice to start the day with friends, doing something that's good for me.

Max picks up her pace. I get the feeling she wants to maintain a safe distance from any sympathetic hugs.

Ginny and I aren't having it. We stop in our tracks and wait for Max to notice, which doesn't happen until she's nearly half a block away. She makes a sharp U-turn and approaches with a scowl on her face.

"Don't tell me you need a break already," she says.

"We're not tired," I say.

"Just curious," Ginny says.

"Keep up if you want to hear the story," Max says and takes off again. I feel like a donkey being led by a dangling carrot.

"I told them to come and say goodbye," Max says. "I don't know how much longer Harold has. They need to see him before he goes."

"Good for you," Ginny says.

"They didn't realize how bad things had become," she says. "I suppose that's my fault. I didn't want them to think I needed help."

"Of course they want to help," Ginny says.

"Children are a blessing." Ginny's catchphrase slips out before I can stop myself. "When they're not being assholes."

The ladies laugh and I join them.

"What are we going to do when it gets too cold to walk outside?" I ask as we merge onto the pathway that leads through the park. Now that school's back in session, there are just the little ones on the sand and swings. Their parents and nannies hover nearby, trying to decipher between screams of joy and pain.

"We live in California," Max says. "It's never cold outside."

"We could go back to water aerobics," Ginny offers.

"Think Lina would let us back in her class?" I ask.

"Maybe we could arrange for Max to take over," Ginny says with a sly wink.

"Be a shame if Lina had to give up the class," I say.

"Nothing serious, of course," Ginny says. "I don't want to see her physically injured."

"Of course not," I say. "But a bad performance review . . . that can really tank you."

"People are so quick to be offended these days," Ginny says, shaking her head in mock sympathy. "One sexually explicit song gets put on your playlist and poof! You're canceled."

"You two are awful," Max says, picking up her pace.

We laugh, but I can see we're all thinking how to make it happen.

Acknowledgements

I suppose the first person I should thank is the scammer who convinced my mother to send him a gift card for $200. Like Proust's madeleines, he triggered a flood of emotions (mostly anger) that fueled the writing of this revenge fantasy.

Then I should thank my mom who let me turn this embarrassing incident into a novel. Although my mother's story happens to many, it's hard to admit you've been scammed let alone turn that experience into a 300+ page novel. I'd also like to thank Channing House, my mom's retirement home, a wonderful place filled with kind people, none of whom are international crime bosses (as far as I know.)

My agent, Natanya Wheeler came into my life just when I thought I'd never publish another book again. She has been a tireless advocate for this book and kept me going through every rejection and revision. I couldn't ask for a better partner to help me navigate the arduous path toward publication.

My editor, Luisa Smith, is a superhero. A woman who is so wise and funny and hard working, she makes me feel like a lazy sloth (If she were editing this acknowledgment page, she'd point out the redundancy of "lazy sloth" and encourage me to come up with a more original simile). Honestly, I have no idea why she wanted to work with me given her bona fides but I'm eternally grateful that she did. If you enjoyed this novel, it's because of her.

Thanks to the team of incredibly talented people at Mysterious Press, Charles Perry, M. Lisa Liu, Michael Pintauro, Julia O'Connell, who turned these Microsoft Word pages into the beautiful book you hold in your hands.

I am lucky to have people in my life who are willing to read early drafts of my book and offer me both encouragement and criticism. Chief among these is my sister, Sheila, who I send the earliest, most terrible versions of my books to and who responds like a teacher counseling the parent of a disruptive student ("He's got a lot of energy! Let's try to focus it in more positive directions.")

Larkin Ryder was incredibly generous with her time and counseled me on cyber security to make Jeremy sound like he knew what he was talking about. I'm so lucky to count her as a neighbor and friend, even when she scams me out of my hard earned cash on poker nights.

Later drafts of this novel went to Donna Tracey, Anne Battle, Lyn Fairchild Hawks, Parker Peevyhouse, Mary Taugher, Eileen Bordy, Ann Gelder, Cheyenne Richards, Kim Ratcliff, Matthew S. Rosin, Maricia Scott, Harriet Garfinkle, Prudence Breitrose, and Carolyn Schwartz, all of whom provided great feedback along the way.

Robie Livingstone allowed me to use the names of her entire family in this book, including her cat. Her friendship and support has been such an important part of my life as a writer, karaoke singer, and human being. The fact that we're still friends after making smoothies at the Good Earth is one of life's greatest gifts.

Writers need emotional support (this writer needs lots of it) and for that I turn to a cadre of incredibly gifted people who provide much needed therapy on a semi-regular basis. Thank you Wednesday Waffle Club Members: Stacey Lee, Misa Suguira, Randy Ribay, Kelly Loy Gilbert, and Parker Peevyhouse for sharing your struggles and successes and for making me feel less alone in this weird life as a writer.

Thank you to Lisa, Jeff, Charlie, Marié, Cooper, Caitlin, Ed, Ellen, Juan, Sheila, Rachel, Edu, Rickey, Marisa, Alex, Alessandra, and Daniel. The best family of funny, generous and talented people I could hope to be a part of.

Finally, there's Kathleen and Henry, neither of whom has read a single line of prose I've written, but who are there for me every day and give me a reason to go into my he-shed every morning, sit down in front of the computer, and type, even when I've got nothing to say. You are my everything and to acknowledge all you've meant to me would take volumes.